FOOLS rush in

A CARTWRIGHT
BROTHER ROMANCE

Lilliana ANDERSON

INTERNATIONALLY BESTSELLING AUSTRALIAN AUTHOR

FOOLS RUSH IN

A CARTWRIGHT BROTHERS ROMANCE

LILLIANA ANDERSON

Cover design by *Ember Designs*

Editing by *Hot Tree Editing* and *Making Manuscripts*

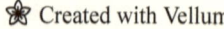 Created with Vellum

For you

If you read Fool Me Twice, you'll know that this series started as a dream that had me in fits of giggles. Everything about the series is crazy and outlandish, but it's *fun*, which is why I really love writing it.

All up, there will be five stories for five brothers. Why five? Well, I have five kids myself, so the number seemed right to me.

There is so much in this book. I read it again the other day and had a moment where I thought 'Holy fuck, how does this stuff come out of my head?' I literally have no clue. I just go into my head and write down what I see, kind of like watching a movie and describing it. Maybe I'm crazy, maybe I'm just really awesome.

So, this one is Sam and Alesha's story. If you read Holland and Nate's, I'll be really interested to hear your opinions. In the following pages, you're going to get the chance to see everything you didn't get to experience in book one. You'll get to see why Alesha pulled back, what kind of person Jasmine really is, and of course, you'll get more Toby, more Kristian, and more Abbot—it can totally be read as a standalone, so if you didn't read book one, don't worry.

This book is all about perspective and finding your own path. Alesha is thrown into the deep end of the Cartwright lifestyle so her experience with them is very different from what you might expect.

Now, I should probably say something about not condoning the actions of the characters within and stuff like that. But, we all understand it's a work of fiction, so I'm going to just leave it here so you can dive in.

I really hope you enjoy, *Fools Rush In*....

CHAPTER ONE
AT FIRST SIGHT

OUR BREATH CAME in pants as we burst through the door, lips locked, hands pulling at clothing, desperate for skin.

"I need you, Alesha," Sam whispered, his lips soft as they nibbled at my ear. "I need my wife."

I can't believe I'm finally married.

"Oh, yes," I moaned as his fingers danced over my skin, pulling the long zip of my wedding dress until the beautiful beaded bodice came undone and revealed my ample bosom, heaving with desire. "I want you too. I want my husband." I never thought I'd be so head over heels in love with a man I just met. Especially a man I knew to be a criminal. I was a good Christian girl, who was supposed to abhor the bad and seek to guide them to redemption. But I wanted Sam to be bad. I wanted him to show me how to be bad too. I could be a bad, *bad* girl. "Oh, Sam!"

"Oh, Alesha. I've wanted you from the moment I saw you crawling across our lawn with your arse in the air. You're everything I've ever wanted in a woman. Having you as my wife is a dream come true for me." With a low growl, he buried his head in my amazing cleavage, his large hands cupping my big boobs as he spoke between kisses. "And your breasts, they're amazing. You're perfect in every way."

Damn right, I was perfect.

Wait.

None of that actually happened.

Well, it *kind* of did.

It happened in a dream I had earlier today while on the plane from Melbourne to the Cook Islands. It was a great dream. A little over the top with the dialogue and the size of my breasts—I actually only had nipples on pancakes— but it *felt* good. As for the rest of it, I had a hope that it could somewhat come true. One day. I longed to be desired in that way, longed to be touched and adored by a man who would look at me the way Nate, Sam's older brother, was looking at Holland, my best friend. Unfortunately, that day was not today. Instead of joining hands with a doting groom who was smiling at me and whispering about how beautiful I looked, I was standing by a swampy-smelling waterfall, my feet sinking in mud while the literal man from my dreams stood in front of me, swaying slightly because he was so incredibly drunk.

Am I really that unappealing that he needs to be intoxicated to go through with this wedding?

It was a horrible hit to my already low self-esteem, and it made me wonder if the other option Holland and I had been given was possibly the better choice. You see, we'd stumbled upon something we shouldn't have, seen more than we should. Things got incredibly complicated, and in the end we were given two options—marriage or death.

You won't need many guesses to work out which option Holland and I went with.

"Do you, Alesha Ward, take Samuel Cartwright to be your lawfully wedded husband?"

Welcome to our shotgun wedding. In attendance were four out of the five Cartwright brothers, two of whom were grooms: Nate, who was marrying Holland, and Sam, who was marrying me. The other two, twins Abbot and Kristian, were witnesses. Also joining us was their mother, Jasmine—she was the one who wanted to kill us. I could rattle on for hours about the intricacies of the plot that brought us all to this moment, but I think Holland could tell it better (possibly in a book all of her own). So, you're going to have to settle for my no-frills version of events. And with all eyes on me, I was struggling to remember what the hell I was supposed to say, let alone how we got here.

Wait, what was the question again?

Oh, that's right. Do I want to marry Sam?

I glanced over at Holland, seeking a familiar face, needing her support. But she wasn't any help at all. While she looked beautiful in a cream wraparound dress with flowers pinned in her blonde hair, she also looked like she might throw up, or worse, run and leave me here all by myself. Many best friends dreamed of having a combined wedding, but somehow for us, that dream had turned into a nightmare—a nightmare filled with incredibly attractive men, mind you, who were all staring at me expectantly.

"I…." The question hung in the air, everyone waiting for me to spit out my answer. It was only two words, but when you didn't really mean them, they were so damn hard to say.

Could I marry Sam? With his dark hair and ice blue eyes, he was the hottest man I'd ever been able to form a sentence around. He was taller than me, buff as fuck, and he was *charming*. When we met—which was a nice way of saying 'when Holland and I were captured'—Sam put me at ease in the midst of that awful situation. That was a miracle in itself, because normally I could barely speak around any man, let alone one who had a face most sculptors would cry over. He'd put an arm around my shoulders and offered me a beer, and somehow the social anxiety that had crippled me for most of my life just melted away like magic—although, the fact I'd been running for my life moments before, and my fight or flight instincts had kicked in, might've also had something to do with it. But I was calm around him, even twenty-four hours later, and that was a huge deal for me. I was *never* calm around members of the opposite sex. Never. So maybe, just maybe, this guy was the cure to my social anxiety. Maybe, just maybe, I was *supposed* to meet him the way I did Everything happens for a reason, right? Well, that's what the old ladies at my church said, anyway.

My head was spinning, searching for reasons, for signs. But I didn't have time for any of that. I had to give an answer. They were waiting.

"I…."

I should just marry him, right? Statistically, arranged marriages worked out better than love matches. And you never knew, we might just be a match made in Heaven.

Maybe.

Lord, give me strength. Help me choose.

Based on everything I've said so far, you probably guessed that Sam was not a 'good guy'. In fact, he was the very definition of a 'bad guy'. The man was a thief. Part of a band of five brothers who cleaned out people's houses for a living and sold off their belongings.

That was actually how I met Sam, through his thievery. He and his brothers had cleaned out Holland's apartment *twice*. I know, I know—how the hell can the same people rob you twice? Well, Holland and I had been best friends since we were eight years old, so I knew better than anyone that she was a special kind of crazy and rarely thought things through before she acted. She was convinced she would do a better job tracking down her robbers than the police would. And she'd been right. She found them, dragging me—the faithful sidekick—along in the process. *Her* lack of forethought was the precise reason we were standing in a bug-infested swamp about to marry men we barely knew.

The heat pressed in around us, making my dark hair stick against the back of my neck. I could barely breathe through the humidity. "I…."

Holland had been so good at tracking down the thieves that we now knew exactly who they were, where they lived and where they stored their goods. Because of that knowledge, we were too dangerous to let go. It was either marry into the family or spend the rest of eternity in an unmarked grave. A crazy conundrum for any person to have.

Honestly, if I were the Cartwrights and two crazy chicks came barrelling into my life, knowing all we knew, I would've ended them then and there to save all this wedding drama. But then, I *did* have access to a crematorium through my job as a mortuary beautician, so getting rid of a body would be a lot easier for someone like me.

No digging deep holes and worrying about search dogs finding some nice soft ground….

I had to admit that I took some sort of comfort in knowing that these guys were more willing to marry us than to kill us to protect themselves. I suspected it was Nate's weird connection with Holland that had been the primary driving force behind this irrational scheme to save our lives, and once again, I was sucked along by association. I couldn't imagine Holland would want anything to do with Nate if he let his family kill her best friend, so I was 'saved' along with her, given a brother to wed. I guess that meant they weren't really *that* bad, right? I presumed it meant once we took their name, we couldn't go to the authorities, because we could be considered associates. Or maybe they had some kind of ulterior motive I hadn't considered.

My mind wouldn't stop reeling.

"Alesha," Jasmine hissed. I swallowed hard.

No matter what spin I put on all this, one fact remained true—I wasn't ready to die at only thirty-two. I'd done nothing with my life, barely had the chance to live yet. There was only one *real* choice available to me. Only two words between me and my own salvation. If only I could spit them out.

"I. Do." The words burned as they passed my lips, the effort taken to force them out removing all the air from my lungs.

Great, now I'm married to a criminal.

Relief crossed Sam's features, which surprised me since he seemed so drunk. Then I sucked in a large gulp of air, trying to stop myself from passing out over the reality of what I'd just agreed to. I just said "I do". I was married to a man I barely knew, and my father, who was the most religious man I'd ever met, was going to kill me. *Dear God, save me from my father's wrath. Let him understand that I'd never do anything to upset him on purpose. Grant him the gift of compassion towards his only daughter.* I didn't want to be cast out of my own family just because my wedding didn't follow the right protocols.

Just as my silent prayer ended, divinity answered with a solid middle finger as a bug flew right down my throat, choking me with its malaria-riddled wings.

"*Uck.*" My eyes went wide as I coughed and leaned forwards, grabbing Sam's shirt, begging for help as I tried to spit the horrid creature out, my feet sliding on the slick and spongy ground.

"Whoa!" Sam grabbed my elbows in an attempt to steady me, but the ground was too wet, too soft, and our shoes provided little grip. We tilted forwards, then back, desperate for purchase, our hands gripping tighter when our feet failed us. Then we went down with a squelch, mud splashing up and coating the stark white of my slip dress. The fairy tale was definitely over. I was either going to scream or cry.

Holland, my most favourite person in the world, stared at me in shock, her honey-coloured eyes opened wide. She looked so beautiful, so curvy and confident. I expected her compassion, needed her sympathy, or at least her hand to get out of the mud. Instead, she pointed at me and laughed. "You should see your face!"

———

"Bathroom is in there." Sam pointed to the door inside

our hotel room as he started unbuttoning his muddy shirt, peeling it from his well-muscled chest. The sight made my mouth go dry and my feet glue themselves to the floor. *I'm married to that?* Despite all that I knew he was, Sam was a beautiful man who sent my heart all aflutter every time I looked at him.

"See something you like?" he asked, a half grin kicking up one side of his mouth.

Immediately I dropped my chin, my gaze hitting the floor as my cheeks heated. "I'm sorry," I mumbled, heading for the bathroom. I was so completely out of my depth in this situation. There was no handbook on how to behave when marrying into a crime family. *Maybe watching some mobster movies would give me some pointers.*

"I'm happy to come in there and wash your back for you." Playful. He was playful. All man. Too much man. Too sure of himself. Too knowledgeable. And I... I was too nervous. What was I supposed to do?

I shook my head and scurried away like a mouse, locking myself in the bathroom where I immediately caught sight of the catastrophe in the mirror.

"Good Lord," I gasped. So. Much. Mud. The entire wedding party had reacted to Sam's and my fall with laughter and a mud fight. At first, I was devastated— weddings weren't supposed to have mud fights in them. But then weddings weren't supposed to be rushed either. I could sook about it, or I could roll with the punches and have fun with everyone else. I chose fun. And while the mud fight lightened the mood, it absolutely destroyed my dress and made me look like some kind of swamp monster. Not pretty.

Stripping quickly, I got into the shower stall and turned on the water, wishing I'd waited for a moment when the icy cold hit my skin and I let out a small shriek.

"You all right in there?" Sam called through the locked door, startling me for a second time. I was already a nervous person, and the stress of the day was definitely adding to that.

"I'm fine. The water was cold. It's fine now."

"Sure you don't want me to wash your back?"

I smiled to myself, holding my hands under the warming water. "I can manage," I called back. He seemed to enjoy teasing me, and I think I liked it. It felt light and fun to me, just what I needed to stop being so nervous around him. I'd struggled with attraction before, not knowing what was expected of me, but he'd been kind and affectionate from the get-go. Twenty-four hours. It wasn't a lot of time to get to know someone, and I honestly wasn't sure if he was attracted to me or if he was just playing the kind of game his family seemed fond of. The Cartwright brothers were experts at seducing lonely women. When Holland was robbed the first time, the police told us it was their MO—they preyed on the lonely and lived like kings as a result. Was that the case here too?

I ran my arms under the water, watching the mud rinse away while wondering if I called out "yes, you can wash my back", would Sam come into the shower expecting to have sex with me? After all, that's what married couples did. The thought made me nervous. But not as nervous as the thought of him laughing and not wanting to come in at all. What if he *was* only joking? What if he didn't want me in the slightest?

Once clean, I wrapped myself in the thick white towel

the hotel provided and wished I'd thought to bring my suit-
case in with me so I didn't have to go out there to get
changed. *This could get really uncomfortable.*

Staring at the door, knowing Sam was on the other side
waiting for his turn in the shower, I took a deep breath. *I
can do this. I can walk out there almost naked in front of
my husband.* There was a certain expectation for a woman
on her wedding night, and perhaps it would be a good test
to see if he actually was interested or had simply been
teasing me all this time.

Was I ready for that revelation though?

Clutching the top of the towel, I cracked open the door
and peeked out. He was sitting on the end of the bed in just
a pair of boxers, the TV remote in hand as he flipped
through channels. Lordy me, that man was stunning. All
muscle and taut skin that called out to my fingertips,
begging them to touch. I'd been in his arms during the
playful games he'd included me in the night before—
swimming in the pool, playing billiards with his brothers.
He'd stayed close to me the entire evening, made me
feel safe.

I was a good girl. But I wanted him. Did that make me
bad, knowing what I knew?

"It's all yours," I said, my voice catching a little in my
throat.

Grinning, he immediately stood and dropped the
remote on the bed, reaching me in only a couple of strides.
The man was enormous. I was five-ten, and he was almost
an entire head above me. Plus his shoulders were crazy
broad. I could fit three of me across him. And he looked
after that body. He was made to seduce, and everything
about him made my skin buzz.

"Thanks, peaches," he said, chucking me lightly on the chin as he walked past and closed the door.

Peaches?

I was standing there *naked* save for a towel, and he *chucked* me on the *chin*? A sour taste filled my mouth and twisted my lips downward. *Am I that undesirable?*

Hearing the shower turn on, I moved over to the cupboard where our suitcases were waiting. I wasn't really sure what was in mine since the twins had been dispatched to 'grab some of my things'. When I placed my hand on it, I wondered if they'd packed anything at all. The bloody thing was empty. *Oh shit.* I didn't even know where the clothes I'd arrived in went.

Please let there be something in this cupboard.

Taking hold of the handles, I willed my clothing inside it, then pulled, sighing with relief when I found the shelves filled with familiar items. It looked as though Abbot and Kristian had been quite thorough in bringing a little of everything I owned. My biggest disappointment was the lack of a make-up bag. I hated going bare faced, and it looked as though I had no choice in the matter.

Grabbing a pair of white cotton briefs—I owned *nothing* sexier than cotton—I pulled them up my legs, still holding my towel over my chest for modesty despite being alone. It was something I'd always done. Nakedness wasn't something that was ever acceptable when I was growing up, so I barely saw myself naked, let alone anybody else.

I pulled out a matching cotton triangle crop that did little more than cover my nipples so they didn't show through the fabric of my clothes. I didn't need any under-wire or support because my chest was non-existent.

Holland often referred to me as Olive Oyl because I was so straight up and down. All the curves had skipped me and been bestowed upon her. It's why she was the one who got all the guys—not only was she funny and outgoing, but she was voluptuous too.

Pausing before I put my dress on, I took a moment to really look at my body. It was like somebody stuck a head on a rake. My face wasn't much better, basic brown hair and eyes too big for my face. My mouth seemed too small by comparison, and my nose was a little on the crooked side. There was also a tiny gap in my front teeth because my father believed in accepting what God gave you, so no braces in my house. I'd lived life with a whistle gap instead. *Acceptance of what God gave me. The problem with that is He gave me nothing significant at all.* When I looked at myself, all I saw was deficit. No gifts.

With a sigh, I turned away from the mirror. It was no wonder Sam had walked straight past me. He probably had some beautiful busty blonde he'd visit on the weekends, and if I was lucky, he'd be discreet. He wouldn't need me, the mousy brown-haired whistler for the itty-bitty-titty committee.

His flirting, his hugs, his kindness? Probably generosity towards his frightened, pathetic new pet. He simply felt sorry for me.

And here I was, his wife. *God, what have I done?*

Pulling my dress over my head, I thought back to the conversation I'd had with Holland on the plane that brought us from Melbourne to the Cook Islands. She was in a panic over our impending nuptials and I'd told her not to worry, that Sam and I were in love. "It was love at first sight," I'd said. "We're waiting for the wedding night." It was a bold-faced lie, and I wondered why in the world I'd said that to her instead of being honest. Maybe it was to help her stress less by not worrying about me. Maybe I wanted her to think I had something that she didn't for a change. *Maybe you said it because you've always been jealous of her, and you wanted her to think you were happy and in love,* a little voice whispered in my head. A thump resounded in my chest as the words rang true.

I'd always wished I was more like Holland. More beautiful. More sensual. More passionate. Just *more.*

Yes, I was married to a gorgeous man. A man who was *way* out of my league, who'd essentially swooped in and pulled me from my dreary life and into the excitement of his. It's what I'd been wishing—no, *praying* for. But given that I'd barely earned a quick glance from Sam as he walked past me, being me wasn't looking so great. I wondered how long I could continue to live my passion-less life. I was so tired of feeling unwanted.

CHAPTER TWO
THE GIANT FISHBOWL

"NATE AND HOLLAND aren't down yet," Kristian said, sipping some sort of amber liquor as he leaned against the bar and ran his hand over the top of his cropped hair. Based on his movements, he seemed stressed, or maybe just tired after a long day of travelling and tension. Even regular weddings did that to people, so I wasn't surprised to find him in a less than jovial mood after ours.

As the youngest of the five Cartwright brothers—by four and a half minutes, a fact his twin, Abbot, announced gladly not long after I'd met them—Kristian was probably my favourite after Sam. I hadn't known him for much longer than the day and a bit that I'd known the rest of the family, but so far he seemed fun-loving with a serious side that we were seeing more of since we'd arrived in the Cook Islands. He was focused but didn't turn into a jerk when things didn't go according to plan. And lately, nothing was going according to plan. All of our lives had been turned upside down over this crazy 'wed or die' plan. It had all happened so fast that I wasn't even sure what I thought about it yet. I was scared but I was also excited, unsure and overwhelmed. The fact that I knew I was here simply because I wanted to keep breathing meant I couldn't do much more than float along, doing whatever was needed or expected so I didn't end up with a backhand to the face like Holland had received when *she'd* expressed a little defiance.

"What about Abbot and Jasmine?" Sam looked around the bar, trying to find them in the faces of the other tourists in the hotel.

Jasmine was their mother, the matriarch who, from what I could tell, was the determined leader of this merry band of thieves. She was tall, slender, elegant and very intimidating: a six-foot blonde with Audrey Hepburn's grace mixed with Katharine Hepburn's looks and attitude. Although, I had to wonder if Nate, the second oldest of all the brothers, wouldn't rather the control shifted to himself. He seemed a little... hungry, that was probably the best word I could think up to describe him. From the way he carried himself to the way he looked at my friend, he never seemed satisfied. Out of all the brothers, he seemed to be the most restless.

As far as genes went, all five brothers *looked* like brothers. All of them were tall and broad, with dark hair and varying shades of blue eyes, tan skin, and bodies that made your fingers itch. Besides age, their personality and style seemed to be the only thing that set them apart. When I'd been given the choice to marry into the family for my protection, I'd been offered the hand of Toby, the oldest of the brothers. He was just as hot as the others, and for what I was being offered, he seemed nice enough. But he didn't set my heart on fire the way Sam did. I figured if I was going to be forced to marry a Cartwright, then I at least wanted to choose which one.

For the first time in my life, I'd lifted my chin and said, "No." Then I told Jasmine I wanted Sam. Without even asking him, Jasmine had smiled at me and agreed, like I'd somehow impressed her. I never saw the moment when Sam was informed of his new fate. *What did he really think about having to marry me?* I had zero clue, and I wasn't even sure I wanted to find out. Especially since there wasn't much we could do about it. What was done was done.

"They're outside having a smoke." Kristian waved the bartender over. "Order a drink and take a seat. I reckon we're gonna be here a while. You want something floofy, darlin'?" His eyes landed on me, taking a moment to graze the length of the simple floral maxi dress I was wearing. It was modest but pretty. It had always been my favourite church-going outfit, although I normally wore it with a cardigan. "Spaghetti straps are not appropriate for the Lord," my father always said. And I always did what my father said. Well, when he was watching, anyway.

"Floofy?" I responded, not exactly sure what Kristian meant.

"Yeah. You know, the ones that come in big glasses with fruit and umbrellas and shit sticking out of them. Isn't that what girls drink when they're on an island?"

I slid onto the stool he pulled out for me. "I suppose. But I'm happy for whatever."

"No, darlin', not whatever. If you're gonna be a Cartwright, you have to make decisions like one. Be precise. What'll it be? You can have anything you want." He gestured across the bar at all the colourful bottles that lined the well-lit shelves. I didn't really know what I wanted. I tended to drink whatever was on offer or whatever Holland was drinking. I very rarely drank alone, so I didn't buy alcohol for myself. Plus I didn't like to create waves or call attention to myself by being picky.

Going with the flow was how I lived my life. Even my job hadn't been my idea. I was studying beauty therapy after high school when my uncle, who's a funeral director, had an opening for a mortuary beautician. My family basically decided I would fill that role. I guess I didn't *mind* that my father and uncle set up the job without consulting me, since it paid well and all, but it would've been nice to be asked. I kind of had my sights set on working in Chanel, or behind one of the fancy make-up counters at David Jones. You know, a job with actual breathing people.

"Here, peaches." Sam placed a cocktail menu in front of me, pulling me from my thoughts. "Pick whatever tickles your fancy, and don't look at the cost." Then he rested his hand between my shoulder blades, his fingers moving lightly, creating tiny electrical currents beneath my skin. It felt so good and I wanted to lean in to him, but a resounding thought rang loudly in my mind: *He touches me intimately in public and chucks my chin in private.*

This whole situation was messed up and confusing. I needed to stop trying to figure it out or else I'd drive myself crazy.

Just go with the flow like you always do. Everything will be fine. Even if Sam doesn't want you like a husband should want a wife, he still seems like he's planning on being kind to you. It's not like he's beating you in private and acting all sweet and caring in public.

Oh God, what if that's what he's going to do in the future? What if I don't meet his standards and he goes all Patrick Bergin in Sleeping with the Enemy *on me? Every time I hear him play a certain song, I'll know I'm in for it? Please no, I don't want to live like that!*

"Peaches?"

"Huh?" I snapped my head up, my entire body flinching as I turned to face a bemused-looking Sam.

"See anything you'd like?" He gestured to the menu I was clutching in a death grip between my fingers.

His hand moved up to the back of my neck as he leaned a little closer. *Oh no! It's starting already!* I winced a little, bracing myself before his threat entered my ear. "You can have *anything* you want," he whispered, gently sliding his hand down until it rested on my lower back.

I let out a breath. *Did he just proposition me?* It was times like these that I wished I had a little more life experience. I couldn't read his signals properly, and my mind was flipping between thinking the worst and hoping for the best.

I needed a drink. Actually, I needed about seven hundred and ninety-two drinks.

Keeping my breathing even while trying to focus on anything but the significance of his touch, I scanned the menu. When I couldn't stop my brain from overanalysing every moment from the past twenty-four hours, I just chose the first cocktail to jump out at me. I didn't want to make the bartender wait any longer than he already had. "I'll take a Mai Tai, please," I said, figuring it was probably the perfect cocktail to go with our Polynesian setting in the Cook Islands anyway.

"What size?" the bartender asked.

"Size?" *They come in different sizes?*

"Standard, tall or fishbowl."

Just as I was about to open my mouth and enquire about the exact size of each vessel, Kristian and Sam both leaned forwards and said, "Fishbowl," in unison.

The bartender grinned and I simply shrugged. "Fishbowl it is." I laughed, allowing myself to relax just a little. *Let the boys have their fun. I'll just sip it so I don't get too drunk.*

I may have thought Sam was the most beautiful man on two legs, but I wasn't stupid. I didn't know these people and needed to keep my wits about me.

"Itsh so delish-i-ness." I slurped the straw along the bottom of the giant fishbowl glass, digging out a red cherry with my fingers and shoving it in my mouth. Boy, was I feeling light-headed.

OK, maybe I was *a little* stupid.

We'd been waiting at the bar for so long that I'd managed to *sip* away a literal fishbowl-sized drink. I was beyond drunk. I was hammered.

"Mai Tais are the besh-t. Fuck beer. I'm never saying yesh to one of those dirty sock-tasting things again." My eyes went wide as an idea struck me. "Ish that actu-actually how they make beer?" I gasped and turned to Sam, trying to make my mouth move around my words. "Do you think that if I went to a dish— distillery and opened a vat, I'd find a whole bunches of sweaty socks and gym shoes inside?" I covered my mouth and started giggling. It wouldn't surprise me.

"All right." Sam chuckled and pulled the straw I was chewing from between my teeth, placing it back in the glass bowl and pushing the whole thing away. "I think we need to get some food into you."

"Ohhh yes! Do they make burgers in this place?" I think I yelled every syllable, and when I whipped my head around to look for some indication that I could get a burger, I almost fell off the stool. Luckily, Sam caught me. My cheeks burned as I found myself pressed against his chest, and I couldn't help but breathe deeply and take in his manly smell. "You are so very handsome, and you smell like freshly cut grass and salty air and soap," I whispered under my breath. At least I hoped it was under my breath, because that would be an odd thing to say out loud.

"We'll get you the biggest burger they have. Even if they aren't on the menu." His voice sounded like a smile. *Sigh.*

"Fine. We'll eat," Jasmine said with a sigh of her own as she looked at her watch. "They're obviously not coming down and honestly, I'd rather not dine with that woman anyway."

That woman was my best friend.

"She's not that bad," I said in her defence, righting myself with the help of Sam's strong hands and feeling bold from all the liquid courage I'd imbibed.

Jasmine regarded me with her cool eyes and I shrank back, almost hiding behind Sam. She was the one who had backhanded Holland when she got a little mouthy before the wedding. Her entire cheek had swelled up because of it. I was horrified but quickly realised that Jasmine wasn't to be crossed. Self-preservation 101.

"I'm sorry," I said in a rush, suddenly sober after the

adrenalin spike my fear caused. "I shouldn't have said that."

She pressed her lips into a fine line. "I should think of all the people in this world, you'd have the biggest reason to be angry with Holland right now. Don't forget, she's the one who put you in this position."

"This position isn't so bad." The moment the words left my lips, I wished they hadn't. I'd said them thinking it might show Jasmine that I was tougher than I seemed. But the delivery wasn't quite right, and I think I ended up coming across as the ultimate clinger instead, so desperate for the attention of a man that I was actually happy about a forced marriage.

What the hell is wrong with me? Why can't I think before I speak? And it wasn't even that I was happy about being married to the hunk of spunk by my side—OK, I kind of was—it was more that I was trying to be hopeful. Sitting in a corner and crying wasn't really going to change anything. I could accept what was happening, or I could fight it the way Holland had been fighting it. And all that had done was earn Holland a whole lot of animosity. I hated to imagine what would happen in the future if she continued to fight the family's rules. No, fighting didn't work. It never worked.

Jasmine took a moment to look between both Sam and me.

"You think you're a good match for my son?"

Oh God, what a question. I didn't even know how to answer that and instead moved my mouth around like I was doing an impression of a goldfish to go along with the giant bowl I'd just drained.

When I didn't answer, she looked at Sam, the question in her eyes now directed at him. "Well?"

Sam placed his hands on his hips. "You're the match-maker, Jasmine. You should know," he said, a slight sound of annoyance in his normally happy voice.

What does that mean? Is his annoyance directed at me or at her?

"I suppose we'll have to wait and see, then." Jasmine's eyes landed back on me as if daring me to admit I'd chosen him. Frankly, I was surprised he didn't already know. "Won't we, Alesha?"

"I guess so," I whispered, ducking my head so I was looking at my feet, shrivelling back inside myself.

It was then that Sam's hand moved to the back of my neck and his fingers pressed lightly.

"Let's get you fed, peaches. We'll worry about the rest of this shit later."

Looking up at him, I took a breath and nodded, feeling added strength and sobriety from his touch. He smiled and I melted like the pathetically lonely thing I was.

Taking my arm, he guided me into the hotel's restaurant while I walked on unsteady feet, my mind worrying.

I think I need another drink.

CHAPTER THREE
MY EXORCIST IMPRESSION

"WATER."

Did someone put sand in my mouth? I moved my tongue around, trying to produce some sort of moisture. I felt *awful.* So awful that the deady-bones—as we in the funeral industry respectfully called our deceased clients— probably had a better pallor to their skin. *What the hell happened to me last night?*

"Steady." I didn't recognise the deep voice at first. It spoke quietly somewhere to the side of me, and felt kind of good in contrast to the screaming in my brain. When I forced my eyes to open, memories came flooding back to me.

"Oh. That's right." I closed my eyes again. "I'm married."

Sam chuckled. "Why don't you drink this? I don't have any painkillers, I'm sorry."

"There should be some in my handbag," I rasped, my throat scraping with each word. I took the offered glass and sipped at the water. At first my stomach refused, but I persisted and got a few mouthfuls down. At least my mouth felt better.

"Here." Sam returned from my bag and handed me two Panadol.

"Thank you." I took them and swallowed some more water before he took the glass from my hand. "What happened last night?" I croaked, lying back on the soft pillows and pressing my hands against my throbbing temple. The movement caused the sheets to rub against my body. My *naked* body.

"What?" I grabbed the sheet and peeked beneath it. I was starkers. Naked as the day I was born. "Did... did we, um...?" I didn't *feel* any different down there, but still... no clothes. I met Sam's eyes and cleared my throat. "Why am I naked?" I clutched the sheet beneath my chin to preserve what little modesty I had left.

"We didn't consummate our vows, if that's what you're asking. You drank way more than you could take, then threw up on your dress and passed out while I was cleaning you up. It was easier to put you to bed naked than to try and dress an adult-sized rag doll."

Oh dear. I dragged the sheet over my face, my whole body burning in humiliation. Just once I'd love not to feel so stupid. Insipid. Ashamed.

"I ruined our wedding night," I groaned. "You should just leave me here to die alone. It's what I deserve. Marry your pretty blonde girlfriend instead. She'll make you happy and probably manage to keep the towels even in the bathroom."

"I have no idea what you're talking about." Sam pried the sheet from my grip so he could see my face, laughter in his voice as he spoke. "There's no pretty blonde girlfriend,

Alesha. And I don't know what even towels are. Does that mean they're folded the same?"

"It's when the designs match when they're hanging on the rack."

"Why would anyone care about that?"

"Because everything is supposed to be perfect."

Laughing through his nose, he placed his hand on the top of my hair, his thumb brushing the skin on my forehead as he shook his head. "You're a little bit crazy, aren't you?"

I pressed my lips together in a withering smile. "Sorry you married me yet?"

Still smiling, he shook his head. "Shockingly, no. Not yet. I'm kind of partial to blushing brunettes with no filter and gorgeous brown eyes."

"You actually *like* that stuff about me?" My eyes about bugged out of my head. "Wait. You *are* talking about me, right?"

He laughed again. "Yes. I like you, peaches. I wouldn't have agreed to this if I didn't."

Pressing up on my elbows, I sat up, keeping the sheet tight around my chest as a deep furrow etched between my brows. "But you haven't even kissed me. Well, besides the wedding… and a few times on my forehead."

Sitting back, he met my eyes with a serious expression. "You're shy. I don't want you to feel pressured."

"Pressured?" I laughed. "I was given the choice to marry into your family or face the consequences. There isn't much more pressure than that."

"Precisely. That's why I'm not going to force myself on you. As it is, you're flipping between blurting whatever's on your mind and cowering like someone hit you.

Let's spend time together and when the time is right, things between us will happen naturally."

Things will happen naturally. My experience with the opposite sex was limited to a single awkward moment in the back of a car that happened over a decade ago while we were both so drunk we could barely string a sentence together. I didn't have *any* experience within a relationship. I had no clue what to think when guys made comments like that. It sort of sounded like a stalling tactic or a brush-off to me. I mean, I was no expert, but what kind of a man didn't want to have sex with a woman he was supposedly attracted to? He was either some sort of saint, which we both knew he wasn't, or he was lying. I might've been naïve when it came to the inner workings of the male mind, but that didn't mean I was stupid and would fall for any sort of line he fed me.

"I'm kind of partial to blushing brunettes with no filter and gorgeous brown eyes." Right.

He couldn't say he liked me in one breath then tell me he wanted to wait in the next. It felt like a paradox to me. If he didn't want me, he'd just have to come out and be honest about it. That way I could put any hopes I had in a box inside my mind, lock it up tight and work with what was right in front of me. Honesty was the only real language I spoke and understood.

I took a deep breath, summoning all my courage so I could say what was on my mind. "I wouldn't feel pressured," I whispered, dropping my gaze so I didn't have to see the reaction in his eyes. I had a horrible feeling he was going to laugh at me. He was so beautiful, and I was so basic.

There was a pause before he spoke, one that stretched

far longer than I was comfortable with. When I couldn't take it anymore, I looked back up and found him studying me intently.

"Have you ever been with a man before, peaches?"

My already crimson cheeks heated to a scarlet red. "I…I, um, sort of. Yes."

"Sort of?"

"I've, um, I've fooled around. A little."

"So, you've been kissed?"

"Yes."

"Touched?"

"Yes."

"Where?"

"Um…."

"Your breasts?"

Swallowing, I nodded.

"Any lower?"

Our eyes locked as my heart stuttered in my chest. "I don't want to have this conversation anymore," I said in a rush, gathering the sheet around my body as I scrambled to get off the bed. The moment my feet hit the ground, I rushed for the bathroom, only to be jolted to a stop when the damn sheet wouldn't disconnect from the bed. "Why won't this work?" I growled, tugging harder and leaning back to put the weight of my body into it.

"Alesha. Stop."

I continued growling and tugging.

"Alesha. It's OK."

"No." Tug. "It's." Tug. "Not." *Rip.* The sudden release of the sheet sent my body in a spin, my toes teetering like an uncoordinated ballerina before I lost my balance and landed on the hardwood floor with a thud.

"Ow." I coughed, the air having been knocked from my lungs when I suddenly became horizontal. On the plus side, the ceiling was quite pretty.

"Can you breathe?" Sam's beautiful head came into view as he stood over me, surveying the extent of my injuries.

"Yes," I responded, digging my elbow into the floor so I could sit up.

"Whoa, whoa." He quickly crouched beside me, his hands at my arm and my back to assist me. "Is your neck OK? Your back?"

I pulled away. "I'm fine. I'm just...." I groped for the sheet around my chest but only touched skin. "Sitting here with my tit out. Oh God, look away!" I placed one hand on the side of his face to push him away while the other hand adjusted the sheet.

"Peaches, there isn't a single part of your body I didn't get an eyeful of last night. And I've got to tell you, if I weren't such a gentleman, I would've done a hell of a lot more than just look."

"Maybe you should have. It's what husbands do with their wives, isn't it?"

He looked at me like I'd just spoken Klingon. "What? No. How were you raised? Husbands don't fuck their unconscious wives, especially not when that wife is a virgin. There has to be consent, Alesha. Sex is something to be enjoyed by two people, not taken by one." His entire face seemed upset with me. "No, Alesha. Just... no."

Seeing his features scrunched up, directing his disgust towards me, caused my stomach to twist and lurch. Once again, my mouth had preceded my brain and I'd put my foot in it, but even worse, Sam just called me the V-word. *How did he know?*

"I need the bathroom," I gasped, scrambling to my feet and rushing through the door. I had just enough time to slam it closed and lock it before I launched myself at the toilet and wretched into it. Everything was coming apart. He wasn't supposed to know, wasn't supposed to find out. It was embarrassing enough to be thirty-two and yet to be deflowered without having the one guy who was supposed to be obligated to do that deflowering find out and put the brakes on the physical side of our relationship. *Does that mean he's freaked out? Or that he thinks I'm a freak?* I hated this, hated that I was so pathetic and so inexperienced and clueless and everything else that was wrong with me. I hated being me.

Just as I flushed, a light tap sounded on the door before Sam spoke through it. "I'm sorry, peaches. I shouldn't have reacted like that."

I stood in front of the mirror and splashed cold water on my pale face. I didn't trust my mouth not to offend him again. It would be better if I just stayed silent.

"Are you OK in there?"

Silence.

"Alesha?"

"I'm fine."

"Will you let me in?" When I didn't respond, he let out a sigh. "Fine, we'll do this through a locked door, then. What you said back there, about me... doing things to you while you were passed out drunk. I need you to understand that I would never touch you without your OK or do anything to you that you weren't comfortable with. That's not what I'm about. And I really hope you've never been treated that way yourself."

"No," I replied.

"No, what?"

"I've never been treated that way." I'd never been treated *any* way. Drunken kisses and groping at my breasts were as far as it got before my date puked and passed out. That was the entirety of my sexual experience.

He breathed a sigh of relief. "That's good."

Is it? As far as I was concerned, it was humiliating.

"How did you know?" I said over my shoulder.

"About what? You being a virgin?"

"Yes."

"I had a fair idea, but you confirmed it last night."

"I told you?" I had never told *anyone*. Not even Holland knew. It was my most closely guarded secret. I wasn't even planning on telling Sam, figuring I'd just fake it until I didn't have to anymore. What possessed me to blurt that information out?

"Yeah." A slight chuckle bounced along with the word. "You kept slapping my hands away when I was undressing you."

"Oh God. I want to crawl into a tiny hole and never come out again."

He laughed more openly at that. "It wasn't that bad. It was kinda adorable, actually."

Adorable? *Adorable?* Kittens and puppies were adorable. Vomiting women, not so much.

"I'm sorry."

"It's OK. I didn't mind taking care of you."

That wasn't what I meant. "I'm sorry that I'm not the kind of woman you're probably used to."

"Alesha." I could hear the pity in his voice by the way he drew my name out.

"I need to shower. I'll meet you in the dining room for breakfast."

He started to speak, but when I flipped the shower on, the pounding water drowned out his words, along with his pity for his thirty-two-year-old virgin bride.

I'm never going to be enough.

CHAPTER FOUR
OH MY MY

"HEY." Sam stood from where he'd been sitting and pressed his palms against his jean-clad thighs. "You OK?" He placed one hand on my waist and pressed a soft kiss on my cheek.

Instead of answering, I looked around the hotel dining room, noting the large table he'd selected that was vacant except for him, his coffee and an open newspaper. "Where's everyone else?"

"No one else is down yet."

"Maybe they all had fishbowl cocktails too."

He grinned. "Possibly." Then he pulled me a little closer and inhaled. "You smell good."

My breathing hitched as my hands landed instinctively against his chest. "There's mango in the shampoo." I closed my eyes, not wanting to look into his eyes and see any sort of remnants of our previous conversation.

"I like it." Then, before I could do anything else, his mouth connected with mine, his hands shifting from my waist so his arm was wrapped around me, holding me up as he kissed me so passionately that I arched my back. For a moment, I wondered if I should kick my leg up in the air to put on a show for the other patrons, but all I could really do was hold on and kiss him back because man, could he kiss. He kissed me like the heroes do in books and in movies—with everything he had. Well, that's how it felt anyway. I hadn't been kissed enough times to know if it got any better than that.

When he set me back on my feet, I felt a little light-headed. "Wow," I whispered.

Looking into my eyes, he held my face in his hands. "I love the fact that I'm going to be your first."

"Can we please not talk about this," I said, trying to pull away from his grasp and avoid any further embarrassment. I mean, who in this day and age was still a virgin at thirty-two? I didn't want to address it. I just wanted him to pop my cherry and get this awkwardness over and done with. *Devirginise me, dammit!*

"Don't run away again." He caught me around the waist with one arm and held a finger under my chin to keep me from looking away. "Don't look away either."

"Can't we just forget that you know?"

"Why? Are you embarrassed that you've saved yourself?"

"Well, it's not like I did it on purpose. I just never had the opportunity." Having an overbearing, uber-religious father on top of being socially awkward—someone who worked well with the dead—hadn't exactly created windows of opportunity.

His grip around me tightened, and the finger under my chin shifted to tuck my hair behind my ear. "I think you're perfect," he murmured, his ocean blue eyes drinking in every feature of my face. "You're pure, innocent. A ripe peach, untasted and ready to be picked."

"Yes," I gasped, wanting badly for him to pick me and taste me and do any number of things that men and women were made to do together. I wanted it all. With him. Now would *not* be too soon.

He grinned, then leaned forwards and sucked my bottom lip between his teeth teasingly. "Women like you are a gift, and I want to take my time unwrapping you. Can you let me do that, peaches?"

"Yes." I nodded. Now I totally understood why he gave me that nickname. I didn't really know what I was agreeing to, but being unwrapped by him seemed like a pretty sweet deal to me.

"Good," he whispered, kissing me softly. "I'll teach you everything I know."

"I can't wait," I said back to him, my knees weak and my body aching with wanting. There was years' worth of anticipation inside me. I wasn't delicate and really didn't want to wait at all.

"You gave me your word!" The strong voice interrupted the hormone-induced, lust-filled moment and caused the entire dining room to speculate in quiet murmurs.

"What the…?" Sam frowned, squaring his shoulders as he released me and looked towards the sound. Two men were arguing.

"Is that Nate and Abbot?" I asked when I heard another voice say something about "not touching her".

Touching who? Has something happened to Holland? To Jasmine? I hoped Holland wasn't in trouble again.

"You were supposed to keep her safe." The words

weren't spoken as much as they were growled. I thought it came from Nate, but I didn't know him well enough to pick his voice yet. Then I gasped when something hit a wall and someone grunted.

With a quick glance at each other, Sam and I rushed towards the sounds, the sense that something big was going down overtaking me. We arrived in time to find Nate slamming his fist into Abbot's face.

Oh my Lord! I gaped in horror, watching blood run down Abbot's chin. Sam's arm went straight around me as he pulled me against his chest protectively, keeping me a safe distance from the ruckus. But not before I saw Nate punch Kristian in the face too. *Poor Kristian!* Nate's eyes looked wild as he practically foamed at the mouth.

What is going on?

"What are you doing, brother?" Sam demanded, his voice stern but even. I'd never seen anything so frightening in my life and turned away, burying my face in Sam's shirt.

Nate didn't respond. Instead he turned his attention to Jasmine and *growled* at her. "If you lay another fucking hand on my wife, I'll forget you're a woman and make you pay like a man."

Oh, now I know what this is about. When we were getting dressed for the wedding. Holland made some drunken taunting remarks to Jasmine, which was when Jasmine backhanded her. Nate must've seen the bruising, or perhaps Holland dobbed Jasmine in. Either way, this was insane. Nate looked ready to attack his own *mother*.

"Then tell your wife to get with the program. She's either with one of us, or she's a liability." Jasmine's chin tilted up, a defiant set to her jaw. She wasn't backing down.

Neither was Nate. His hulking frame seemed to curl around her menacingly, his voice taking on a tone that sent chills down my spine. "Holland is not yours to order around. She is *mine*. Do you hear me? Touch her and I don't care who you are to me, I will destroy you without mercy." Jasmine's eyes went wide as Nate withdrew his threatening stance. Then he turned and addressed the rest of us. "Don't forget that it's *you* who needs *me*, not the other way around. Touch my wife again—any one of you, for any reason—and I'll make you pay. I promise you that."

Then he turned and stalked off, leaving the rest of us stunned silent. My mind though, was never silent. Like Sam, Nate had been forced to marry Holland. I'd never seen such fury in someone's eyes, but to think that anger had been because Holland had been hurt? As much as I despised strong-armed tactics, Nate had been nothing short of fierce in his defence of my friend. He scared the living crap out of me, but at least he was willing to fight for her honour. I had to wonder if I'd ever inspire that kind of emotion in Sam. Would he ever fight for me?

"You're shaking." Sam's arms tightened around my frame.

"I'm fine," I insisted. "But we need to get them cleaned up. Why don't you get some ice and meet us in Abbot's room? Jasmine and I can help them get there."

Sam looked at his mother with a quirked brow, as if asking 'Is that cool with you?' Jasmine nodded and together we took the twins upstairs, Abbot sporting a split lip and Kristian a cut brow.

"Why didn't you hit him back?" I asked Kristian as I pressed a damp cloth over his eye.

He winced a little from the pain, then met my eyes. "Because he's right. We need him more than he needs us."

"That doesn't give him the right to hit you and get away with it."

He shrugged. "He had to hit someone. If he did nothing, it would mean hurting his wife was OK. Would you prefer that?"

Never. Violence was never the right answer.

"I'd prefer it if no one got hit at all."

"Sometimes fists speak louder than words."

Sam arrived with a bucket of ice, placing a handful inside a napkin and handing it to Kristian. "Think you'll be able to see out of that tomorrow?"

Kristian chuckled a little and shook his head. "Nah, mate, he got me good. Eye's already closing up." He pulled the ice away from his face and showed Sam the swelling on his eye.

"Always has had a good right hook on him. What'd you do, anyway?"

"He didn't do anything," I answered for him, taking his hand and guiding the ice back to his eye.

"I just told him that I didn't know how his wife's face got bruised."

"Which is true," I said. "He wasn't even in the room when it happened."

"When what happened?" Sam asked, looking between us.

I dropped my gaze to the floor. I didn't want to be the one who dobbed in his mother.

Kristian didn't volunteer the information either.

"Somebody had better tell me what the hell is going on," Sam boomed, causing me to jump slightly and close my eyes against the sound. I hated yelling. When I was small and my parents would fight, I used to take all the toys out of my chest and climb inside it with my blanket, then close the lid to muffle the sound. Once, I fell asleep in there and they thought I'd run away. When I woke up, there was a policeman in the living room asking for a recent photo of me. Boy, did I get a whooping over that. I couldn't sit for a whole day, plus they took my toy chest and cut it down as firewood. I just sat on my bed and blocked my ears after that.

"I hit her," Jasmine confessed as she entered the bathroom with a bloodied washcloth in her hands. "She wouldn't shut the fuck up, so I made her. She obviously went crying to Nate over it."

"Nah," Abbot said, leaning against the door frame with his own bag of ice against his lip. "I don't reckon she did."

"Then how did he find out?" Jasmine said.

Tugging his unruly shoulder-length hair behind his ear, Abbot bounced a shoulder. "I don't know. But he came down last night demanding to know what happened. She told him she fell, and he didn't believe her." He nodded towards Kristian. "We backed up her story, but he didn't seem to believe us either."

"Yeah, he put a hole in the wall in our room as a warning. Said it'd be us if he found out we were lying," Kristian added.

"Guess he followed through with his threat, then," I said.

Kristian nodded. "Maybe he kept at her and she cracked, told him the truth. He's had this massive caveman boner for her since they met. He'll do anything to keep her. I suggest we give them some space. He'll calm down. He always does."

Once the twins were cleaned up and Jasmine seemed to relax—with the help of a hefty glut of whiskey in her morning coffee—Sam took me outside for a walk along the beach so I could clear my own head.

"You were pretty great back there, jumping in to take care of the wounded the way you did. I can see why Jasmine thinks you're going to fit in well with the family." He stopped and picked up a shell, throwing it sideways into the water so it skipped along the surface.

"She said that?" After her comment the previous night, I wasn't sure what she thought of me at all.

He nodded, then threw another stone. "Said you'll make a good wife and mother, that she sees you being good for us. She's looking forward to having another woman around the house."

My mind was stuck on the part about being a mother. They expected me to produce *children?*

"And what do you think about all that?" I asked, trying to keep my slight panic hidden.

He looked at me for a moment, then took my hand, lacing our fingers together. "I think you're a hell of a lot stronger and smarter than anyone has ever given you credit for."

I smiled and caught my hair in my free hand, stopping the chocolate strands from whipping me in the face. "Is that a compliment?"

He pulled on my arm a little, guiding me until we were toe to toe. Then he lifted my chin and looked into my eyes. "Yeah, peaches, that's a compliment," he said, just before he brought his mouth to mine. I hesitated, then slowly slipped my arms around his neck and curled my toes in the sand. *God, I love it when he kisses me.*

"Thank you," I murmured when he released me, leaving my cheeks flushed and my legs shaky.

"For kissing you?" He grinned as if he thought that a funny thing to be grateful for.

I guess he's never been hard up for a willing pair of lips to kiss.

I nodded. "And for being nice to me. I know this probably isn't how you imagined getting married, and I know I'm not the ideal choice for a man like you. So I appreciate that you're giving this a chance when you could just as easily be callous and resentful."

He released a slow breath. "Why do you keep putting yourself down like that?"

"I'm not," I argued. "I'm just being honest."

"No. You're being self-deprecating. I've told you that I like you. I've told you that I think you're rare and perfect. Do you think I'm lying to you?"

"No, I just… I think you're being kind."

Placing his hands on my arse, he roughly pulled me flat against his body, his hardness pressing into my soft lower belly. *Oh my.* "Does this feel kind to you, peaches? Or does it feel *hard?"* He ground his hips to further punctuate his words. *Oh my my.*

"H-h-hard," I gasped, my mouth suddenly super dry.

"So, when I tell you that I think you're gorgeous and that I *want* you, do you believe me?" He rolled his hips again.

I closed my eyes. "Y-y-yes. I b-believe you."

"Then I don't want to hear you putting yourself down

or doubting what I think of you again. If I say I like you, if I say I want you, if I say I'm ecstatic that I'm going to be the first man inside that tight little snatch of yours, then that's exactly what I mean. I won't lie to you, Alesha. We might be thieves, but that doesn't mean we're bad people."

"OK," I whispered. "I'm sorry."

He took a hold of my chin. "Don't be sorry. You're a Cartwright now. You don't have to be sorry for anything."

CHAPTER FIVE
I STOLE A UNICORN

HAD I known that I'd soon be on my honeymoon with the sexiest bad boy on the planet, I would've been a little more discerning in my recent underwear and swimsuit purchases. Everything I owned was, in a word, practical. There wasn't a shred of lace or silk anywhere. It was all basic cotton for comfort, and my bathers were black with a high neck and a zip up the back so when I did laps at the local pool, my straps didn't fall down. I didn't do sexy. I'd never had reason to. Before now.

Standing in the warm tropical water in a set of nanna bathers while I tried not to fall over my tongue at the sight of Sam's naked chest only served to remind me exactly how out of my depth I was. I wasn't the girl who got the guy. I was the girl who read the books about the girls who got the guy. This couldn't possibly be my life.

So what if he was a criminal? He was gorgeous, he was fun, and he was kind. I *wanted* him. I wanted him from somewhere deep inside my blood. So he lived on the wrong side of the law? So bloody what.

Wait. So what?

What am I even thinking? Of course it mattered that he was a criminal. It *should* matter. *Shouldn't it?*

But what if it didn't? Now that was something to ponder. Did I seriously not care about the whole family of thieves thing? When I was with him, I didn't care about much more than when he was next going to touch me. The times I did think about his chosen vocation were during these quiet moments when the walls of my new reality wavered, when I felt that perhaps my meeting him was just a dream. That was when I ran through the facts, when I told myself I should care. So maybe I did care that he was a thief, and maybe I didn't. Either way, I was a part of it now.

This was my life.

"Ready, peaches?"

I took a breath, meeting his eyes as I pulled my mask over my head. "As I'll ever be."

After getting past the drama of the morning, Sam and I gravitated towards activities more fitting of a newlywed couple on their first island adventure. No, we didn't start bunny humping in our room (get your mind out of the gutter). We booked a snorkelling adventure instead. Right now, to add to my sexy bathers, I was also wearing a giant pair of flippers, half-face goggles and a snorkel. Say it all together, ladies and gentlemen—se-xy! That's right, walking like a duck with my eyeballs sucking out of my face and my lips protruding around a plastic tube was as alluring as it got.

Somehow, when Sam put the exact same gear on his body, he *did* look hot. There wasn't a single way in the world to make that godlike man look unattractive. Go figure.

Gliding forwards in the water, we followed along the reef, watching colourful fish dart in and out of the brilliant coral. At one point, Sam took my hand as we swam along together. It was like floating through a dream in which I ceased to be me. The Alesha I was, the one who lived in Melbourne, worked with the dead and constantly worried what her father thought wasn't in the water with me. I was someone else. I was Peaches.

Pointing ahead, Sam directed my attention towards the ocean floor where a ray was shuffling about in the sand and kicking up a dusty cloud. He signalled to dive down farther and we released our hands, taking a deep breath and angling ourselves towards the ray.

Keeping at a respectful distance, we watched it shuffling, most likely hunting out a food source. It kind of reminded me of a little puppy playing in the dirt and I couldn't help but laugh—which was probably a bad idea under the water, because I couldn't really coordinate holding my breath while laughing and ended up sucking in some air. Except there wasn't any air, only water, and people can't breathe under water.

Needing oxygen faster than a crack whore needed a hit, I powered myself towards the surface, bursting through to take great gulps of air, blissfully easing the burning in my lungs.

"Holy crap," I gasped, pulling the goggles from my eyes and wiping a hand over my face. *That was close.*

"You all right?" Sam popped up only seconds later, a concerned look creasing his brow as he removed his gear.

"Yeah." I looked towards the beach. "I just ran out of breath."

He placed a hand against the side of my face, his thumb caressing my cheek. "You scared me."

"I'm OK." *Albeit horribly embarrassed.*

Bringing his body closer, I felt the warmth of his chest and then his mouth pressing against mine, kissing me softly with just a tiny bit of tongue. I could taste the salt of the sea as I wrapped my arms around his neck to deepen the kiss. He made me nervous and eager. I wanted to experience what it was like to be this new woman, the object of Sam's desire.

"Maybe it's time to head back," Sam suggested when we gave our lips a brief pause. Then he kissed me again as if he couldn't stop himself. I had to wonder if he really wanted me as much as he claimed, or if he was just excited by the fact that I was still a virgin. To me, it was an embarrassment. But to him, it was arousing. I didn't really get that about men. Why would having sex with a nervous girl who was likely to bleed everywhere be a turn-on? Wouldn't it be better to sleep with a woman who knew what she was doing and could therefore rock your world? For example, I read once that when Marie Antoinette married Louis XVI, they were both virgins and had no idea what they were doing. It was rumoured that the reason she couldn't get pregnant was because they were doing it in the wrong hole (that's her butthole for the ill-informed) and the moment they started using the right one, she was pregnant pretty much straight away. Talk about awkward! I didn't understand the allure of that much cluelessness.

"Mmm, I'm hungry," I responded against his lips,

because I was. We'd missed breakfast, and it was well past lunch.

Pausing his exploration of my mouth, he looked at me and smiled. "I like you, peaches. I like that you know what you want."

There was a lot I wanted that I didn't say out loud. If he heard half the thoughts that went on in my mind, he'd probably run for the hills.

"I don't mind you either."

Heading back to shore, we didn't waste any time returning our equipment before we headed up to our room, holding hands the entire way. This would be the first time that Sam had shown any sort of affection or intimacy towards me behind a closed door.

I could finally lose my virginity tonight.

That was a funny saying, 'losing one's virginity'. It was spoken about like it was an actual thing instead of an experience, and to speak of losing something implies that you want it to be found. Did anyone want it back once they got rid of it? Based on what I'd seen a couple of porn stars do, I'd say no.

As we walked down the hallway towards our room, I stole a glance at Sam's face. He must've felt my nerves because he gave my hand a squeeze and said, "Relax, I plan to feed you."

Did that mean he planned to feed me his cock? I'd seen some guy offer his dick as a substitute for food before. Holland and I had gone through a phase in our teens where we watched Internet porn, then discussed what we'd seen. It was both out of defiance and curiosity, because my dad wouldn't let me be a part of the sex-ed classes at school, and since my mother had taken off by that stage, Holland felt it was her duty as my best friend to inform me. Somehow, I didn't think 'devouring pork swords' was covered in class.

"Why don't you grab a shower, and I'll call room service. Anything you prefer? A burger?" He grinned, and I had a vague memory of demanding a burger from him the night before.

"Yeah, but only if it has bacon on it. And lots of fries. You can't have a burger without fries."

"Duly noted." He grinned, then picked up the phone, dialling through to reception. Once he connected, I turned and headed for the bathroom. "Peaches," he called after me, his hand covering the receiver as he beckoned me closer. I kept moving until I was standing directly in front of him. Then he gestured for me to turn around while he waited for whoever was on the other end.

Curious, I did as he asked, then almost stopped breathing when I felt his fingers on the zipper of my bathers, pulling it down to where it ended just below my shoulder blades. I held my breath the entire time, each release of the teeth like an incredibly slow seduction. *Do it!* my brain screamed. *Take me and get this stupid rite of passage over with.* I honestly didn't want to draw it out. The faster we busted past that hymen of mine, the faster we could get to the good stuff. Every account I'd ever heard or read said it was better the next time, and I was growing impatient.

He pressed a tender kiss against my skin. "Enjoy your shower," he said before turning his attention back to our food order. "Yes. Room 318." As he relayed our order, he smiled at me and nodded towards the bathroom. I hadn't moved yet, still buzzing with anticipation for something, *anything*. I wanted more than kissing and teasing. "Go." He shooed me away with a laugh and I did as I was told, an automatic response that was a result of incredibly strict parenting.

As I turned on the shower, I thought for a moment about my father. He was going to be furious with me. Not only did I get married without inviting him, but I didn't do it in a church, and as far as I knew, the Cartwrights weren't the religious type. He wasn't going to take the news of his only daughter's nuptials well at all.

I did my best to put the thought of his reaction out of my mind. I'd been allowed to call him to let him know I was leaving the country—a call I had to make on speaker with a couple of Cartwrights listening in, a precautionary tactic to make sure I wasn't reported missing—but I wasn't sure if I'd get to see my family again when we returned to Australia. I didn't know how strict my imprisonment disguised as a marriage really was.

Stop thinking, Alesha. There are no answers here, and Sam is waiting. Focus on him. Just him.

Shutting off the water, I stepped out of the shower and looked around. Once again, I hadn't brought anything to change into. If I had some sexy sort of negligée, that would've been perfect. But since I didn't, the hotel robes and nothing else would have to do. It seemed to work well for Julia Roberts in *Pretty Woman*.

When I opened the door, my heart thumping a little faster than normal, Sam came straight for me, placing his hands on my hips before moving into the bathroom. "God,

I love that mango smell." He went straight for the shower and turned it on, holding his hand under the spray for a second to check the temperature. "You planning on watching?" he asked, pulling his worn T-shirt over his head and baring that beautifully defined chest of his.

I didn't look away, but I did blush. "You left the door open."

He grinned. "That's because you're standing right against it." Hooking his fingers in the waistband of his board shorts, he met my eyes with quirked brow. I had to swallow a lump in my throat, but I still didn't look away. "OK then." He shrugged and pushed his shorts and anything he had on underneath them to the floor, then stood there in all his glory, hands on his hips.

"Holy mother of God," I gasped, my eyes no doubt wide with shock. "You have a small child's arm for a penis. And that hasn't even grown yet, right? I mean, it's going to get"—I gulped—"bigger, isn't it?" Maybe I could handle being a virgin for a *bit* longer.

"It is," he responded—looking incredibly pleased with himself, I might add.

"It's going to split me in two!" I blurted, horrified. That wasn't normal. Men didn't have appendages like that in real life, no way. I'd seen hundreds of penises during my job, but they were all flaccid and, er... dead, so I'd tried not to look. The hard and living ones I'd seen had only been via porn, and since they were only on a small computer screen, even the biggest porn dicks didn't look that big. His thing looked like a cannon. A real-life motherfucking cannon.

"It won't split you in two." He chuckled. "You'll

stretch. But don't worry, I'm not giving you this until you're ready for it."

I couldn't stop staring at it. "I am not ready for *that*."

He chuckled again, making the damn thing bounce along with his shoulders. I couldn't get over the size of him. Staring at it, I was transported back to the time our school had gone to a petting zoo where they had a donkey that let its dick hang low and swing while it nibbled on hay and violated the innocent eyes of a bunch of eight-year-olds. *That's* what it reminded me of. A donkey dick.

"Jeez, peaches, you're lucky I've got such good self-esteem or I'd develop a complex." He stepped into the shower cubicle and closed the door. It was clear though, so I could see right through it.

"I'm sorry," I started. "I didn't me—"

"Cartwrights don't apologise, Alesha." He opened the shower door just enough to pop his head out and look me in the eye. "Own what you say and do, and never take someone else's shit on board. You're the only person who knows the real truth behind your thoughts and actions, and as long as you can live with yourself, that's all that matters."

"Is that what you tell yourself to justify what you do?"

Rubbing shampoo through his dark hair, he held his head beneath the spray and spoke to me while he rinsed. "We take things that don't belong to us and sell it for our own profit. That doesn't make us bad people, it makes us opportunists. We aren't hurting anyone. They're all insured."

"Is that something you check first?"

"Yep." He shut off the shower, and I grabbed a towel and held it out to him. He dried off his hair first. I tried not to look but failed, staring at the movement of his cock with his body. The way it swayed was slightly hypnotic. If he clicked and told me I was a chicken, I'd probably start squawking. "It's how we know who to hit and what to take."

With a quick shake of my head, I made myself look at his eyes. "Why Holland?"

He wrapped the towel around his hips. *My Lord, this man can wear anything and look good.*

"She wasn't the mark. Nate went rogue on that one."

"What do you mean? Who was the mark?"

"He was in that bar looking for someone else. But he saw Holland, got a massive boner over her and threw the plan out the window."

"Well, who was he looking for? One of the girls in the hens party?"

"You could say that."

The night Holland and Nate had met, we'd been out at a karaoke bar because of a bachelorette party for my cousin. Holland loved karaoke and got up on stage when-ever she could. She was good, like *really* good. And when she'd finished her song, Nate had approached her and talked his way into her bed. He'd seemed so nice and genuine that I was shocked when she told me he robbed her the next morning. That night was the catalyst of all the events that led us right here, right now, married to virtual strangers. Hot strangers, but strangers nonetheless.

"What do you mean? Who—" That's when it hit me. The police had told us that the Cartwrights preyed on *lonely* women. "Oh my God." I took a couple of steps back. "It was me, wasn't it?" It made sense. I was single, I had some pretty cool stuff at my place, and I was insured for it all, having recently changed insurance companies too. "Of course it was me."

Suddenly, my knees gave out and I dropped my weight on the closed lid of the toilet. They'd never wanted me. They'd just wanted my stuff. Holland was the only reason I was here. Had their plan worked out, I'd just be another statistic, another notch in the success column, and they'd have moved on without giving me a thought.

I was a job. A fucking *job*. I felt sick. God, I was the worst kind of joke. "I am so fucking pathetic."

Sam was in front of me in a flash, kneeling at my feet and gathering my hands in his. "What did I say about putting yourself down? The way all this worked out, I'm glad it wasn't you. If you'd gone home with my brother and given your virg—"

"I wouldn't have." Despite feeling shell-shocked over the fact that I was their target, I had no doubt that they would've failed. I didn't respond to Nate the way I responded to Sam. He never would've made it back to my house.

"You say that now, but that guy can talk any woman into his bed. I've seen it."

"Well, I would've been the kryptonite that would turn him from lady killer to mere mortal. If he'd approached me, I would've clammed up. At best, I'd have embarrassed myself and bolted. That's just what I do around men. I can't talk to them."

"You talk to me."

"That's because you're special."

He frowned a little. "Because we're married?"

"No. From the moment I met you, I don't know why, but you make me feel safe. And you don't freak out when my weird comes out of my mouth. I don't feel so awkward when I'm with you."

"And you felt like that instantly?" I could understand why he was questioning it. In his presence, I had been quite verbal, verging on outgoing. My shy only really kicked in around the rest of his family.

I nodded. "From the moment you put your arm around my shoulders and offered me a beer."

"Huh." He seemed to mull the information over in his mind for a moment as a slow smile crept over his face. "So let me get this straight. If my brother, the man with the golden tongue, had approached you in that club, there's no way you would've gone home with him?"

"That's right," I said with absolute conviction. *I wouldn't have been able to form a word, let alone invite him home with me.*

His smile grew wider. "But you probably would've left with me?"

I felt the blush creep over my cheeks as a smile fought with my lips. "Probably."

His eyes positively shone with delight. "You're a unicorn."

"What?" I couldn't help but laugh.

"No woman resists my brother. I believe you're the only one who can. Therefore, you're a unicorn."

"Maybe I was just made for you to find?" I suggested. It was cheesy and wishy-washy, but maybe it was also true.

Reaching up, he brushed the backs of his fingers against my flushed cheek. "To *steal*. I'm a thief. I stole you. I stole a unicorn. And now you're mine." He grinned and then pulled me to my feet, kissing me the way I always longed to be kissed. He held me with both hands cradling my face like I was the most precious thing in the world. He made me feel safe. He made me feel special. He made me feel *wanted*.

If this was what it was to be stolen, I never wanted to be recovered. I wanted to stay gone.

"I AM STUFFED," I said, flicking a fry onto my plate because I couldn't face eating anymore. I leaned back and ran a hand over my belly.

"For a skinny girl, you can certainly pack it away." Sam wiped his mouth with a napkin, then scrunched it up and dropped it on his room service tray. "I can't eat any more either."

"Want to compare food babies?" I asked, leaning back on the bed against the pillows, lifting my top enough so my stomach poked out. I'd since pulled on a pair of pink cotton panties, my blue-checked sleep shorts and a white singlet. I'd skipped the bra because the top had one of those shelf bras in it and I didn't need the support.

"Is the pope Catholic?" He grinned and slid up to me, placing his hips next to mine. He was only wearing a pair of burgundy boxers and briefs. I didn't think it was normal to wear briefs under boxers, but my guess was that if he didn't wear the briefs, that third leg he had going on would constantly hang out the bottom.

"I think mine is bigger," I said, pushing my stomach up so it was as round as possible.

"Nope, I totally win this one. Your little pot has nothing on this keg." Filling his stomach with air, he pushed it high enough that mine was but a hill to his mountain.

"That's cheating."

"Let out your breath and then tell me you weren't doing exactly the same thing." Rolling onto his side, he laid a warm hand over my belly, sending a thousand little zings all through me. I sighed from his touch and my stomach deflated. "I knew it." He chuckled, his fingers moving lightly against my skin.

It felt amazing to be touched. I turned my head to face him. "Will you kiss me, Sam?"

I didn't need to ask twice. His mouth tasted mine, gentle lips and probing tongue. Then I let out the tiniest moan, which caused him to groan and deepen our connection, his tongue diving farther, his hand sliding to my hip and gripping tighter, pulling me flush against him.

With my fingers in his hair, I responded as best I knew how. I was eager, perhaps too eager, because when those endorphins kicked in, I couldn't stop myself from making all these crazy-sounding noises or from rubbing my body against his. He groaned back and slid his hand beneath my top, fingers pressing into my back like he was trying to bring me even closer.

I rolled my hips.

"Peaches." The word came out as a moan, and it sounded like a good kind of moan, so I did it again. He was so hard, and I wasn't talking about his muscles. I could feel him pressing against my thigh. I liked that I was doing this to him. "Jesus," he groaned, his hands going back to my hips and digging in a little. It kind of hurt, but in a good way. The slight pain felt like his answer to the aching need that was building inside of me. *Why haven't I been making out with guys all my life? This is amazing and so much better than that drunken moment ten years ago.*

Which was when it hit me: it wouldn't have felt this way with anyone else. It felt this way because there was something special about the man I was with. Simply put, he felt right.

"I want more," I gasped, hooking my leg over his and rocking myself against him. I needed some sort of pressure to ease the throbbing need I was experiencing.

He hummed in this really sexy way, then rolled onto his back, bringing me with him. I spread my legs wide, straddling him while our mouths stayed joined, moving, licking, sucking and nibbling. I didn't want to stop kissing him. He tasted so good that I thought I'd rather die than be forced to stop.

"Ohhh," I moaned when he positioned my hips so his hard length was pressed perfectly against my ache. He reached up and slid his fingers into my hair, brushing it back from my face as he held me still then looked into my eyes. He rolled his hips. My eyes lost focus and my mouth fell open. "More." I placed my palms on his chest and ground myself against him, his long shaft feeling so good against that empty yearning. I couldn't stop myself from moving, needing the friction so desperately.

"That's it, peaches. Take what you need from me. Let yourself go."

There was this insane kind of feeling going on in my head, like a thick cloud of desperation driving my movement, urging me to grind against him, faster, harder, until…

"Holy fuck!" My entire body shook, an explosion occurring between my legs as whimpers leapt out of my throat. For some reason, my breasts ached, and I couldn't stop myself from grabbing them and arching my back while my hips rocked and rocked until the spasms in my core turned into tiny euphoric waves. A warm and fuzzy feeling buzzed all over my skin as a dopey smile curled my lips.

Then I opened my eyes and reality set in.

"Oh my God," I gasped, releasing my breasts and scrambling off Sam's lap. "What the hell was *that*?" I was so embarrassed. It was the first time we'd made out, and I'd just dry humped him and grabbed my tits. What did he think of me?

"That," he said with a grin before he sucked gently on my lower lip, "was the hottest fucking thing I've ever seen."

"Really?" It didn't feel hot in the aftermath. It felt out of control and over the top.

He pulled at his bottom lip with his teeth and nodded. "Incredibly hot. Watching you lose control like that. Mmm, it was a beautiful thing to witness. Was that your first orgasm, or have you—"

"Masturbated? No. No way. I never…." My eyes were wide as I shook my head. Then I met his eyes and a smile spread over my lips. "I had an orgasm." A sudden giggle burst past my lips, and I covered my mouth with my hand.

"Yeah you did. It was so hot I almost blew in my pants watching you."

"You mean you didn't have one too?" The idea

shocked me. I thought guys always had one. Did that mean I'd done something wrong?

Sliding his hand into my hair, he pulled me closer so he could kiss me. "Let's just focus on you for now. I can wait."

"But that doesn't seem fair. Don't you want to... finish too?"

He ran his fingers through my hair. "Sometimes the reward is in the build-up."

"If you say so. But I don't want to be one of those selfish lovers. I've heard about them, and I want to give just as much as I receive."

It was a dead serious comment, but for some reason Sam found it the funniest thing. He laughed and gathered me in his arms, kissing my head before telling me to get some rest.

His breathing seemed to even out fairly quickly, but I couldn't quite relax while lying in bed with my head and hands resting against the most divine-looking chest I'd ever seen. I wriggled against him, trying to get comfortable while also trying not to let my hand wander down, down his chest and to his boxer area. I wanted to know if he was still hard or if it would still go down even if he didn't come, and it was making my hand itch with curiosity.

"Sleep," he commanded when I wouldn't stop wriggling.

So I closed my eyes and tried my best to do just that. But I couldn't. I could only think about the hot hard male lying next to me, and the gentle throbbing taking place between my thighs.

"Sam?"

"Yes, peaches?"

"Will you kiss me again?"

When he didn't answer right away, I grew a little worried, but then I noticed the sheet lift right above his crotch and I knew. There wasn't going to be much sleeping tonight.

"I'M READY," I rasped, my body aching so delectably that I couldn't stand it anymore.

Sam paused his tongue's torture of my nipple, but his fingers continued moving inside me. It felt so good. I wanted more, more, *more.*

"Not yet."

"Please. I want to." I moved my hips against his hand, a night filled with orgasm after orgasm having left me feeling greedy. I knew there was something I was missing, and I wanted it. Now. I didn't want to be patient. I'd been patient all my life.

His mouth returned to my nipple as he added an extra finger, pushing a little deeper, stretching me a little farther. He made a soft rumble in his throat that sounded like plea-sure, and I loved that something we did elicited such a response.

I moved against his hand, whimpering and gasping. My lady parts had never known such attention. I felt like an addict, each orgasm spiralling me closer to obsession.

Then he pressed this part inside me that caused my eyes to roll back in my head. "Oh yes." It turned out that I was quite vocal too. Sam seemed to like it; he made that rumbling noise a lot when I told him what I wanted. He even asked me questions to keep me talking.

"You like that?"

I nodded. "I do."

"How about this?"

I felt myself stretching more as it seemed like he was adding yet another finger and massaging my internal walls with firmer strokes. The aching was sublime.

My hands flew down and wrapped around his wrist. "Oh, God, *yes!*"

His mouth captured mine, my cries of ecstasy muffled in the kiss that started aggressive then became tender as the tremors subsided. I'd lost count of how many orgasms I'd received.

"I love making you come," Sam whispered against my lips. "I adore that I'm the only man who's ever made you moan and writhe under my touch."

"When do I get to be the one to make you come?" He had so far seen and explored almost every part of me, yet he remained in his boxers. I didn't think that was fair.

He grinned and kissed me some more. "So impatient." Kiss. "So curious." Suck. "So insatiable." Nibble. "You still want more?"

"Yes." I slid my hands down his back, dragging my nails over his flesh before pausing at his waist, tucking my fingers beneath the cotton. "I want to see it. I want to feel it, and…." I felt a little nervous saying the next part.

"And?"

"I want to taste it."

He inhaled deeply, his breath shaking as though he was struggling with his control.

"Please, Sam. I want to do it all. I want to know what

it's like to have you inside me." I moved my hand to the front of his boxers and boldly massaged his hard length.

"Oh, peaches. You know what you do to me. I've been showing you how much I want you all night."

"Then take me. Please. I want it all. I don't want to wait."

Pulling back, he looked deep in my eyes. "I don't want to hurt you."

"You won't. You said it yourself, I'll stretch, right?"

"Yes, but it's your first time. It's going to hurt no matter what."

"I know, but I want it. I want to feel my husband inside me."

He dropped his forehead against mine and drew another ragged breath. "Your husband," he repeated, testing the word out on his tongue like a foreign dialect. "Say it again."

I rolled my body beneath him, speaking in gasps. "I want to feel my husband inside me. I want you to make me yours."

"Mine," he said. "Only mine."

"Yes," I whispered, pulling him closer. "My first. My only."

He released a moan as he sat back and hooked his fingers into the waistband of his boxers. "If it gets too much, you say stop and I'll stop, OK?"

"OK." Nervous and excited butterflies flapped about in my stomach and fluttered in my chest. This was it. The moment I'd been waiting for. I felt no fear over his size anymore; his expert touch had seen to it that I was relaxed beyond words. Now I was desperate to please him.

"Look how excited you are." He chuckled as he

stepped off the bed and pushed his boxers and briefs to the floor. When he stood back up, his cock stood proudly with him. And I couldn't help myself, I licked my lips. "That's a better reaction than when you saw it earlier."

"That's because I was shocked last time. This time I knew what to expect."

He placed a knee back on the bed. "I like this reaction much better."

As he knelt before me, I met him in the same position, our naked bodies pressing together as we kissed.

"Tell me what you want," he said.

"I want to touch you," I whispered against his lips.

"Then touch me."

He groaned as I slid my hands down his chest, lower, lower. I felt his stomach jolt beneath my fingers, heard his breath catch as I stroked lightly up his shaft, then saw his cock jump when I wrapped my hand around its girth. My fingers barely touched it.

"Is this OK?" I asked, moving my hand up and down.

"It's more than OK." His voice was thick, his eyelids looking heavy.

Leaning down, I inspected his long, thick member. It kind of reminded me of an eyeless worm, but a massive one like those sand worms from *Dune*. I was fascinated.

"Can I lick it?" There was a small bead of arousal on his tip, and I really wanted to know what it tasted like.

"As long as you don't try to break it or bite it, you can do anything you like."

With my eyes on his, I held his dick in my hand as I gave it a long, slow lick right over the swollen head. It tasted salty, like kissing him in the ocean had.

"Fuck, you're so beautiful."

It was the first time he'd said that. He'd called me gorgeous, but it had felt more like a comment on my personality than how I appeared in his eyes. But in that moment, as his fingers caressed the side of my face, I felt as though he really meant it. I felt like he *saw* something in me I'd never known existed. *Beauty*.

I smiled then licked his tip again, sucking a little before I parted my lips as wide as I could and took him in my mouth. I'd barely gotten past that ridged part where the helmet became the shaft when his fingers tightened in my hair and he hissed, "Stop," through his teeth.

"Did I do something wrong?" I asked, releasing him immediately.

He shook his head, then climbed over me until I lay back beneath him. "Not a thing. You're perfect." He sucked my lip. "I just won't last long that way. If I'm going to come, I want it to be inside my wife."

A huge grin spread across my face, and I shifted my legs so I could open them for him. He'd called me his wife. "I want that too."

With his eyes locked on mine, he reached between us and ran his tip against my seam. I was finally going to understand what all the fuss was about. Foreplay had been amazing, but this—him inside me—was what I'd been waiting for. I was more than ready.

"Relax. I'll go slow, and we can stop at any time," he assured me.

Releasing a slow breath, I nodded and placed my hands against his firm chest. "I trust you." I could feel his heart raging beneath his skin. *Could he possibly be as nervous as me?*

I felt him push in slightly. I sucked in my breath with the accompanying burn. He was so big. I felt too tight.

"You OK?" He stilled and I realised that my nails were digging into his skin. I willed myself to relax, then nodded.

"I'm OK."

He pushed a little more and I felt myself stretching, and stretching. The burn was a little less, but it was still there, along with this wonderful feeling that I didn't know how to describe yet. All I knew for sure was that I didn't want him to stop. I wanted him to push farther, deeper.

"More," I gasped.

He pushed again, and a sudden piercing pain flashed, then burned. I cried out. *What the hell?* He stopped moving and leaned down to kiss me, slowly, softly, a hand caressing my face while the other kept him braced above me.

"I'm sorry. Do you want me to stop?" His voice was almost a whisper, filled with concern as well as desire and his strained control.

"Cartwrights don't apologise," I gasped, causing him to chuckle lightly, breathlessly. "Don't stop. I want you to keep going."

His push was torturously slow, giving my body the time it needed to fully adjust both to his length and his girth. It was a strange sensation, uncomfortable and inde-scribably good all at once, with my body aching for more still. The moment he moved back and forth a touch, I knew it was friction I was craving.

"Yes," I said with a shaky voice, clinging to him while doing my best not to clench around him.

He moved a little more and I moaned, the burn becoming a memory, taken over by a wonderful pressure that built with each languid stroke of his cock against my insides.

"I don't know how long I can last," he ground out. "You feel so fucking amazing."

"So do you," I gasped. "Oh God, so do you." I moved my hands across his chest, resting them on his arms as I looked into the eyes of the man who was connected to my body in the most pure and carnal way a man and woman could join. *One flesh.*

As he moved inside me, I couldn't escape the teachings instilled in me from a young age, that marriage was sacred and the most intimate of all human relationships, uniting a man and a woman with a promise and then a consummation where they became one flesh, a new kinship forming from the most intimate of human bonds. For the first time in my adult life, I was glad I'd waited, glad I'd kept my virginity for this one perfect moment. I could feel myself changing, opening for him, bonding to him. He was my new reality.

"The things I want to do to your body, peaches," he grunted, his hot breath washing over my skin as his mouth moved along my collarbone, trailing up my neck. "But you're so sweet and innocent. So *sweet.*"

When his hips ground against me and his cock pressed a little deeper, I gasped and arched my back. I didn't feel so innocent anymore. Despite my romantic thoughts, my body was full of wanton craving.

"I don't want to be sweet," I said, words mere gasps and whispers. "I don't want to be innocent either. I want you to take me, Sam. Do all the dirty things to me you imagine. I want it. Please, make me dirty. So dirty."

"Fucking hell," he groaned, pistoning his hips. In and out, in and out. "You are so fucking hot. I can't hold on."

Neither could I. The pressure built and built. I felt set to explode.

"Oh God. Sam." My fingers dug into his arms.

"Alesha."

He said my name as a sigh and then shuddered over me, his hips continuing to move until I did the same, my internal muscles gripping him tight and causing him to hiss and shudder some more.

Staying inside me, he kissed me languidly until the pulsing in our connection subsided. Then he ran a hand over my hair. "You are amazing. Brilliant. Sexy."

I grinned. "You weren't so bad yourself."

"I barely made it past the first couple of strokes. That dirty stuff is going to have to wait for another time."

I blushed a little as the words I'd spoken in the throes of ecstasy returned to me. "I may have gotten a little carried away with the talking."

His fingers gripped my hip and squeezed. "Oh no, peaches, don't you take it back. I have every intention of turning you into a *very* dirty girl."

Placing my hands over my face, I couldn't suppress my giggle. Talking about that now that the lust haze had cleared felt a little like teasing. I met his eyes. "Stop. You can't tease me over the things I say when you're balls deep inside me."

"You mean like I am now?" He wriggled his hips a little, grinning.

"Yes. And any time we're naked. I can't be held responsible for what comes out of my mouth."

With a hum, he took my mouth in his. "I love the

things you say when you're naked. They're pure and true, just like you are."

"They just pop out. I feel silly for saying them."

"Don't. It's hot. I love it. And I'm really going to enjoy making you my dirty girl." He grinned and tickled my side lightly until I giggled and squirmed. Then he kissed me, caressing the side of my face. "Are you OK?"

I released a contented sigh and nodded. "I'm more than OK." I smiled, running my hand down his chest. "I'm actually kind of perfect."

CHAPTER SEVEN
THE FAMILY BUSINESS

"I NEVER THOUGHT it would be that amazing. Especially not the first time."

"*You* were amazing," Sam said, kissing me again before slowly pulling out of me. It was an odd sensation, and I felt the need to squeeze my pelvic floor the moment I was empty.

"Let me get something to help you clean up," he offered.

As he hopped off the bed, I felt it, this warm seeping feeling of something coming out of me. I tried to squeeze harder but I could still feel it.

Oh no. Is that... blood? Did he actually tear me with that big cock of his, and now I'm bleeding everywhere?

I sat up suddenly, almost too afraid to look but forcing myself to assess the carnage so I'd know if I needed immediate help. *What's the emergency services number in the Cook Islands?*

"What the...?" What I saw on the sheets wasn't blood at all, but this milky-coloured gunk that was streaked with pink. *Did that come from me?* "Oh, yuck," I muttered, looking around the room for tissues or something to clean it up. I had no idea if that was normal or not. Holland had always regaled me with detailed tales of her sexual encounters, but she'd never mentioned *this*. I wanted it gone before Sam saw it and never wanted to touch me again.

Too late.

"I don't think you bled much," he said when he re-entered the room with a washcloth in hand.

Desperate to hide the mess and having nothing to wipe it away with, I shifted to the side and covered it with my thigh.

"Is that normal?" I asked, trying to assume some sort of sexy-looking pose so I didn't look like I'd just given birth to a glob. I went with my knees to the side and an arm over my head. It felt very 'draw me like one of your French girls'.

Sam knelt on the bed, then tapped my top knee. "Open."

A coy smile spread across my lips. "Why?"

He lifted the washcloth. "So I can clean you."

My cheeks burned over the thought of letting him wash my private area. "Oh. No. I can do that." I reached for the cloth but he held it out of my grasp.

"It would be my pleasure." He pulled on my knee a little but I clamped my legs shut.

"Nah." I wrinkled my nose and shook my head.

He laughed. "There's no need to be embarrassed, peaches. It's my mess too."

When I took a moment to meet his eyes, I saw both

determination and kindness in them. He obviously really wanted to do this.

"I can clean myself," I said again.

"I know, but I want to take care if you. Can you let me do that?"

Taking a deep breath, I slowly lifted my knee, granting him access to the massacre between my thighs. Strangely, he didn't even flinch. *Maybe this is normal.*

"You might want to lie back and press your knees together next time. You have semen all over your thigh." He lifted my leg and wiped away the streaky goop.

Semen. *That's* what it was. *Of course.* I felt so relieved.

"Why isn't there a bunch of blood?" I asked as he was finishing up. "I thought I was supposed to bleed."

"Not everyone does. There was a little, but it was mostly mixed in with that load I shot inside you." He gave me a half grin and a wink.

"That's really crass." I giggled.

"Yeah but you like it." He gently pinched my arse and I giggled again.

"You know, I think I like everything about you, Sam."

He seemed surprised as he set the cloth aside and lay on the bed beside me, his eyebrows lifting as if he thought it was a strange thing to say.

"Should I not?" I asked as he tucked his hand behind his head.

"I don't know. You just surprise me."

"In what way?"

"In every way. You've taken all this extremely well."

I flipped over to my stomach. "Worried you've married someone slightly insane? Think I might boil your bunny?"

I was smiling as I said it, but his eyes found mine quickly. "I'm joking." I laughed.

"I don't think you're insane. A little crazy maybe, but not insane."

"That makes it so much better." There was sarcasm in my tone, but I didn't take any offence. I'd never claimed to be normal.

He turned his body to face mine and started running his fingers up and down my back. I closed my eyes.

"That feels really nice," I said, happy to move on to other things, like sleeping for instance.

He kept his fingers moving soothingly, but it was like I could hear his brain thinking, so I knew we were going to keep talking. "I guess I just don't understand why a girl as sweet and amazing as you could be interested in what I have to offer. I mean, I get that you weren't given a hell of a lot of choice, but you're just so… cool with it."

I opened my eyes again. "Would you rather I hated you?"

He shook his head slowly, his expression telling me that the idea pained him.

"Would you rather I was scared and crying all the time?"

His expression remained the same as he shook his head again.

"Then what would you have me do?"

"I don't know. But we barely know each other. I wonder if there will come a moment when you stop for a second and take a look around, only to realise that this isn't what you want."

"My whole life has been something I don't want."

"What do you mean?" His expression morphed into

concern, and it took a moment for me to realise why he reacted that way.

"I don't want my life over, if that's what you're thinking. It's just that I've *never* really been given a choice. I'm the girl who does what she's told. I'm the best friend's sidekick. I'm the daughter who never complains. This marriage is probably the first real decision I've ever made for me. Granted, the alternative wasn't the best option, but at least I had a choice. I even got to choose you." When his expression grew curious, I elaborated. "Jasmine told me that if I wanted to live, I could marry Toby. I said no, that I wanted you. She agreed."

"Huh." His hand stopped moving and he rolled onto his back, raking his fingers through his hair.

I pushed up onto my elbows. "Does that bother you?"

He lowered his hands and rested one on the curve of my arse. "Honestly?"

"Yes."

"I don't know how I feel about this entire situation. I mean, I like you. A lot. When you and Holland busted into our property, I thought you had a lot of spunk in you. I thought the way you fought Toby off was the most entertaining thing I'd seen in a long time. Then I liked you more as the evening went on. Did I want to sleep with you? Yes. But did I think I'd found my future wife? No. I'm thirty-five, and the thought of getting married has never crossed my mind. But Jasmine says jump and we say how high."

"Is that the only reason you agreed to marry me? Because she told you to jump?"

He ran a single finger up the centre of my spine. "I agreed because I liked you and the alternative was...." He paused and frowned. "I didn't want that to happen to you. You didn't deserve that."

"So you wanted me more than you wanted me dead?"

"That's very blunt, but yes. I wanted you, and I didn't want to be responsible for ending your life."

"Have you ever killed someone before?"

"Never." His response was so fast that I was sure killing would never be a part of his job description. I felt glad over that. I'd witnessed too many sorrow-filled loved ones at funerals over the years. The people who were taken suddenly and violently were always the worst.

"Have you ever seen a dead body before?"

"A couple of drownings at the beach but never close up. Nothing like you would've seen."

"Do you find that odd about me?" I asked. My job had always been a fantastic man repellent.

"Well, I think we've already established that you're a little odd." He tapped me on the nose, then added, "In the best possible way."

"You're the one who married a stranger because your mum told you to. If I'm odd, then what does that make you?"

He smiled. "Completely mental. A little spontaneous."

"You weren't nervous about going through with it?"

"You couldn't tell?"

I scrunched my nose. "You were kind of drunk."

"A better man might apologise for that," he said.

"But you're a Cartwright so you won't."

He grinned. "You're catching on quick. But yes, I was nervous and I hit the liquid courage a little too hard. Nate and I both did. It was a lot to take in. One day he's playing a game of cat and mouse with a girl he was into, and the next everything blew up in our faces and we needed to marry that girl and her friend to save them. We might be criminals, but we have hearts."

"What made Jasmine decide death or marriage was the only answer?"

"I don't fucking know. Women's logic, I guess."

"That would mean I'd understand it."

He chuckled and rolled onto his back, looking up at the ceiling. "I wasn't part of the conversation, only the result. But from what I gathered, Nate was the one who brought up the marriage idea."

"So it was a 'keep your friends close and your enemies closer' kind of deal?"

"Maybe." He didn't seem convinced, and I had a moment where I felt that Sam was just as lost as I was, always going along with choices that weren't his. Would he be the one who would look around one day and not want me anymore? Or would he always do what he was told out of loyalty? He seemed very loyal.

"Why don't you tell me about *your* family," he said after a moment of quiet, obviously tired of talking about his own.

I sighed. "There isn't a whole lot to tell. There's my dad—he's a funeral director. He's incredibly devout and believes that all lessons in life can be learned from scripture, and that as long as we have the Bible in our lives, we don't need anything else. There's my brother. He's the golden child who married his high school sweetheart and followed my dad into the family business by becoming an embalmer. He has two perfect children on top of that. My mother, well, she's a whole other story. Dad says I take after her. Possibly because I've always pushed boundaries as far as he was concerned. Mum left us when I was ten. I guess marriage and children weren't for her, but opiates were, so at least she found her calling." I gave him a broad smile, even though her leaving was something that pained me greatly. Because of her abandonment, my father became ten times stricter. I wasn't allowed to go to parties, couldn't talk to boys, or have any semblance of freedom. I had to sneak around and lie just to have even a snippet of fun. Holland was always my partner in crime, ready with the perfect cover story to feed my father. I'd have had no life growing up without her creativity.

"Your mum's an addict?"

I nodded. "Didn't guess that about me, did you? I've pretty much been under lock and key ever since she left. Dad is petrified that I'm going to do the same thing. He even chose my career path. I wanted to do beauty, so he organised a job for me at my uncle's mortuary with them, doing make-up for open casket funerals. That way he could keep an eye on me."

"I hear there's quite an art to making them look peaceful."

"There is. I basically have to recreate their expressions from photos, like a painting on an uneven surface. People look very different when their spark is gone." I met his eyes, impressed that he even knew.

"I'll bet you're really good at it. I see you excelling at everything you try to do."

The comment seemed honest enough, but it made me uncomfortable nonetheless. I didn't think I had ever excelled at anything in my life. I wasn't even second best at anything. I dropped my head and let my shoulder-length hair fall over my eyes. Then I took a breath and brushed it all back before looking at him again. The movement acted as a curtain being drawn and then pulled back to reset the scene—aka my emotions, my mask. Then I was smiling again.

"Why don't you tell me more about your family?" I suggested.

"What's there to say that you don't already know? There are five of us. We're all in our thirties, still act like we're in our twenties. And we steal shit. Pretty much sums it up."

"I doubt that's all there is to it. For instance, how did you become thieves in the first place? Jasmine is your mother, but where's your father? Is he still around? Do you all have the same father?"

"We have the same father. He's currently serving a life sentence or two in the state's maximum security facility."

"A life sentence? Was that from stealing or doing something much worse?"

"A job went bad and people died. But he started out like us, got Jasmine into this life. As we grew, she got us into it. It's the family business."

The family business. Did that mean I'd have to become a thief too?

"Do you like it?"

"Stealing?"

"Yeah."

He shrugged. "It's what I know, what I'm good at. Do you like putting make-up on dead people?"

I shrugged. "It's what I know, what I'm good at." He caught my gaze and we both smiled.

"Ever wish you could run away and start all over again?" he asked.

I considered him for a while before giving my answer. "I'm pretty sure I just did."

"Maybe. Or maybe you've just moved from one controlling family to another."

Maybe.

"Ever wish *you* could run away and start again?"

He reached out and ran his fingers through my hair. "All the damn time." His honesty made my heart stop.

"Can I ask you a favour?"

"What's that?"

"If you do decide to run, will you take me with you? You can drop me off somewhere random, but just make sure you take me. I don't want to be left behind to die."

His eyes moved from left to right, studying me, while thoughts I could only guess at ran through his mind. Then he leaned closer and pressed a kiss to my shoulder. "Cartwrights don't run, even when we feel like it. We also don't leave people behind. I promise to protect you, Alesha. You're mine now. That makes you one of us."

I wasn't exactly sure what it meant to be one of them. It seemed like there were a lot of rules. But with Sam by my side, making me feel as amazing as he had already and offering me his loyalty, I figured I'd be just fine with the rules.

Lucky I was really good at doing what I was told.

CHAPTER EIGHT
I GET IT NOW

"TOBY." Jasmine immediately wrapped her arms around her oldest son's neck when he met us at the door of the Cartwright house in Torquay. It was this massive white-rendered two-storey home situated on a secluded slice of land just outside the city centre. There was a swimming pool, a tennis court and a three-car garage beside the main house facing the curved driveway. The gardens were all immaculately maintained, the trees surrounding the property tall. The entire thing screamed money and a desire for privacy. You could probably wander around outside naked and no one would be able to see you beyond the thick trees and bush.

"How was the trip?" The question was directed at her, but his eyes found me and then searched the remaining faces. His expression told me he came up empty. Looking for Nate, perhaps? None of us had seen him since the outburst at the hotel, and we hadn't seen Holland since the wedding. Jasmine said they'd flown back early and were probably at Nate's house. Everyone else seemed fine with that, but I was worried. She had been so scared and upset before the wedding, and I wished I'd had a little time with her afterwards to find out how she was feeling now.

"Worse than expected," Jasmine announced, sauntering into the house after handing Toby her bag. He frowned, then rolled his eyes.

"The surf was good," Abbot teased, slapping his big brother on the back as he walked past.

"So was the fishing." Kristian followed, slapping Toby on the opposite shoulder.

Toby shook his head in response. I assumed surfing and fishing were two of his favourite things.

"How were things here?" Sam asked, lugging our bags through the door on one arm.

Toby shrugged. "Quiet. Nothing out of the ordinary."

"Good."

"And how about you?" Toby's clear blue eyes landed on me. I wasn't sure what to think of him. Out of all the brothers, I'd had the least interactions with him. While he shared in their good looks and oversized build, he seemed a little more intense than the rest; he studied his surroundings more and stayed quiet in the noise of the house. I felt that Jasmine was the closest to him and trusted him most. I wondered if that meant I should be more careful around him, or if it meant that I could trust him too. Time would tell.

"What about me?"

"How are you?"

A nervous feeling fluttered about in my stomach. Did he seriously want to know, or was he asking in a general way to be polite?

"I—"

"She's fine." Sam's arm slipped around my waist, and he guided me through the door ahead of him. *I guess I'm fine.* He gave me a little nudge so I stepped in ahead while he stopped and spoke quietly to Toby.

I heard Toby ask about the damage to the twins' faces and the mention of both Nate's and Holland's names.

"I'll meet you in the kitchen," Sam said, obviously not wanting me listening in to whatever he wanted to say. I took a quick look around and headed in the direction I recalled walking the last time I was here—the day Holland and I trespassed on their property and got caught. The day my life completely changed.

Everything felt different now that I knew I wasn't allowed to leave. Not horrible, just different. I hadn't seen my father in almost a week, hadn't received a lecture on the way I conducted myself, or been made to feel that I wasn't living up to my potential. Here, I didn't feel like I was a lost cause. So yeah, I felt different, better, and I didn't want to go back to what I was before, even if I could.

"Coffee's brewing," Jasmine said as I entered. She was pulling mugs out of a cupboard and lining them up along the counter. "How do you take yours?"

"White with two sugars, please."

She took out an extra cup and placed it on the end of the line before she met my eyes and smiled. "Same as me."

Not thinking the comment needed much of a response, I simply smiled in return, then headed to the fridge and got the milk to make myself useful. I was never good at sitting still. When I was young, my mother used to say I had ants in my pants. We would laugh and she would tickle me, telling me she was trying to tickle my sillies out. Life was so much better when she was around, and I'd missed her every day since she left.

Sometimes I thought I saw her in a crowd. Of course, it was never her, though after twenty-two years and only a child's memory of her face, I didn't think I'd recognise her if she was standing right in front of me. Actually, I didn't even think that would be a possibility. I had a feeling that my mother died long ago and my father just never told us. Possibly to protect us, possibly because he couldn't face it himself. Either way, I still wondered about her.

The coffee percolator hissed and gurgled, spitting out the last of the coloured liquid into the pot. Jasmine finished adding sugar to each cup, then filled them all with coffee. I uncapped the milk and followed along behind her, the only words exchanged when she told me that Toby preferred his black.

One by one, the Cartwright brothers filed into the kitchen, picking up their mugs without having to ask which one was theirs before disappearing into various corners of the house, obviously intent on relaxing after travelling all day. Sam stood next to me and hooked one finger into the belt loop of my jeans, holding me in place. It was such a subtle thing to do, but I loved the possessiveness of the action. It made me feel like he wanted me.

"Elixir of the gods," Sam moaned after he'd taken his first sip. "I really needed caffeine."

"I think we all did," Jasmine added. "Remind me the next time we book a holiday that I hate travelling."

"Sure thing." He chuckled, watching her over the edge of his mug as she picked up some mail and left the room. Then he set his mug down and turned to me. "Want to see my room?"

A smile crept across my face. "That depends. Do you have any cool toys in there?" The moment I said it, I realised how it could be taken and blushed. "I meant, like, action figures and stuff. It was supposed to be a joke."

He lifted his hand and ran his thumb lightly over my cheek. "I'm sure I can find something in there that will interest you."

Taking my barely drunk coffee out of my hands, he set it on the bench next to his, then led me up the grand staircase to the room across from the guest room I'd stayed in on my first night here. He'd slept in there with me but on the floor, kind of blocking the door. I didn't sleep much that night.

When he pushed the door open, I found myself in a large room painted a soft grey with white edging. The carpet was thick and a darker grey than the walls, and there was more furniture than one room should really have—a king-size bed, a desk and chair, two bookcases and a TV unit dominated by an LCD TV and a couple of gaming consoles. There were posters of surfers on the walls, a couple of women with enormous tits and round arses looking sexy on the beach or holding a surfboard as well. Besides that, there was one really beautiful framed photo of five kids standing at the edge of the surf, looking out to the setting sun. I couldn't make out any features because the boys were silhouetted, but I figured it was Sam and his brothers. It was the prettiest part of the whole room.

"So, I guess you really like surfing," I said, pointing out a poster featuring a curvaceous brunette arching her back while lying on a surfboard.

He followed my gaze. "Shit. I should probably take that down."

"You don't have to," I said, closing up a little. Those posters made me feel inadequate. I didn't look anything like those women. "It's your room. You can have whatever you want on your walls."

"Well, it's your room too, now." He moved around the room and tore down all the busty women, scrunching the shiny paper in his hands. "And this shit really doesn't need to be here anymore. They've seriously been up since high school."

"You've kept your room the same since high school?"

"Not really. I haven't always lived here. But my room has always stayed the same, and sometimes it's just easier to stay at the house."

"You have your own place?"

He tore down the surfing posters too, anything that wasn't in a frame.

"Not exactly. Toby and Nate are really the only ones with property of their own. The rest of us kind of share the family portfolio when it suits."

"So we'll be living here with the rest of the family?" Their house seemed like it was always busy and noisy. I wasn't sure if I'd like that or if I'd crave the peace and quiet I was used to. I'd been on my own for a long time.

"Yeah, we're staying here." He looked around the room to make sure he had all the posters, then tossed them into a wastepaper basket. He moved to stand in front of me and took a hold of my hands. "Maybe we can redecorate."

I took a deep breath and looked around. This was my new home. We were in our thirties and living with his family like we were all in our teens. OK. I could deal with that. If Sam kept looking at me like he wanted to undress me, I could probably handle anything.

We'd had a wonderful few days in the Cook Islands, and I was feeling a little high on sex and pheromones. Still, my married life was beginning in what still looked like a teenage boy's bedroom. "Can I paint the walls pink and get a sequinned bedspread with fluffy pillows?" I asked, keeping my voice serious.

His eyes widened, and he blew out a burst of air as he struggled to maintain an impassive expression. "If that's what you really need to feel comfortable," he said diplomatically.

"I don't want pink walls and sequins, Sam." I laughed. The fact that he'd actually agreed to that really warmed my heart.

A relieved sigh caused the tension to leave his shoulders. "Thank God."

"And I don't particularly want to change your room." I looked around again. It was a large room, but if it was going to be the place we spent most of our time in, it might get a little cramped. "You know, if there's some reason we can't stay in a place of our own, I have a whole house we could live in."

"There's no reason. It just works better when we're all here." His response was quick and clipped. It gave me the impression that there was more to it than convenience —like maybe we had to stay here because of me. That made sense, when you broke it down, I wasn't exactly a free woman. I was living in a glorified prison, and I needed to remember that. Sam might say that I'm a Cartwright now, but I had no doubt that my existence within the family would be tenuous until I somehow proved my worth.

"OK, then I do want to change it a bit, but only

condense it so some of my stuff can fit in here. We *can* go and get some of my stuff, can't we?"

"Of course. I'll take you tomorrow. We can pack up all your clothes and whatever you feel you can't live without. Then we'll work out how to fit it all in here."

"And I just leave everything else behind?" Reality was creeping through my carefully composed façade. I'd worked so hard for that house, for my things. Were they going to clean it out and sell it all, or would it just sit there and fall into disrepair?

"For now. We'll work out what to do with it later."

Disrepair it is.

"And what am I supposed to tell my family?"

"What do you want to tell them?"

Pressing my lips together, I tried to work out what I could tell Dad without him flipping out. I'd been doing this on and off over the past few days, and there wasn't really much I'd come up with. "I'm considering writing a letter to tell my dad that I joined the Peace Corps and am already on my way to the jungle. Failing that, I'm thinking that faking my own death might work too."

He laughed. "Have you considered telling him you got married and are moving in with your husband and his family?"

"No." I drew the word out so it lasted for a few seconds too long.

He chuckled, but it wasn't because he thought I was funny. "Why don't you want to tell him that? Is there something wrong with my family? Well, besides the obvious."

"You, um… aren't Christians."

"Excuse me?" He seemed visibly shocked.

"He won't be happy that I married a man who wasn't religious enough to get married in church. He's very... traditional." For years, he tried to set me up with single men who he deemed appropriate from within our church, but when none of them worked out, he shook his head and said, "There is no one for you," before he gave up on me, relegating me to the position of his spinster daughter forever. I didn't mind. It was easier than being forced to make conversation with men I had nothing in common with.

"Are you upset we weren't married in a church?"

"No," I answered quickly. "I don't believe the way he does." I prayed sometimes as a knee-jerk reaction, but I didn't really believe anymore, especially not since my mother left and everyone we knew responded with 'only God can save her now.' I didn't think she needed God to save her. She needed people to care enough to make sure she got the help she needed.

"So you don't care that I'm not religious?"

"No. Just my father will. And also my brother. And my uncle. And everyone else in my family. Maybe not my niece and nephew though."

"You're saying that your family will be prejudiced against me because I'm not a Christian?"

"That's exactly what I'm saying."

"Isn't that very *un*-Christian of them?"

I shrugged. "It's just the way they think." And it made sense to me. One of the reasons I didn't want to marry anyone from Dad's church was that we fundamentally believed very different things. Surely going into a marriage knowing we'd be so intrinsically different would be asking for a divorce. I wanted to marry someone like-minded, someone who understood me. *And I married a thief. What does that say about me?*

He raked his hands through his hair and paced back and forth a couple of times, clearly exasperated. "So, let me get this straight," he said when he stood still again. "You would rather tell your father you died than introduce him to me?"

Oh dear. When he put it that way, it sounded really horrible.

I opened and then closed my mouth, not knowing what to say. I really needed to quit talking. Sometimes honesty wasn't the best policy.

"Um...."

I pressed my palms together, sweaty and a little nervous. I almost didn't want to respond, knowing that whatever came out of my mouth, be it a truth or a lie, wasn't going to fix the situation.

"Well?" he asked, looking at me expectantly.

Letting out a sigh, I sat on the edge of the bed and rubbed my palms against my knees. *Fuck it.* "Yes," I said, going with honesty.

The muscle at the side of his jaw ticked as he stood there staring at me, his blue eyes locked on mine while God only knew what flew through his thoughts.

"Get your things," he said finally.

"What?" *Is he dumping me?*

"Your things, your bag, whatever shit girls grab before they walk out the door. Grab it and let's go."

"What? Why?"

"Because you're taking me to meet your father."

"Now?" My eyes went wide. "Noooo."

He wrapped a big hand around my upper arm. "Yes. Let's go."

I set my jaw. "Fine. But don't say I didn't warn you."

———

SAM DROVE a flashy-looking Range Rover that was a dark metallic red with a really fancy black and grey leather interior. It smelled new.

"Is this car stolen?" I asked after about half an hour of keeping a lookout for cops.

Sam's grip tightened on the wheel, and I heard the leather creak beneath his fingers.

"That would be kind of stupid, don't you think?"

I shrugged. The only thieves I'd ever known had come from movies and TV. Take Jimmy-Steve from *Shameless* as an example—he drove around in stolen cars all the time.

"I wouldn't have asked if I thought it was stupid." I looked at my hands, my voice a little quieter than before. I hated it when someone made me feel bad for asking questions. I had an inquisitive nature and rarely let a curiosity pass me by. Asking questions was how I learned things about people. I'd always thought it was normal but had learned later in life that most people would just pretend to understand, because asking too many questions is considered rude. That made zero sense to me but explained a lot about why humans struggle to understand each other—everyone was just pretending to know.

Well, I wanted to be sure. So I asked.

Sam reached over, letting out his breath before he took one of my hands. "I wasn't calling you stupid. I—" He stopped abruptly, seeming so close to an apology that he knew he shouldn't deliver. Then he took his eyes from the road for a moment and changed tack. "For all intents and purposes, we run a legitimate business. We don't bring anything we take into our own lives. That's too risky."

"So what, you just put it all in that storage facility to be sold off?"

He took a moment before he responded with a simple "Pretty much."

"Does that mean yes? Or that you aren't telling me because you don't know if you can trust me?"

He just looked at me, telling me it was the second one.

Fine. Be that way.

Slipping my hand out from his, I folded my arms across my chest and looked out the window. I knew I hadn't really done anything to earn the trust of the Cartwrights in the few days I'd known them all, but the fact that I knew enough to get them all sent to prison and hadn't once used the hotel phone or taken advantage of an unguarded moment to run meant I understood my place— if I kept quiet and behaved, I'd be just fine. I wasn't about to do anything to jeopardise my own safety. It kind of stung that he wasn't forthcoming, I guess I figured that since I already knew so much, the rest of it was just semantics, but whatever.

"I can't tell you about the business, peaches." His voice was soft and felt nice in my ears. I closed my eyes as a surge of emotion shot up from my chest and pressed against the back of them. I didn't understand what it meant, just that I couldn't handle him shutting me out and then treating me with kindness. The two didn't seem to line up in my mind.

"It's fine," I responded, keeping my gaze on the passing scenery. My voice came out a little thick.

"You're upset with me?"

"I'm fine." A tickle beneath my eye told me a tear was falling. I swiped at it quickly, hoping he didn't see. I had no clue why I was crying.

"You don't look fine."

"You should be looking at the road, not me."

Clicking on his indicator, he pulled off the main road and stopped the Range Rover.

"We don't have to do this," he said, putting the car into Park. The engine idled.

"Do what?"

"Visit your father. It's obviously got you stressed, and I was being an arsehole getting my nose all out of joint over the religion thing."

"Yeah, well what do you think you're going to do? Force him to like you? He's not going to understand no matter what we do, or how long we leave it. But we're going to have to do it eventually if you don't want him to report me missing and get the cops involved, so we might as well get it over and done with now. We're almost there."

As much as I hated my father's scrutiny, I knew it came from a good place. He cared about his children and wanted what he thought was best for them. He just did it in a really crappy way that involved laying the guilt on thick while using his strict interpretation of the Bible to convince us that God would send us to Hell if we didn't obey our parents. It wasn't until Holland went through a rebellious teen phase and dragged me along with her that I even started to question my father and the things he'd been teaching me. That was when there became two sides of me

—my father's Alesha, and Holland's version of me. I was never sure which one I really was and often wondered if my true identity was still struggling to break through. Did I even have a true identity, or was I capable of only being someone else's version? Perhaps there was no real me at all.

Sam had said he'd liked the girl he first met running across his front yard. That I'd had spunk. Would he be horribly disappointed when he saw the me my father knew? The girl who bowed her head and watched her toes more than she looked into eyes? Was that what I was more worried about than Sam actually meeting Dad?

"I'll try to come up with something," Sam said, then put the car in gear and merged back into the traffic. I didn't like his chances. My father didn't suffer fools gladly. He could sniff out a lie a mile off.

When we arrived at the funeral home about half an hour later, my nerves twisted my stomach.

"This is it?" Sam looked upward, taking in the imposing building. One would think a funeral home would more closely resemble the Addams family residence, but my uncle's looked nothing of the sort. It was built specifically for the business in a blond brick with a dark tiled roof. The gardens were manicured with sweet-smelling flowers and perfectly trimmed bushes that lined a concrete walkway leading to the main door. If it didn't have a massive sign out front saying 'Eastern Funeral Services', you'd peg the building as a community centre, or something a little more fun like an RSL club.

"This is it." I took a deep breath and unclipped my seat belt, preparing to face the music.

"Wait," Sam said, jumping out of the car and jogging

around to my side. "What kind of husband doesn't open his wife's door?" He stood grinning as he held his hand out to help me.

"How very chivalrous of you." I smiled, placing one hand against his chest. *Lord, I love to touch his chest.*

"Ready to go in?"

I looked towards the building and shook my head. "No. But I'll do it anyway."

Catching my face in his hands, Sam pressed a lingering kiss against my lips, causing my head to lighten and my toes to tingle—among other parts of my body. "After we do this, I promise I will never make you do something you don't want to do again. This was really shitty of me."

Yes it was, but it needs to be done.

I released a heavy breath. "Let's just go in."

"Alesha." My aunt Miranda looked up from the reception desk she often manned as we entered. "You're back." She smiled, but there was an accompanying annoyance in her eyes. I'd left them without a make-up artist for several days. Replacing me at short notice wouldn't have been easy, so she was understandably pissed. "And who might this charming young man be?" She had a real smile for Sam.

He held out his hand. "Samuel Cartwright, ma'am."
Wow, she gets the full formal introduction and everything.

As she took his hand, I noticed my aunt blush a little. *Those Cartwright boys seem to have that kind of power over most women.*

"And how do you know our Alesha, Sam?" she asked when she reluctantly took her hand back.

"I'm her—"

"Where's Dad?" I jumped in before Sam could say

anything more. There was no way I was breaking the news to her before I'd told my dad. It would be yet another thing he'd never forgive me for.

"Downstairs with Trevor. We had two new clients come in today. Tragic accident. You'll have your work cut out for you if they want a viewing."

"OK. Thank you." I grabbed Sam by the hand and pulled him to the side door that opened straight onto a narrow staircase leading to the basement, where the bodies were stored and my brother and I performed our work.

I was thankful to Sam for not making me feel bad about cutting off his conversation with Miranda. There was no way I would have been able to explain without being overheard. Sound travelled easily in this facility. "You might see a body," I warned as we alighted the stairs.

"Consider me well informed," he said, following along behind me.

"Dad?" I called out when I heard familiar voices. Trevor was talking about turning a tap, and Dad was questioning the order in which he wanted things done. Typical. My brother had performed the embalming procedure on hundreds of bodies over the years. My father had performed precisely zero, yet he still felt he knew best.

"Leesh?" The nickname came from my brother's mouth.

"Nice of you to join us," Dad said, keeping his back towards me as they came into view. "You'll find we're likely too busy to talk since one of our workers decided to take a last-minute trip without giving any notice."

"Dad had to do Mrs Hill's make-up himself. She looked horrifying." I met Trevor's laughing eyes and he gave me a sympathetic smile. Despite his perfection in my father's eyes, I didn't hold anything against him and actually got along with my brother quite well. It had felt like we only had each other growing up, so there was no space for sibling rivalry.

"How bad was it?" I asked, trying to fight a smile as I imagined the job he would've done.

Trevor produced a wide-eyed manic smile that could have been mistaken for the Joker on a bad day. I put my fist against my mouth to stifle my laugh.

My father didn't seem to find it funny. "You don't need to be here, Alesha. Unless of course you're here to do some work," he added, fidgeting with the tubes attached to the pump.

"I actually came to introduce you to someone," I started, which was when he decided to turn around and actually look at me. Then he did a double take when he saw Sam standing beside me. I'd be lying if I said it wasn't entertaining to watch his eyes move up, up, until he finished noting the entirety of Sam's size.

"Young man." My father nodded politely at Sam, pulling his disposable gloves from his hands. Then he looked at me. "Why did you bring him down here? We have a body out. Have some respect."

"He can't see the body from where he's standing, Dad. It's hidden by the curtain."

"Still." Then he gestured for us to follow him to his office.

I gave Trevor a wave and he mouthed, "Are you OK?'. I nodded and motioned that I'd talk to him later, even though I wasn't sure if I'd be able to follow through on that promise. I had no idea what kind of contact I'd be allowed to have with the people I cared about once this visit was over. Would I be able to call them? Visit? Could I see them on holidays and birthdays? Would every moment be supervised? My head throbbed from all the questions bursting inside it.

"What is all this about?" Dad asked, looking fairly put out once we were inside. He pulled his glasses from his face and started cleaning them with his handkerchief.

I decided to jump right in. "This is Sam, Dad. My husband."

His cleaning motion stopped. "I beg your pardon?"

"Samuel Cartwright, sir. I'm married to your daughter." Sam held out his hand, and my father didn't even register it.

He's in shock.

"But," Dad blustered. "But… but how?"

I opened my mouth to tell him a fairy-tale version of how we met, but Sam jumped in first.

"My church group was spending the day taking under-privileged kids to the beach—kind of like a big brother program. One of the kids got scared of the surf and tried to run away. Alesha saw him, saw me calling after him, then caught him before he could get too far. We got talking, and sir, I fell for your daughter then and there. I was honoured enough that she agreed to have dinner with me. You won't believe how honoured I felt when she agreed to be my wife too. We got talking about our dreams and then we thought, why wait? God had obviously brought us together for a reason, right? So we flew to the Cook Islands, got married in this quaint little church that opened out on the beach, and sealed our union under the eyes of the Lord." *Oh dear.* "It was beautiful, sir. My only regret is that you weren't there to see it."

When Sam finished, my dad was dead silent. He finished cleaning his glasses, then slid them back on before he looked at me. "Is this guy for real?" He obviously didn't believe a word. I didn't blame him—that story was probably even more far-fetched than the truth.

"Um…." I glanced at Sam, who widened his eyes slightly, silently telling me that I should back him up. And I should back him up because he was my husband, and wives were supposed to honour their husbands, right? But then, children must also honour their parents. So who came first?

Sam's brow twitched like he couldn't believe I wasn't immediately rushing to back up his story, but he didn't understand. He wasn't raised the way I was. The guilt over lying to my dad would consume me until it ate a hole through my insides. But then I had to share a bed with Sam, become a part of his family and live by their rules. They had their own moral code. It didn't align with the way I was raised, but it worked for them. It would work for me too.

I was a Cartwright now. I had to remember that, had to act like it too.

I took a deep breath before I answered.

"The boy was running towards the road. I had to step in. Sam and I have been inseparable ever since."

Sam's expression softened. I'd chosen him.

I feel sick.

My father still didn't sound convinced. "So you two just ran off to some island and found a priest to marry you? Just like that?" He clicked his fingers.

He really doesn't believe us. "Yes," I said. "Just like

that. We didn't want to wait. I'm sorry if this has upset you."

"Upset me? Losing the chance to walk my only daughter down the aisle? Being unable to participate in the tradition of giving that daughter away to a man I believe worthy of her hand?" His voice rose with each word. "I'm not upset, Alesha. I'm furious. I do not condone this… this impulsive and wanton behaviour." He lifted his hands and gestured that he wouldn't discuss this anymore. "You will have this marriage annulled."

Sam held up his hand. "With all due respect, sir, you're out of line."

"Some Christian boy you are. Sweeping a naïve girl off her feet, then whisking her away from her family. You didn't even have the respect to ask me for *my daughter's hand.*"

"Alesha is an adult who is capable of making her own decisions," Sam argued, staying surprisingly calm.

"What are you, one of those Pentecostals? So free with your interpretations of His word, singing in your fancy stadiums while you all look like you're on drugs," Dad growled, his face turning red while angry spit foamed at the corners of his mouth.

"Dad!" I gasped, horrified at the way this had escalated. "How dare you speak to him that way. He's done nothing to you."

"He's taking my daughter away," he returned without missing a beat. "How could you marry a man you just met? How could you be so irresponsible? This isn't how I raised you. He must have brainwashed you somehow. This isn't you. You belong here, Alesha. With us."

No I don't. I never belonged.

There was a long pause where we just stared at each other. There was nothing I could say, no way I could explain any of this away to make him feel better. I couldn't tell him the truth, couldn't assure him that this wasn't what I'd wanted, that I'd done it to protect my life, and his, and Trevor's and everyone else in the family. The happy by-product was that Sam wasn't a bad man. He treated me kindly when he could have been horrid, and he cared enough to try and make my father believe he was the kind of man he'd want me with. It was a bullshit lie, but the kindness was within that lie. The kindness was in the caring.

Sam's hand caught mine, his voice gentle when he spoke. "I think we should go, Alesha."

I blinked twice at the contact, shocked out of my turbulent mind, then gripped Sam's hand a little harder, borrowing some of his calm strength. "He's a good man, Dad. If you give him a chance, you'll see that too."

"The man is a thief. He stole my daughter from me and took her innocence. I see no good in him."

"Dad." My mouth fell open, further words failing me. It seemed like such a horrible thing for him to say, while at the same time he'd hit the nail on the head. Sam had done all of those things. But he was wrong about one thing: Sam *was good*. I knew that in my heart.

"Come on, peaches. It's OK. I get it now."

He slipped his arm around me as I turned away from my dad, from my brother, from my entire family.

"If you leave, Alesha, don't ever come back. You won't be welcome around any of us."

I looked back over my shoulder, seeing my father one

last time. "I love you, Dad." They were my last words to him. Then we left.

I'm sorry.

Wait.

I thought about Sam's earlier words. A Cartwright had to own their shit. So I wasn't sorry for what *I'd* done, I was sorry that my father's arrogance and parochial attitude would lose him a daughter.

I guess it didn't matter how much access I'd be allowed to have with my loved ones since I wasn't welcome anymore. The realisation felt heavy on my heart as I leaned a little closer into Sam's side, the man who was currently the only family I had, the only one who hadn't turned me away.

"WHAT THE HELL WERE YOU THINKING?" Jasmine's voice travelled up the staircase where I sat listening to her berating Sam. The moment we walked in the door, she started. I felt like a teenage girl all over again.

"You asked me to marry her so she'd stay quiet, not be her prison guard."

Jasmine felt that taking me to pack my things and meet my family was a colossal error in Sam's judgement.

"She could've told them everything. Escaped. Called the cops. Signalled that she was in danger."

Sam scoffed. "Not from me."

"You think this is some joke? That girl could ruin this family with what she knows. I expect you to keep her *here*, not go parading her about town."

"You're insane. She's not going to talk."

"How can you be so sure."

"Because she's had plenty of opportunity already, and she hasn't said a word."

"Perhaps she's just biding her time?"

"I don't think she's like that. I thought you liked her. She's a sweet girl, Jazz."

"Sweet." She said the word like it sickened her, and it made me realise that it wasn't a compliment. Sweet, nice, cute: all words that meant a person was simply OK, but nothing special. I felt so out of my depth.

"Yes, sweet. Just leave her to me. I said I'd take care of her, and I will. But you need to trust me to do it my way or you aren't going to get what you want."

Do what? What does she want? I don't understand. Listening made my stomach ache. I wished Holland was there for me to talk to. I needed desperately to talk to her about everything that had happened since the wedding. But she wasn't there, and I was afraid for her. Not for the first time, I wondered, *What have we gotten ourselves into?*

"Causing waves already?" Toby lowered himself to the step next to me as Jasmine reminded Sam that there was an easier way to deal with me if I became a problem. I felt my eyes prick and pressed my palms hard against my thighs.

"We're not going to let that happen," Toby assured me, placing a hand on my shoulder. "Jasmine's old-school. They solve their problems with violence and threats. My brothers and I like to get a little more creative."

"Is that why this is happening? Because you're *creative*?"

"This is happening because Nate is obsessed with your friend. You got offered the same deal."

"So it's a marriage by default."

He shrugged. "You like him though, don't you?"

"He's too beautiful for me."

"Let's skip the part where you try to claim you aren't pretty enough and stick to the facts."

"You don't think I'm pretty?"

He laughed, but I wasn't joking.

"You know you're pretty, Alesha. All pretty girls know it, you're just raised to pretend like you aren't."

That was the thing, I really wasn't pretending, I didn't see pretty when I looked in the mirror at all. I focused on my hands.

"You haven't answered my question," he prompted. "Do you like Sam?"

I turned and met Toby's eyes. Compared to his brothers, who were varying degrees of surfer chic, Toby was as clean-cut as it got. His dark brown hair was neatly trimmed and styled, his jaw cleanly shaved. There wasn't a wrinkle in his clothes. He looked as though he'd be more at home in a boardroom than in a band of thieves.

"Yes, I like him," I admitted, even though I was fairly sure that fact had been painfully obvious since the moment I'd stepped foot inside their house.

"Then focus on that. Let us worry about everything else." His empathy surprised me, seeming at odds with the stoic man I'd witnessed him to be thus far. Was this the kind of man Toby really was? Kind? Soft-hearted? He gave me a reassuring pat on the knee before he got up and headed downstairs, leaving me sitting there with my head against the wall, my brain aching and my heart sick.

I'd been OK until today. I'd convinced myself that as long as I did what I was told, everything would be fine. But it wasn't fine. I'd lost everything that was mine. Now I was stuck in someone else's house feeling like an unwanted refugee. I was a yo-yo. This sucked.

Tears flowed from my eyes. I wanted to go home. I wanted my best friend back in her home too. I wanted to be pathetic and single again. I couldn't do this. I couldn't just give up my family and shift into this one. My father was right, this wasn't me. I wasn't the girl who ran off with some guy and lived happily ever after.

I don't belong here.

Then where do I belong?

My stomach dropped. I didn't feel like I fit into my old life either. I was lonely, pining for a life more exciting than the one I had, for companionship, for a man. Everything I'd asked for had been dropped into my lap. But at what cost?

I'm so confused. What do I do from here?

"Praying?"

I opened my eyes to find Sam walking up the staircase, nodding to my clasped hands on my knees.

"Worrying," I replied, separating my hands and flattening my palms against my thighs.

"About?" He stopped right before he reached me, his face just above my eye level. He reached out and gently wiped at my tears, the gesture overwhelming me to the point where my face crumpled, but I immediately reined it in. *Get a grip, Alesha.*

"This. You. Me. Us." I shrugged. "What we've done and our reason behind it. It was impulsive. And wanton."

"Those are your father's words."

"But they're true, right? Our marriage is a sham. It's baseless. Something we both did because we were told to. How puerile can two people be? My God, I've done everything I was told to. All my life I've been the good girl. And look what it got me? Your mother wants to kill me.

My father doesn't want to speak to me. I have no job, no friends, no contact with the outside world. You said I'm not a prisoner but I am. I fucking am." I stood and turned on my heel, rushing for our bedroom where I planned to slam the door and continue crying on my own in peace. But Sam was faster and grabbed the door before it slammed, then caught me before I made it to the adjoined bathroom and locked myself in there.

"Let me go!" I screeched. "Let me go! You don't want me. You should've just let me die." I beat my fists against his chest as I shut my eyes tight and willed my emotions to just go the hell away. I didn't want to feel this way, it was too real.

I heard a squeak. Then shock flooded my system as ice-cold water rushed over my head. When I opened my eyes in alarm, I realised that Sam had corralled me into the shower cubicle and turned on the water.

"Calm the fuck down," he growled. I pushed at his chest, spluttering as the water rushed over me. But he was holding too tight, his expression set firm. I gasped, then sobbed, feeling weak, my fight draining out of me. I slumped against his chest, my hands grabbing at his shirt, holding fistfuls of fabric as I opened my mouth and released a silent howl.

"I get it, peaches," he said, holding me up when I struggled to stand. "It's OK. I get it."

The water changed from ice cold to warm, then comfortably hot.

"I get it," he said again, kissing my wet hair. "It's OK."

That's when something new came over me, something desperate and crazy.

I grabbed either side of his face and pressed my mouth

to his, kissing him forcefully. It took a beat for him to respond, but when he did, it felt just as hungry and fierce as what I had building inside of me.

I pulled my shirt over my head. He did the same, and our mouths collided again. I removed my crop while he forced open the buttons on my soaked jeans, our mouths struggling to stay connected as we wrestled with the denim. With me naked, he palmed my breast and squeezed, pushing me back until my skin hit cool tiles.

"Do you want me?" he asked, his voice thick as he kissed and nibbled, gripped and pinched, his mouth on my throat.

"Yes," I gasped, my hands on his shoulders, fingers digging into his muscles. "Yes, I want you." *How could I not?*

He groaned as he gripped my thighs and lifted me off the ground like my weight was nothing to him. Then he caught my nipple between his teeth, sucked back until I hissed, then lowered me onto his shaft.

"Oh God," I shouted as my insides opened to receive him. My body froze, unable to move until our connection was complete, my focus on him and how he filled me so entirely.

"You're fucking perfect, peaches." His breath washed over my throat as his hips began to move. Every fibre of my being was suddenly alive as the urge to burst built. "So tight. So wet. Amazing."

My eyes pricked again at his words, my mind struggling to believe they were true but loving them anyway. I slid my fingers in his hair and clashed my mouth against his, wanting to feel him, taste him, pull him into my body to chase the whispering away. I was stronger than this, stronger than the girl who was crying on the stairs. I could chase all my worries away, I just had to focus on him—the beautiful, manly, glorious Sam. He felt like a dream, yet somehow he was my reality. I just had to believe.

Believe.

Did Sam believe in me? In what we had? He'd chased me down instead of letting me go like many had before. Did that mean he really did see me as his? That he really did see me as amazing as his ecstasy-laden words proclaimed? Oh, I wanted that, the sense of belonging. I wanted to be his. Only his.

"Sam!" I threw my head back, thumping it against the tiles as my orgasm tore through me. Sam shuddered and groaned into my neck, his cock pulsing inside me as his chest heaved from the effort of our tryst.

He kissed my shoulder. "Feeling better now?" He flashed a grin, then ground his hips a little against mine, his length still firm.

"A little," I teased, running my thumbs over his brows as I looked into his kind eyes. "I'm sorry I'm such a mess."

With a smile playing on his lips, he shook his head. "What'd I tell you about apologising?"

With a sigh, I closed my eyes. "Cartwrights don't apologise."

"And are you Alesha Cartwright, or are you still Alesha Ward?"

I held up my hand, catching sight of the gold band on my ring finger. "I'm Alesha Cartwright."

"Then be who you need to be. I've got you, OK?"

He had so quickly and completely become my entire

world, this giant of a man, this thief with an honourable heart, that I had no choice but to believe his words as true.

I nodded. *Believe.*

He had me.

And he wanted me too.

CHAPTER TEN
GOOD ENOUGH

I SET my fight aside again after that night, pushing my questions and worries into the dark corners of my mind so I could go back to doing what I did best: going with the flow. I'd made a choice to side with my husband, and I was going to do everything I could to make sure that he didn't regret sticking his neck out for me. I made myself available to him whenever his desire emerged—which was often, and *not* something I was complaining about. And when we weren't together, I made myself as useful as possible around the house, helping with cooking and cleaning while learning everything I could about each member of the family. Jasmine wasn't the easiest person to get along with, but after years of living with my father's difficult personality, I figured I could adapt to anyone. I found that she took great pride in her cooking, so asking her to teach me was the 'in' I needed to get her to view me in a kinder light. I knew my efforts were working when she made a comment about her life being easier now that she and I were sharing the load.

The brothers weren't anywhere near as time intensive, since they were like puppies and just liked it when you fed them. They were easy to talk to because they all had a common interest in surfing, often getting up before dawn to catch the best waves together, so I just spent my down-time reading the surfing magazines I found lying around the house so I understood what they meant when they spoke about carving and A-frames.

"You know, Leesh, I can teach you," Kristian said over lunch the Monday after I'd been living with them two weeks. Every meal so far was a family affair, and that day, Jasmine had shown me how to make her chicken and vegetable soup with fresh herb bread rolls. It was delicious, and she seemed pleased that I was learning fast.

"To surf?" The offer took me by surprise. I'd never pictured myself on a surfboard before.

"Why not? Saves you being stuck around here all day."

I tucked my hair behind my ear and moved my spoon through my soup. "I don't know. I don't have a board, or even the slightest idea how to start." I glanced at Sam to gauge his response. I was tempted—leaving the confines of the property sounded like Heaven—but he was looking at something on his phone.

"No phones at the table." Jasmine grabbed it from his hand and placed it face down.

"That was work."

She inhaled slowly, then lifted his phone and looked at the screen. A second later, she handed it back to him. "Have you spoken to Nate?"

"I have."

He has? I had no idea. The desire to enquire after Holland burned in my chest.

"And when is he coming back?"

"He's not. Says he and Holland are staying at the beach house for good."

Oh. Disappointment bloomed inside me, replacing the burning questions.

Jasmine's jaw tightened at the news. "What about work?"

"He'll be ready," Toby put in, lifting his eyes from his food. He sat at the head of the table with supreme confidence, the small Boston terrier they'd named Rogue sat at his feet silently, knowing who his master was.

Jasmine's icy eyes swung to him. "You've spoken to him too?"

Toby nodded once. "He'll be ready," he repeated.

Jasmine sucked a slow breath in through her nose, then stood without finishing her food. She seemed upset, and it was my instinct to get up and follow her to make sure she was OK. But when I moved, Sam clapped his hand over my forearm and shook his head. "Give her a moment," he advised, his hand moving to my thigh, fingers stroking lightly beneath the table.

Our relationship had continued to grow in passion, and it was hard to get enough of each other in the moments he was home and not out working. Those moments seemed few and far between most days, leaving little time for anything else to develop between us that wasn't associated with taking our clothes off.

"So what do you say, darlin'? You wanna learn surfing or not?" Kristian asked.

"I don't know."

Sam threw a piece of bread across the table, hitting Kristian in the head. "Quit hitting on my wife."

Kristian laughed. "I'm not hitting on her."

"Then quit calling her darlin'."

Kristian continued laughing and I grew a little warmer on the inside, enjoying the hint of jealousy from Sam. "I'm just offering Leesh the chance to get out of the house. You can't keep her locked up here forever."

I didn't want to be locked up forever. Since the excursion to meet my father, I hadn't left the property once. I could go out and swim laps in the pool, even go running around the perimeter, but I couldn't pass the tree line. I needed to be in sight at all times, like a minimum-security prison.

"Take her now, then," Sam said. "Should be flat at Winkipop since the swell was only four feet at Rincon this morning. Just take good care of my girl. I've grown quite fond of her." He leaned closer and kissed my shoulder, skimming his hand a little higher on my thigh. "Why don't you go up and get changed?" he instructed. "Give me a minute with the boys."

"Sure." He squeezed my thigh and I stood, taking dishes into the kitchen before I headed upstairs to get my bathers on.

Jasmine's voice caused me to freeze in my tracks. She was standing at the farthest point of the kitchen, one hand on the benchtop and her back to me, a mobile phone pressed against her ear.

"I just want us to be a family," she said, pausing as she listened to the voice on the other end. "That wasn't my intention. She was being insolent... I understand... Yes... Please, Nathaniel, just come to dinner. I can make it up to her. I'll be nothing but nice."

Well, that answered who she was talking to. It didn't

surprise me that it was Nate on the other end since she'd seemed so hurt that Sam and Toby had spoken to him when she hadn't. She obviously liked to keep close tabs on her sons, much like my father always kept tabs on me. The difference being that Jasmine wasn't pushing her sons away, she was doing her best to bring everyone back together, despite her obvious dislike towards Holland. *If only my father could be the same way.*

Not wanting to interrupt what was possibly meant to be a private conversation, I ducked my head and slid my bowl into the dishwasher as quietly as I could. Jasmine heard though and turned to face me with a start.

"Sorry," I mouthed.

She held up her hand like it was no bother, then signalled for me to wait while she finished up. "Tonight, then," she said, just before she lowered her phone and hit the End Call button. She sighed, then met my eyes. "That was Nathanial. He and Holland will be joining us for dinner this evening. What does she like to eat? I'm to make her feel as welcome as possible."

"She likes roast lamb and potatoes au gratin. She doesn't really have a favourite vegetable, but she's not picky."

She walked over to the fridge and looked inside before sighing. "I'm going to have to go to the supermarket." She turned back to me. "Would you like to come?"

"Oh." I felt horrible refusing her when it was the first time she'd offered to take me somewhere. "I'm actually supposed to have a surfing lesson with Kristian."

"That's fine," she said, looking at her watch. "If you can be back by four, that'll give us enough time to prepare the food."

"OK." I grinned. I didn't know why, but the whole interaction made me happy. I was going to the beach *and* my best friend was coming to dinner tonight. I turned and almost skipped away.

"Alesha?" she called before I made it to the stairs.

"Yes?"

"Do you like it here?"

I placed my hand against the archway that led to the stairs and crossed my feet at the ankles. That was a hard one. If I gave her the answer I thought she wanted, she'd probably know I was lying and call me on it. But if I told the truth, I risked insulting her and ending the tenuous relationship we'd already established.

I went with something in the middle. "I don't hate it."

She nodded, her expression unchanged. "Enjoy your surf lesson."

"Thank you," I said, spinning around and rushing up the stairs, taking them two at a time. I was excited to be going somewhere and doing something where I wouldn't have to worry so much about my behaviour for a couple of hours. Kristian was super easy-going, and I figured the lesson would be fun and relaxed.

Once in the bathroom, I wriggled out of my jeans and underwear, then pulled off my T-shirt and crop top. I was just reaching for the swimsuit I had drying on the towel rack when the door cracked open and Sam appeared.

"Jesus," I gasped, grabbing for the nearest towel and covering my nakedness from his sight. "You scared the life out of me."

"When are you going to quit being so modest around me? I've seen everything you're hiding several times over." He grinned and looked at my towel-covered body.

"In fact, I'm picturing it all right now. That towel is hiding nothing from my memory."

My cheeks burned. "I don't know. It's just a habit, I guess." I held the towel a little tighter, my body trembling as he stalked a little closer. It wasn't that I was scared of him, it was just that he made me nervous. Despite the amount of time we'd spent together, despite his assurances, despite his obvious hunger, I still felt unsure of him. I felt unworthy.

He stopped right in front of me. "You aren't this modest when you're screaming my name."

"That's different," I whispered. "My heads all cloudy then."

He dropped to his knees in front of me, gripping my hips. "I'd like to make it all cloudy now."

"I'm supposed to be getting ready."

Parting the opening of the towel, he pressed his lips at the point where my thigh met my hips. "You are. You're getting ready for me." He tugged at the towel, pulling it away from my body dramatically.

Oh my.

"But Kristian's waiting." I didn't even know why I was still protesting—my pussy was already aching for his touch.

He slid his hand up my stomach, fingers pressing against my chest and then raking back down as he peppered kisses over my thighs, his hot breath fanning over my juices. "Let him wait. You're *my* wife, and I want you now."

He hooked one of my thighs over his shoulder and lifted me just high enough that my pussy was aligned with his face. Then his tongue swept between my folds and I moaned. *God, he does amazing things to me.*

Unable to keep both feet on the ground, I lifted my other leg and Sam pushed it onto his other shoulder before rising to his knees, my back sliding against the wall as I held onto his head for balance.

"My God," I gasped as he sucked back harder, his tongue moving inside me and then back to suck against my clit, the rhythm and pressure causing my insides to tighten and swell. I could feel my orgasm only moments away. "It's happening. Sam. I'm right there. Oh. Fuck." I exploded, my hips bucking against his mouth as his tongue sucked and swirled, speared and tasted. I could barely see from all the stars.

When the raging pulses subsided, he lowered my feet to the ground, then stood in front of me before kissing me passionately, pinning me against the wall with his body— which was just as well, because after *that*, I could barely stand.

"Get dressed," he whispered, breathless as he withdrew.

"What?" That wasn't how things usually went. My hands flew out and grabbed his shirt. "What about... you know... the rest of it?"

Half of his mouth pulled up into a wicked grin and he kissed me again, causing my head to spin and my chest to hum with desire. "Later," he murmured against my mouth. "It'll give you something to come back to." Then he handed me my bathers and left the room with me standing there naked and a little confused. Did that mean he thought I might try to run? That I was going to get on that board and paddle until I reached Tasmania? Huh. The concept intrigued me.

I knew he was enjoying me in the bedroom. Even with my limited understanding of men, I knew having sex on tap was something guys liked the idea of. But I didn't know how much he was truly into *me,* the person. Did that mean he was in this marriage as much as I was? Or was I just overthinking the entire situation?

I shook my head and pulled my bathers up my legs. Only time would tell. I didn't expect Sam to view me as his soulmate, but I did expect that one day he might grow to love me. I wanted that. I dared not even think it too loudly, but it was something my soul craved—a person to love me, quirks and all. If I could do everything right, maybe Sam would be that guy.

"THERE ARE LITERALLY no waves at this beach. How am I supposed to surf?" I looked out at the gentle ripples that attempted to call themselves waves as Kristian and I carried our boards down the wooden steps.

He chuckled and shook his head. "You wanna learn to surf, or you wanna drown your first time out?"

"Learn to surf," I said, the answer fairly obvious.

"Then this is how we learn."

When we got to the soft sand, we stopped about fifteen metres away from the water where he dropped his board on the ground, explaining what a rail was and how I was supposed to attach the leg rope.

"What we're gonna do is get you learning your positioning and practise your paddling."

"Then will we learn how to catch a wave?"

"No. Then I'll teach you duck diving and turtle rolls."

"Do any of these involve real ducks or real turtles?"

"No."

"Then none of this sounds very fun so far," I said, teasing him a little as I folded my arms across my chest.

He laughed. "Quit being a brat. You've got to put in a bit of work before you can have fun. Now get in the bloody water."

With a smile on my face, I picked up the board he'd loaned me and tucked it under my arm, walking beside him until we were knee-deep in the salty water.

"First, we're working on positioning." He showed me how to place my body on the board, centred so it wouldn't roll too far back or forward. Once he'd made me do that about thirty thousand times, we moved on to paddling, which made my arms burn like a mother.

"No wonder you lot all have such big arms," I commented as I heaved myself and my board on another lap between the two trees I was using as my guide. At the end of each lap, he had me get off the board, position myself correctly and then paddle off again. The lesson had been going for an hour, and I was exhausted.

"Had enough for today?" he asked when I slid off the board and leaned against it, a little too puffed to haul myself back on.

I nodded. "I tip my hat to you. I thought I was fit, but I'm not this fit."

"It'll come with practise." He kindly helped me carry my board back up to the beach, where we took a seat on the sand while we disconnected our leg ropes.

"Thanks for this," I said after a few moments. Looking out over the water was calming. It made me feel peaceful and focused.

"No worries. I could see you getting a bit of cabin

fever. But you think this is something you wanna keep doing?"

"If you can handle my complaining." I glanced at him and grinned, making him chuckle.

"You're OK," he said, knocking shoulders with me. "But we should get back. Jasmine will have a fit if we're not back soon, and Sam will start to think I've stolen you for myself."

"Jasmine I understand, but I doubt Sam would be *that* worried."

Kristian looked at me for a long moment. "What makes you so sure?"

I shrugged. "I don't know. It's not like he chose me."

"You don't think he's into you?"

"Time will tell. The novelty hasn't worn off yet."

"The novelty of what? Being married, or being with a new girl?"

New girl. The comment only served to remind me that there had been women before me. It wasn't something I liked thinking about. Would my inexperience mean he'd grow bored sooner?

"Both."

"Maybe it won't wear off at all."

"When a kid gets a puppy for Christmas, he loves it, feeds it, walks it every day. Then the puppy stops being new, life gets more important and the walking stops. He feeds the dog because he has to, but he does it with a sigh because it's become a job. Eventually he gives that dog to a shelter when it starts tearing the furniture apart because it's bored. He says there's something wrong with it, and he doesn't have the time to fix it. And when that dog gets destroyed instead of rehomed, he isn't sad. He's just glad it's not his responsibility anymore."

When I finished, he just stared at me. "That surprises you?" I asked, trying to figure out exactly what was behind the knit in his brow. Was it shock? Confusion? Was he checking to see if I had a second head?

"Your family must be really fucked up for you to think like that."

I looked away. "Maybe."

Standing up, he brushed the sand from his board shorts, then held his hand out to me. "Maybe you should watch the way Toby is with Rogue. That dog is ten years old, and Toby loves him as much as he did the day he got him. We're all like that. Once you become a part of the family, you're a part of it for life. We *always* take care of our own."

His eyes were sincere, and I wished his words could make me feel better. But when I wasn't enough for my own mother, and my father so readily turned his back on me, how could I be expected to believe Sam and his family wouldn't quit me too? The only person who hadn't given up on me was Holland. But now... I missed her friendship. Her contact. Her strength. Was she even OK?

"Come on." He continued to hold out his hand, stubbornly.

With a sigh, I took it and collected my towel and board, rolling his words around in my mind and holding onto them for a while. It would be nice if they were true. It would be great to truly belong somewhere.

"What the fuck?" Kristian raked his fingers through the sand.

"What's wrong?"

"My stuff. It's gone."

"What's gone? Where?"

"I don't fucking know." He dug more furiously, widening his search. "My keys. They're gone. I had them under the towels. Fuck." He stood up and looked around the beach, then squinted up to the staircase that led up the cliff. I followed his gaze and saw a flash of light hair. Someone was running. "Shit," he hissed, taking off at a sprint towards the stairs.

I gathered our towels and the boards and followed him as fast as I could, my mind in a panic. What if they took the ute? How would we get back? Jasmine was expecting us. Sam would think I ran.

Wait.

When I hit the bottom of the stairs, I stopped. *What if I don't follow? What if I drop everything right here and run?* He was on foot. He wouldn't catch me if I was fast. There were multiple beach exits; I could take any of them and flag a car down on the main road. If I left now, I could quit before Sam realised what a mistake it was to marry me, leave before they changed their minds about keeping me around. I could only contain the crazy inside me for so long. It was only a matter of time before I said or did something so far outside the box that I horrified them. That whole dog story was just the tip of the iceberg. Kristian had looked at me like I was mildly insane. So far, only Holland had managed to overlook my… quirks.

Holland.

She was coming for dinner. If I ran now, I'd never see her again. *And what if Jasmine really did follow through with her threat and hurt everyone you care about?* The voice inside my head made a good point.

And what about Sam?

I really, *really* liked Sam, because he was the first man to accept me in any way at all. He told me I was perfect. Beautiful. Was that enough for me in the long run, or could it be more? I wanted it to be more. I wanted to fall in love, wanted him to fall in love with me, painfully, desperately. But I didn't think that could be possible.

You love him already, my inner voice said.

No I don't. I don't. I doubted him—that was how I felt towards Sam.

Bullshit. You l—

"Fucking bitch!" The sound of Kristian yelling in a rage snapped me out of the argument with my inner self. I shook my head, shaking the jumble in there straight before I picked up the boards and started up the stairs.

Forget Sam. Forget Holland. You should run, my inner self insisted.

And go where? Nobody wants me.

You have your house. You can sell it, start somewhere new.

I can't, I responded, rushing up the steps two at a time.

Why?

"Because I'm a Cartwright now," I said out loud.

That's three times. You've chosen the Cartwrights three times now.

Inner me was right, I had chosen them three times. I chose them when I agreed to the marriage. I chose them when I lied to my family. And I chose them when I climbed the stairs instead of choosing to run. They kept telling me I was one of them, I guess now, I had to believe it. I obviously didn't want to leave or I would have found a way.

"Did you see her?" Kristian asked as I reached the carpark.

"No. I was getting the boards." *And contemplating living a life on the run.* It amazed me that he didn't seem to have given a thought to the possibility that I could have taken off.

"Some fucking bitch just stole my car. Now she has my wallet, my phone, my favourite fucking shirt." He picked up a rock and hurled it into the street. It bounced twice, then skidded. "Fuck!"

As I watched him rage, the irony of the situation set in and I couldn't help myself, I started to giggle.

"You think this is funny?"

"You got robbed." Even when I pressed my lips together, I couldn't stop.

"No shit." He ran his hands across either side of his cropped hair.

"You. A Cartwright. *You* were robbed." My giggle turned into full-blown laughter. It was so ridiculous. "The thief gets a taste of his own medicine, and it's *so* sour." I'd moved on to cackling by that point. It was probably a bad idea—Kristian was pissed, and I didn't know him well enough to know if he was dangerous in that state—but I couldn't help it. I'd lost pretty much everything, my mind might as well go too.

"Shit." A slight grin pulled at the corner of his mouth, producing a dimple. "Fuck." He started laughing. "Being robbed fucking sucks."

Tears streamed from my eyes as I leaned forward, struggling to stand. "I hope you're insured." Every word came out more high-pitched than the last. This was the most poetic justice.

"Yeah, I'm insured." He chuckled a little more before he calmed. "Now we have to figure out how the hell to get home. Sam's gonna kill me if I don't get you back."

Wiping my eyes, I looked around and spotted someone pulling a paddleboard from their roof. "Excuse me!" I put the boards on the ground and jogged towards the man.

"Me?" He pointed at his chest.

"Yes. Do you think we could borrow your phone? Someone just stole our car."

"Aw shit, that sucks. Sure, I'll grab it." He turned around and went back to his beat-up Mazda, then returned with his phone.

"Do you know anyone's number by heart?" I asked Kristian. I only knew my father's and the funeral home's from before we all had mobiles. It was one of the curses of modern technology.

"I can call the house. Someone will be there."

While he made the call, I thanked the stranger and made a little small talk about the situation, the surf conditions and the weather. I didn't want to say any of it but thought I at least owed him a conversation since he was rescuing us and all.

I was thankful when Kristian returned and handed the guy back his phone.

"Spoke to Toby. He's on his way."

"Thank God."

After thanking our good citizen, we took a seat on the wooden railing while we waited.

"Was that guy weird to you or something?" Kristian asked after a while.

"No. Why?"

"Because you looked like you were about to shit your-self while you were talking to him."

Charming.

I shifted a little in my discomfort. "I'm just not good at talking to people. Especially men."

"You're fine with all of us."

"Yeah, but you're different."

"We're not men?" He laughed.

"No. I mean, yes, you're men."

"Then how are we different?"

I shrugged, and then the words just tumbled out. "Because you're family, and you treat me like I'm family too." The second part of that sentence was said on barely a breath. I didn't want to be too bold and jinx their accep-tance of me.

A genuine smile spread across his handsome features. "You know, I always wanted a sister."

"Yeah?" A giddy happiness bounced about in my chest.

"Yeah." He nudged his shoulder against mine. "And you can call me Kris. Jasmine is the only one who uses our full names."

"OK, Kris it is. I'd say you could call me Leesh, but you already do."

He grinned. "Guess I already thought of you as family."

"TOBY DOESN'T DRIVE a Range Rover, does he?" I asked as I saw a familiar-looking metallic red SUV turning off the main road.

"No, that's Sam."

"You think he'll let me take lessons with you again?"

Kris frowned for a second. "He's not your keeper."

Isn't he?

The Range Rover crawled to a stop in front of where we were sitting and the hatch opened slowly.

"You get in. I've got the boards," Kris said, grabbing our gear.

Sam got out and opened my door for me. As I walked up, he dropped a kiss on the top of my head but only had a glare for his brother.

"It wasn't his fault," I said, keeping my voice low as I placed a hand on Sam's chest.

"He should've been more careful."

"Should all the people you steal from be more careful too?"

He looked down and met my eyes, his gaze softening. "Don't try and put this into perspective, peaches. I'm trying to be pissed. He was supposed to look out for you."

"And he did. Here I am, safe and sound." I did a little spin, then rose onto my toes and pressed a kiss against his lips. "Thanks for coming to get us." I moved to get in the car, but he caught me by the hand and pulled me back to him, his hands finding my face as he held me close and kissed me until my knees went weak.

"For fuck's sake, we just got stranded at the beach. It's not like you had to rescue her from the trenches in Iraq. She doesn't even have a scratch on her." Kristian slid into the back seat of the SUV and slammed his door.

Sam dropped his forehead against mine. "I don't think he understands how precious you are."

He said all the right words, did all the right things, but so had my mother once upon a time. And she left. Abandoned me to a man who had zero trust in me, who always expected me to mess up. My father said and did the right things too, but it always seemed there was an underlying agenda to his words, designed to manipulate or suppress me. Despite his insistence that I remained within the family's web, he let me walk away with the weakest of fights. All those years insisting I was needed and then *poof,* he no longer wanted me. I had a complete inability to trust the things I saw and heard. I didn't know if I could ever get over that enough to believe Sam when he so sweetly called me precious and perfect. My mind kept adding an invisible 'for now' to everything he said.

With a smile in place of a response, I slipped from his hold and into my seat before he closed my door and got back in.

"Did you see who took your wheels?" he asked Kris, turning around in his seat before he started the car.

"Some girl. Blonde hair. That's all I caught."

"What'd she get besides the car?"

"Phone, wallet, some clothes."

"Got your location switched on?"

"Maybe. Try Snapchat."

Sam pulled out his phone and opened the app, pinching his fingers against the screen and changing it into a map covered with people's Bitmojis.

"I had no idea Snapchat could do that," I said, looking on. Holland and I had downloaded it when it first became a thing, but we just sent each other a photo with some animal filter on it every day to keep our streak going. We'd managed to get to 547, but that would be gone now.

Sam tapped on the one that looked like Kristian, then zoomed in. "Looks like your phone is still on and they're in one of these houses."

"The phone's in the pocket on the door. They probably don't even know they have it."

Sam studied the map for a moment, then looked at Kristian and grinned. "Wanna go steal your car back?"

Kristian pumped his fist in the air. "Fucking yes, I fucking do," he hooted, high-fiving Sam between the seats. "Ready to earn your stripes, Leesh?" He turned to me, his eyes sparkling with excitement.

"What will I have to do?" I asked, genuinely curious but anxious at the same time. The last time I went along with someone's plan to steal their stuff back, I ended up changing my last name.

"Depends on the situation," Sam said. "You might

need to run interference, or maybe just be a lookout. Nothing that could get you hurt."

"OK," I said, even though my stomach tightened.

"You're in?" Kris asked.

"I'm in." I grinned.

Sam took my hand and kissed my knuckles. "That's my girl."

"A true Cartwright," Kris said, beaming proudly.

I grew nervous under their scrutiny. "Are we going to do this, or are you both going to gawk at me all afternoon?"

"Oh, we're doing this." Kris rubbed his hands together as the engine roared to life.

"No one crosses a Cartwright and gets away with it," Sam crowed as he planted his foot and took off, kicking up gravel and dirt in our wake.

About twenty-five minutes later, we found ourselves cruising a residential street filled with very normal, quiet-looking houses. No stolen Holden utes in sight.

"It has to be one of these four houses," Kris said, holding Sam's phone with the Snapchat map as his guide.

"How about that one?" I asked, pointing to the one with the grass that needed mowing and weeds in the over-grown garden. It seemed the most obvious to me—someone who'd steal a car and then bring it back to their own place wasn't likely to be the most house-proud person in the world.

"Yeah," Sam said quietly. "Double garage. Looks like a good place to start."

"I'll go around back, see if there's a way in." Kris went to get out of the car before Sam told him to wait.

"Coms, dude." He opened the glove compartment and

pulled out a walkie-talkie that had a wired earpiece attached. *Impressive*.

Kris put it on while Sam pulled one out for himself, then handed me one too. "Know how to use these?"

I nodded. "Press the button to talk. Release to listen."

He positioned the piece in my ear. "These are even easier than that. Turn it on and when you speak, it activates. We'll do a check once we're out of the car."

My heart was beating even harder than it was on the day Holland and I tracked these guys down. This felt way more serious. "What should I do?"

"Stay here, keep an eye on the property. You see anyone coming out or going in, you let us know."

I nodded. "I can do that." I gripped the walkie-talkie tightly.

"Good girl." He kissed the side of my head, then got out of the car with Kristian, giving him a set of instructions as they walked towards the property. Splitting up, one disappeared down the side of the house as the other passed around the front.

"Everyone reading me?" Kristian's voice entered my ear, followed by Sam's.

"I've got you. You got us, peaches?"

"I've got you," I replied, climbing into the back of the car so I could get a better view of the house. There wasn't much going on, and the curtains were fully drawn. "No activity to report," I added, because it seemed like something I should say in that situation.

"Clear on this side," Sam said. "I can see two people in the house, a male and a female. I'm pretty sure they're fucking." There was a pause, and then he came back on again. "Yep. Definitely fucking."

"Good, they're distracted," Kris said. "Because we're gonna have to get in there. The only entry to the garage is through the house. There isn't even a window to climb through."

"How are you going to get in?" I asked, my nerves starting to make me feel sick.

"Back door. Keep watch. I'm going silent."

"Will do," Sam said. "They look pretty into it. You've got a while."

There was a click in my ear when Kris turned his walkie off.

"Fucking hell," I muttered under my breath, rubbing my hands together to relieve the dampness.

"You OK?" Sam asked.

"Yeah. I was talking to myself, forgot this thing picked everything up."

"You're doing great."

"I'm not doing anything. I'm sitting in a car."

A click. "I'm inside," Kris whispered. "The Ute is here."

"Still fucking," Sam added.

"Clear," I said. I was basically just mimicking what I'd seen in movies.

There was a rustling noise, then a sigh. "I can't find my keys. They're not in the car, and I can't see them in the fucking house." A pause. "Shit."

"Um, dude, do you still use that *Game of Thrones* wallet?" Sam asked.

"Yeah."

"Shit. I see it."

"It's in there with them, isn't it?"

"Yep."

"Shit."

There was no way we could leave any of that behind.

"I've got an idea," I said, pulling the earpiece out and dropping the whole unit on the seat beside me. Then I jumped out of the car and sprinted to the front door before either of them could say anything to stop me.

Out of breath, I rapped my knuckles against the window and pressed the doorbell several times. Then I heard a male voice yelling from inside the house.

"Hold your fucking horses, I'm coming. I'm coming."

He pulled the door open dressed in only a pair of jeans with the top button undone. There were tattoos all over his arms and across his chest. He looked mean. "What's the bloody emergency?"

A dishevelled-looking blonde woman peeked over his shoulder. "Who is it, Johno?" They both peered at me through the fly screen, and I was glad I'd made enough noise that they both came running.

"Thanks God someone's home," I gasped, out of breath from my sprint. "I've been knocking on all the doors and you wouldn't believe it, but no one is home. I tried the house next door, the one across the street and the one next to that." I was rambling, trying to keep them both focused on me long enough for Kristian to get his keys and wallet and get out of there.

"I get it, I get it." The guy, Johno, held up his hands to silence me, but I didn't let that stop me. Kristian kept low, then darted across the living room towards the bedroom. I needed to keep them distracted.

You can do this.

"I'm just so happy that someone is home *here*. You have no idea how much I need to do today. Well, tonight.

There isn't really that much of today left now, is there. Really only enough time to get home and make dinner, which is what's really important to me. I have all the groceries in my car. All of them. And they're coming for dinner, and I'm not going to be there in time. What a nightmare, right?"

"Yeah. Sure. What do you want?"

"Well, as I was saying, there are all these groceries and I need to get them home, but my car, it broke down, and I have no idea what's wrong with—"

"I know nuffin 'bout cars, lady."

Kris appeared in the doorway of the bedroom and gestured for me to keep going. *Come on, brain, don't fail me now.*

"What? Oh no, I don't want you to fix it. I just want you to let me use your phone to call roadside. Silly me left mine on the counter at home. Crazy, right? We have those things attached to our hands almost 24/7, but when you really need it, you've left it behind or the battery has died. But that's life, right?"

Kris darted through the living area again, ducking through an archway that I assumed led into the kitchen, giving me a thumbs up before he was gone from view. I assumed that meant I could wrap things up.

"I'll just get her a phone," the woman said, pulling her dressing gown tight around her body. She was quite pretty, even if she was a little strung out looking. I thought it was a shame that she'd obviously gotten herself mixed up with some sort of criminal element.

Um, hello, Pot, I'd like you to meet Kettle.

The thought threw me for a moment. I was a girl mixed up with a criminal element. I was standing here helping them break into these people's house. It was justified, but still, it was illegal.

"Ah…." I took a step backward, suddenly eager to turn tail and run. "Actually, I think maybe I *do* have my phone. So sorry to bother you." Just as I moved to leave, something fell. Something metal, something noisy, something in the garage.

Shit.

Run.

My movement halted before I even managed to get anywhere as Johno grabbed the back of my hair. "You're not going anywhere, bitch" he growled, dragging me backwards into the house. "I'm not fucking stupid. I know a distraction when I see one."

There wasn't a hell of a lot I could do in the limited space without ripping my hair out at the roots, so I did what I could to keep my footing while trying to remember something from all those self-defence classes I'd taken over the years.

How do you escape a hair hold? I searched my mind, the answer flashing like a slide show in my memory—turn, elbow, knee.

Clutching my hair at his hand, I turned my body to the right and brought my left elbow along with the motion, slamming it into the side of his jaw. He let out an "oof," the surprise making him release my hair and arch backward. I grabbed his shoulders and brought up my left knee, right into his groin. He went down like a sack of potatoes, and I kicked him again for good measure.

"You need to get yourself a nicer boyfriend, lady," I said as I stood over his prone body, adrenaline surging through every part of me. I couldn't believe I'd actually taken that guy out. *I could be the next Wonder Woman!*

No sooner had I delivered my incredibly witty remark than she bared her teeth and launched herself at me, claws out. I braced myself, ready for a catfight, but she was caught mid-air by a strong arm belonging to an even stronger body. Sam.

"That was fucking awesome," he said, looking at poor Johno groaning on the floor while he held the woman under his arm as she struggled and swore.

I blushed. "It was nothing."

"Don't be coy about it." The girl took to flicking her arms and legs back and forth like a frog in the water. Sam didn't even seem the slightest bit bothered. "That was some seriously impressive stuff. Where did you learn to do that?"

"I took some self-defence class a while back."

"You had a great teacher." He shook his head, just grinning at me. The scrutiny made me nervous, and I wished he'd stop looking at me like he saw something special there.

"It was a fluke that I remembered." I waved it off just as the garage door opened and Kristian revved the engine of his ute. It was a copper colour and pretty fancy-looking. Kristian pulled up to where he could see us and wound down the window.

"Got everything?" Sam called out.

"They took a couple hundred out of my wallet, but other than that…." He shrugged. "Who took out the moaner?" he asked, spotting Johno.

"Peaches," Sam announced proudly.

I just shook my head and looked around the living

room. "Where's the money?" I asked the dangly girl. She was trying to push her way out of Sam's grip, still to no avail.

"I'm not telling you shit."

I held my foot over Johno's crown jewels. "If you want to continue having a sex life, you will," I threatened.

"You bitch."

"I'm not the one who stole your shit. Where's the money?"

"We spent it."

"Well...." I walked around the living area. There had to be something that was worth a couple of hundred dollars we could take to make this even. That's when I spotted a MacBook and a pair of Beats. "We'll just take these as compensation for the money and our pain and suffering," I said, pulling the cord from the wall and tucking it all under my arm. "You have a nice day now."

"I'll fucking cut you, you bitch." She struggled some more, and I really wished she was wearing more clothes, because her robe had slipped loose, and those boobs were just everywhere.

Can't unsee. Can't unsee.

"You go. I'll take care of these two," Sam said, nodding towards Kris and his ute.

I hesitated. "You're not...?" *He isn't going to take care of them... permanently, is he?* No. He'd made it clear that killing wasn't in their repertoire, and Toby had backed that up. He was probably just going to make some creative threats, or whatever else they'd do to warn people off.

"Go," he commanded.

Gripping my newly procured items a little tighter under

my arm, I set my jaw and headed out the front, jumping into the ute with Kris. "He'll meet us at home."

"All righty," Kris said, giving his brother a salute before taking off.

I sat there and quietly stewed, my fingers gripping the edge of the MacBook as I ground my teeth together.

I couldn't hold it in any longer. "What is he doing to them?"

Kris shrugged. "Making them sorry they messed with a Cartwright."

"How?"

He glanced at me. "In whatever language they understand."

"I thought you guys got creative before threats and violence?"

"I'm sure he'll be very creative. It's best you don't worry about it. You did the name proud today. I can't believe you took that guy out on your own. And for a girl who can't talk much to strangers, you had bloody verbal diarrhoea."

He laughed and went on for a little longer, but I couldn't listen. The adrenalin I'd been running on was wearing off, making my skin itch. I didn't feel right. I'd acted out of survival then gotten carried away like I was playing some game. But it wasn't a game. They were real people, and I was fairly sure Sam was hurting them.

"Those for me?" Kris asked, bringing me back when he tapped on the metal case of the laptop.

"Yes. They spent the money." I turned and put the items on the back seat.

"Well, don't open it so they can't track it. We'll get our guy to clean it so we can offload it."

"You have a guy for that?"

"We have guys for lots of things."

"What about body disposal?" I couldn't stop the question jumping out of my mouth if I tried.

He glanced at me and quirked a brow. "We don't kill people, Leesh."

"Never? Isn't that why your dad's in prison?"

"He told you, huh? Yeah, the old man got someone killed and he's paying for it. The rest of us are much more careful than that."

His words allowed a little relief to seep into my overly tight chest. I glanced at the time. "Jasmine is going to have a fit. I'm supposed to be helping with dinner," I said, needing a change of subject, needing to focus on something a little more *normal.*

Kris laughed. "She'll be fine. Wait till I tell her what you did today. She'll erect a statue in your honour."

CHAPTER THIRTEEN
SHE DOESN'T GET TO FEEL
SORRY FOR YOU ANYMORE

"DID THEY TELL YOU?" Sam burst through the door and caught me in his arms, pressing his mouth to mine in a desperate kiss that caused me to drop the potato and peeler I was holding.

"About our little ball-breaker here?" Jasmine replied with a grin that lit up her eyes and face. "Yeah. She's a natural. I told you all she'd fit in well."

From the moment we walked in the door, Kristian had started heralding me as the family hero. When I'd returned from my shower, he was still going on. I just wanted to make the potato bake and forget all about it.

Sam released my mouth but not my body, his arm around my waist like we were about to go dancing. "You should've seen it, Jazz. He had her by the hair and I charged in there, about to rip his arm off his body. Then this tiny little thing twisted around, elbowed him in the face and kicked him in the balls. I've never seen anything more beautiful."

"Sounds impressive," Jasmine agreed, a giant smile on her face.

"It was nothing," I argued.

"You're a fighter," Sam stated, pride in his voice. "It's impressive."

"Most chicks freak out," Abbot put in, sticking his head in the fridge on his never-ending quest for food.

"Dinner is in an hour," Jasmine said.

"I'm hungry now."

"Then have this." She picked up a peeled carrot and stuck it in his mouth. He grinned, then bit into it with a crunch. Jasmine shook her head but smiled.

"I need to finish this," I told Sam, nodding towards the pile of potatoes on the counter.

"I'll help." He released me and picked up the items I dropped, rinsing the peeler before he started working on the pile with me.

"I like this domestic side of you," I said, enjoying doing something more with him than having sex. I mean, I really, *really* enjoyed the sex, and since we'd only been together for a couple of weeks, that hunger seemed to always be there. But it was nice to do something a little more... average. I liked *this*. I liked being in the kitchen with the noise and the chaos. It was a togetherness I'd never experienced before, and it made me feel like a part of something. This crowded kitchen was far better than all the space I had to myself when I lived on my own. I didn't miss the solitude for a moment.

Despite being uncomfortable over the events of the afternoon, I couldn't help but let just a little of the pride they felt over my actions seep in. I wasn't used to praise. Egos weren't allowed in my house; only humble, unobtrusive behaviour was tolerated. The fact that I was being applauded for acting in a rash manner was new to me. It made me uncomfortable but happy. Like I wanted to be proud of myself but couldn't stop thinking I should be ashamed. It was a bit of a conundrum.

When preparations were finished in the kitchen, we all dispersed to get ready for our honoured guests. Family was obviously really important to the Cartwrights, and even though Jasmine seemed disinclined towards Holland, she was willing to pull out all the stops if it meant keeping her son happy. In my eyes, that was love.

Sam couldn't wait to get me upstairs, undressing me the moment we were through the door. His lips seared against my skin and his hands were everywhere, squeezing and pulling.

"I can't stop wanting you," he breathed, picking me up before dropping me on the bed. "I want to be inside you day and night. You drive me insane." His fingers danced over my naked chest, teasing my puckered nipples.

"Insane?"

"With desire, with want, with need. I can't get enough." His mouth joined with mine as his fingers travelled down my body and between my legs, teasing me towards climax. "You amaze me."

I shook my head, fighting to keep my thoughts at bay while focusing on the moment, on Sam, on what he was doing to me. He was so complimenting, so kind and loving. He'd given me no reason to doubt him, yet I struggled to trust him. I couldn't just believe the things he said held meaning.

I'm not amazing.

His fingers entered me and his mouth joined in,

causing lights to flash behind my eyes while the pressure in my core built to a mind-numbing crescendo.

"Oh!"

Knock, knock. There was no time between the knock and the opening of the door. "They're only ten minutes— holy fuck. Shit." Chaos ensued as the door slammed. I scrambled for something to cover myself. Sam yelled for Abbot to fuck off.

On the other side of the door came a bubble of laughter.

"What happened?" Kris asked his cackling twin.

"I just saw Sam's arsehole. I need to bleach my eyes," Abbot responded.

"The fuck?" Kristian joined in with his twin's laughter. "What were they doing?"

Meanwhile, Sam had pulled on a pair of pants and burst out the door before Abbot could explain.

Abbot held up his hands. "I knocked," he said through his laughter.

Sam grabbed him by the front of his shirt. "Don't ever walk into our room. Ever," he growled.

"OK, but mate, please tell me you don't still have a hard-on. Because you're standing really close."

That was it for me. I covered my mouth with my hand as my laughter squeaked out and shook my shoulders.

Sam obviously didn't find it as funny as the rest of us. There was a thud against the wall and guttural laughter from the twins. "Just stay the fuck out," Sam warned. Then he returned to the room looking more than a little frustrated, raking his hands through his hair. "You OK?"

Grinning, I bit my lip to contain my mirth and nodded. "Come here," I said, holding out my hand.

"You can't honestly think that was funny," he said, coming towards me.

I got up on my knees and let the sheet drop from my body as I called him with my arms. "You have to admit it was a little funny. Terrible timing, but funny."

"*Terrible* timing."

Smiling, I ran my hands up his chest and into his hair, winding myself around him before sucking on his lower lip. "Forget about them. We only have ten minutes."

A rumble emanated from his chest. "I know this probably isn't a turn-on, but after today and the state I'm in, I probably only need five."

I laughed. "Well, lucky you've already taken care of me today, twice."

He grinned. "I do like to spoil my girl."

"Then give it to me, Sam. Give it to me hard and fast."

"I love it when you tell me what you want," he groaned, moments before his mouth crashed into mine and he gave me exactly what I asked for. Hard and fast.

"THEY'RE HERE!" I practically squealed in delight when a beat-up Ford Ranger pulled into the driveway. Compared to the other brothers, Nate's wheels surprised me—they all had new top-of-the-line rides, whereas his looked like it had seen better days.

The moment I spotted Holland getting out of the truck, I barrelled out the door and practically threw myself at her.

"I've missed you so much," I whispered, hugging her as tight as I could. We'd barely gone a day without speaking since we were kids. Two and a half weeks was too long. I had so much I wanted to tell her.

"I've missed you too," she said, pulling back to look into my eyes. "How have you been?" Her tone told me she'd been worried about me, which was funny because I'd been worried about her. It really pained me that we weren't able to talk to each other all the time. It made the reality of our situation slam into me with full force. Despite how we were being treated, we were essentially prisoners. We couldn't leave without an escort.

I pressed my lips together and held onto her arms. "I'm OK."

She let out a gasp as if it pained her to hear that, then pulled me against her soft body and hugged me so tight I could barely breathe. *God, what was Nate doing to her?* She was beside herself.

Thankfully, Jasmine saw my need for air and interrupted, placing a gentle hand on my back. "Maybe check that the potatoes aren't burning?" she said, and I nodded and headed back inside, where the twins and Sam were starting to carry things to the outdoor table near where Toby was hovering over the rotisserie that had a half lamb on it. I'd thought that was far too much meat at first, but after seeing the way these men put away their meals, I worried that it may not be enough.

"How was the reception?" Sam asked, pausing when he saw me and nodding to where I'd come from. "Frosty?"

"A little," I said with a shrug. "I only caught the beginning of it. Nate hadn't spoken, Holland seemed nervous and Jasmine was being superhostess."

"Sounds about right. Always the prodigal son." He

shook his head and walked away, his hands full of wine glasses.

With the kitchen to myself for five minutes, I pulled the oven door open, the scent of the creamy cheesy potatoes making my stomach growl. This was always one of Holland's favourites. Her aunty made a roast lamb with potatoes au gratin and vegetables every Sunday in winter, and I would score myself an invite as often as I was allowed. She would always let me have seconds, constantly trying to 'fatten me up'.

Using a fork to test that it was cooked all the way through, I decided it was ready to come out of the oven and grabbed the oven mitts to help me handle the huge tray.

"Let me do that." Kris came rushing to my side and took over manoeuvring the heavy pan to the bench to cool. "Smells amazing."

"Thanks. You think I made enough for everyone? This was the biggest tray I could find."

"Probably not." He laughed. "I could eat that whole thing on my own. I'm drooling from the smell."

"Well, you have to share." I gave him a stern look that was mostly teasing.

"Toby says the lamb is good to go. We just need a tray to slice it into," Abbot said, sticking his head into the kitchen.

"I'll bring one," I said, looking back to Kris. "Can you carry the potatoes out?"

"Sure thing, boss." He winked and disappeared with the food with the ease of a dancer. I really needed to get stronger; my arms were screaming after all the paddling I'd done today.

Heading out with the tray, I heard Jasmine's voice coming down the hall. "It's not every day a woman with five sons gets to entertain two daughters." She seemed genuinely pleased about the situation, and I smiled to myself before heading out through the sliding doors to give Toby the tray. As he was piling on sliced lamb, Nate and Holland came out to the table, and the other three brothers greeted them with hugs and cheek kisses. It was a big family reunion.

"You're not going over there to say hi?" I asked when Toby glanced up but went back to carving and stacking meat.

He said nothing at first, just looked over again. "I'll talk to him later."

This was a different Toby. He'd gone all stiff since they'd arrived, and I wondered what was going on between him and Nate besides the obvious. "Do you have something against Holland?" I wondered if that's where his irritation stemmed. He might harbour the same feelings towards her as Jasmine did.

"No." He shook his head. "I just think Nate should've left her alone."

"I guess he did take the game a bit too far. But then so did she."

He looked at me. "Maybe. But everyone else got caught in the middle. Including you."

I shrugged. "I'm OK," I said, uncomfortable from yet another reminder that my position in this family didn't occur naturally.

"Why don't you take that tray over while I finish up," he said, nodding towards the meat.

I made it about four steps before Sam jogged over and

relieved me of the weight. "I prefer peaches, but lamb is good too." He winked and I blushed. We took our seats around the table and the meal took on a life of its own, as they frequently did in this house. I loved the camaraderie, the way the men joked around and Jasmine was always trying to stop them like they were still teenagers. *Men clearly never grow up*.

Everyone seemed to be having a good time, although I noticed that Holland was a little on the quiet side, which was strange because large groups of people were normally her element, and I wanted to share this with her. It was the big noisy family we'd always dreamed of being a part of, but she seemed lost and eager to leave.

When he'd finished eating, Sam's arm slipped around the back of my chair, his fingers playing with the bare skin at my shoulder as he whispered in my ear. "When this is over, I want to take you upstairs and barricade the door shut so I can spend the rest of the night eating you uninterrupted."

My body reacted instantly, and I pressed my knees together to calm the throb.

"Promise?" I whispered, cheeks flaming as I watched his slow nod. I almost jumped out of my skin when Jasmine addressed me.

"The potatoes were delicious, Alesha," she said. "We'll have to add them to our usual rotation. There isn't a scrap left."

"Thank you," I said a little breathlessly when Sam's other hand landed on my thigh and began moving up. I grinned at him and shook my head almost unperceptively. "Down, boy."

He grinned, then nipped lightly at the skin below my

ear. When he moved his hand to a safer position, I glanced around the table to make sure we weren't being too obvious. Everyone seemed unaware. Nate had his arm around Holland and was busy talking to Kris and Abbot about the swell he'd seen from his beach house. Jasmine was happy listening, and Toby was sitting quietly down the end of the table, sneaking scraps of lamb to his Boston terrier. I waited until Holland looked my way, then smiled.

"Will you ladies excuse us for a while?" Jasmine asked when the conversation lulled. "My sons and I have some business we need to discuss."

I glanced at Sam and he nodded, patting me on the thigh before I stood up and started clearing the plates to be of help. Holland stood and did the same, but then Nate grabbed her wrist and shook his head. I frowned and looked at Sam, alarmed. He gave me a look that said 'don't interfere', but I didn't like what I was seeing.

"You aren't a servant," Nate told her.

"Neither is she," Holland objected, indicating me.

Releasing his breath, Nate nodded, then stood and helped clear. My entire body relaxed. Perhaps I read the situation wrong.

"The girls can get that, darling," Jasmine told Nate.

He just kept cleaning. "It'll be faster if we all pitch in. Once all this is clean, we'll talk business. I didn't bring my wife here so she could clean our mess."

Wow. I didn't see a problem with clearing a table to help out while they all talked. Better to get it done now than leave it to later when we were all tired. Besides, it would give me something to do while Holland and I caught up. We didn't exactly have Netflix here, so it wasn't like we could talk shows like we normally did.

"Come on, peaches," Sam said, taking the stack of plates I was holding. "We'll get this done, and then you and your friend can hang out for a bit." He kissed my nose and we all carried everything back to where it came from.

Once everything was right again, Nate handed Holland a couple of drinks, and she and I went to the living room while the brothers and Jasmine went back outside. Sam gave me a wink just before he exited. He made my heart beat ridiculously hard.

Holland still seemed nervous, even though we were alone. She was freaking me out. Had Nate been treating her all right?

"Are you OK?" I asked in a hushed tone as we took a seat on the dark grey leather couch. It was super soft and worn in from countless bodies draping themselves over it. "I've been worried sick about you since the wedding. He hasn't hurt you, has he?" I grabbed her arms and inspected her for bruising. She seemed fine. Why was she acting so cagey?

"I'm fine," Holland said with a laugh, flicking her long blonde hair over her shoulder. "Why would you worry about me? I'm the one worried about you."

"Me? No, I'm great." I wasn't the one shacking up with a guy who gave his little brothers a beatdown and then threatened his mother with the same. "I love it here." Love was probably too strong a word, and I didn't really know why I was selling it so hard, but she'd walked in there acting as though she felt sorry for me from the get-go. I wasn't to be pitied. "I mean, it gets a bit much sometimes having so many people around, and I admit to being a little homesick and bored hanging around the house all the time. But Sam is amazing whenever we're together, and I can pretty much do whatever I want the rest of the time. Kristian is teaching me to surf. Jasmine is teaching me to cook. I'm pretty much perfect." Perfect. Sure. That's what I was.

"So you're living here? Not at Sam's?"

"Sam's?"

"Nate said they all had their own places."

"Nate and Toby are the only ones living on their own. But Toby is here a lot." Toby owned an old boat he enjoyed doing up, and I'd heard him mention a property in passing, but I was fairly sure he was looking at renting it out.

"And you're happy living with them all?"

I shrugged. "I like the noise and the company." That part was true. I never felt lonely in the Cartwright house.

She frowned like I'd just given her the wrong answer. "Wow. So I imagined all the discomfort out there?"

"Discomfort?" What the hell? Did she *want* me to be miserable? She seemed disappointed that I wasn't.

"Yeah, between you and Jasmine, and Toby."

"Toby?" Was she taking drugs? "He's a pussycat."

"Are you sure about that?" She looked at me like she didn't believe me, and honestly it ticked me off. It wasn't OK for her to push her misery on me. She'd put us in this position, and I was making the most of what life had presented me. I didn't need her poking and prodding and looking for holes. She was supposed to be supportive, the one person in my life I could always count on to understand.

"I've just been worried sick about you," I assured her. "After our wedding, Nate went crazy on Kris and Abbot. Kris had a split lip, and Abbot could barely see out of one eye for a whole week. And I saw him yelling at Jasmine." Maybe she'd change her tune if she knew what I'd seen. "Lord, Holl, I was so scared. I thought he was going to hit her."

Her eye twitched. "Did he?"

"No, but he threatened to, held his hand up like he was going to backhand her the same way she did to you. And I thought, 'God help Holland if that's the kind of temper that man has.'"

She shook her head like I was talking crazy. "He doesn't have a temper, Leesh. He was angry because Jasmine hit me and the twins covered for her. I really don't think he would hit his own mother."

That wasn't how it looked to me. "So you're OK?" I wasn't convinced. She wasn't acting like herself.

"More than OK. I'm ridiculously happy. I'm in love with him." This massive goofy-looking smile took over her face.

She's in love with him? Of course she is. Holland always gets the best of everything. Well, I think I did OK out of this too.

"You do? That's such a relief." I forced a wide smile. "We got real lucky with these guys, Holl. I reckon someone was watching over us."

She nodded. "My parents, perhaps."

She always makes everything about her. The thought popped into my head unbidden, my inner voice managing to reveal the underlying cause of my reaction.

I smiled again. Two could play that game. "Or maybe God. Or my mum if she's up there. Lord knows I've prayed enough for a man to whisk me away from my

crappy life." It was true, I had, but I'd forgotten to stipu-
late his criminal status.

"I want the fairy tale," Holland quoted in the worst
Julia Roberts impression I'd ever heard.

It was strange, but as I sat there with the only friend I'd
ever really had, talking about a massive life change we'd both
experienced, my mind kept flashing back to the moment I fell
in the mud and Holland had chosen to laugh at me instead of
help. I could see her in her wedding dress, pointing at me and
laughing like it was a video on repeat in my head. It was the
opening scene to a highlight reel of our friendship, where I
was always the awkward joke and she was always the star.
Had that been why she was friends with me, because I made
her look better? I'd thought we'd been friends because we'd
both struggled with loss and we liked the same things. Except
we didn't like the same things. I didn't even like *Pretty
Woman*. I thought it glorified the objectification of women.

Why was I only just realising this? Ever since Holland
had met Nate, she'd done one selfish thing after another.
And when she fucked up, I was the one who stepped in
and picked her up. Now she was looking at me like I got
the raw end of the deal? I didn't. I got a good man who
thought I was beautiful and a family who actually wanted
me around, never making me feel inadequate. I won the
fucking forced marriage lottery.

She wanted the fairy tale? Well, I was living it. "As far
as men go, it seems we got exactly that." I squared my
shoulders with pride. Becoming indignant really made all
that doubt I normally battled with slip away. Suddenly I
was very sure of my position in this house. I was Peaches.
I was a Cartwright.

She doesn't get to feel sorry for you anymore.

"Yes." She frowned and then nodded towards the back of the house. "But what about the rest of it? Their... business activities?"

I shrugged her question off. She was so hung up on how they made their living. She needed to let it go, because they weren't going to quit any of it for her sake.

"I try not to think about it. The less we know the better, right? That's how mob guys protect their wives."

She smiled. "You watch far too many movies."

"Up until now, they've been better than my life." My life was definitely way more exciting now. I'd never had to take out a car thief before.

She gave me another pitiful look. *Has she always done this?* "You said you're a little homesick. Have you gone to visit your dad?"

That got me. My father's rejection was a sore point, and I had to blink a couple of times to straighten my thoughts. He lived next door to her aunt, so there was no point in lying. If I just stuck to the facts, we could move on. "We went to visit when we got back and he lost it. He's angry with me for getting married without him, and especially because I didn't get married in a church to a good Catholic boy."

"I'm sorry, Leesh."

"Ugh." I shrugged. "He was never going to like anyone I brought home. I always expected something like this to happen."

"He'll come around," she said, patting my leg condescendingly.

"We'll see," I said with a nonchalant shrug of the shoulder. Then I adjusted on the couch, wanting to change the conversation to something, anything else except my quarrel with my father. I smiled when the perfect topic hit me. "Tell me about Nate. I want to know *everything* about him."

Unable to resist talking about herself, her face lit up and she tossed her head back. Then she paused and did something out of character. She asked about me.

"How about you tell me all about Sam. Start with the moment you locked eyes, and don't leave out a thing."

Have I been judging her too harshly? It was possible that my defensiveness over the way she perceived my marriage had made me second-guess the most constant relationship I'd had in my life. I felt awful and almost wanted to ask her for her forgiveness. I took her hands and said, "Oh, Holland, he's wonderful." She'd responded with "So is Nate," and from that point on, we continued to talk about her and how wonderful her new life was.

By the time she left, I wasn't feeling sorry at all. I felt slighted. Again.

"You seem quiet. Everything OK?" Sam walked up behind me and took the brush from my hand, standing behind me and working it through my thick hair. I watched him in the bathroom mirror, his handsome face concentrated on each languid stroke. *God, that feels nice.*

"I'm OK." I sighed. "Just tired."

Nate and Holland had left only half an hour before, and I was drained. She went on and on about Nate's virtues and how he was building her a ladder—why?—and that he was a wonderful cook, delivered as if she thought my husband didn't cook at all. I was really happy for her, truly I was, but I couldn't help feeling put out, dragged down. I had stuff going on in my life too, had found happiness that I wanted to share. I'd been missing her so much over the past weeks, and when we finally got the change to talk, I barely got a word in.

Had I always been the supporting role on the Holland show? And why did I not see or object to it until now?

"You didn't enjoy hanging with your friend?" Sam's hands felt amazing as he ran the brush through my shoulder-length locks. There was nothing more relaxing than having someone play with your hair.

"It was OK. Things are just different now, I guess."

"Because you aren't single and living in each other's pockets anymore?"

"I suppose. But I think I'm starting to see some things a little more clearly."

"Like what?"

I turned to face him and leaned my butt against the vanity. "You know what I keep replaying in my mind?"

He shrugged and placed my brush in the holder next to the mirror.

"Our wedding. More importantly the moment I fell in the mud."

"I was drunk but yes, I remember."

"She pointed and laughed."

He kept his features even except for a light furrow between his brows. "Are you upset by her laughter or the mud fight that followed?"

"Her laughter. She's my best friend. Why didn't she help me up? She should've waited for my reaction before turning it into something else."

He nodded a little, his eyes looking a little faraway and thoughtful before they landed back on mine. "Did you tell her that?"

"No. I just kept sitting there thinking about all the times she dominated the spotlight, and I realised it was all the time. I was nothing more than her sidekick. It's always been about her. You know, when we were in year five, she watched *Strictly Ballroom* and decided her destiny was to be a ballroom dancer. So to prove her point, she entered us in this talent quest and convinced me to dance the male part. She got up there in this beautiful sparkly feather-edged dress and I got up in a coat and tails with my hair slicked back. People called me Alan for weeks. And to make things worse, she tried to do this move where I caught her, and we tumbled off the stage and I sprained my wrist." I ran my hands through my hair in frustration. "I keep looking back on my life, and every time I got into trouble, or felt humiliated or out of my depth was when I was with Holland. Why did I ever agree to do any of those things with her?"

He caught me around the waist. "Because you're a good person, and you've obviously been a great friend."

"I've been an *amazing* friend."

"I think you're an amazing wife."

I pressed my lips together, frowning. "You're just saying that because you want to get in my pants."

His full lips curved wickedly. "I don't need to *say* anything to get in your pants, I just need to touch you like this." He lowered his hands to the curve of my butt and squeezed. "And pull you real close like this." He held me so every curve of my body was pressed tight against the hard plains of his. "Then do a little...." He placed his lips against the base of my jaw, his breath washing over me as he spoke, lightly kissing the sensitive flesh.

I grabbed his giant biceps and gasped. "Yes," I moaned, really enjoying the subject change.

"But if I did all that, I'd be a pretty shitty husband since you obviously need to talk through everything that's troubling you." He was taunting me, I could tell that much. No man understood the inner workings of the female mind, just as we didn't understand theirs. But I knew a distraction technique when I saw it, and I remembered something about feasting on my body behind a barricaded door being mentioned at dinner. I wanted that more than I wanted to dwell on my angst-filled thoughts, just as I knew he wanted that more than he wanted to listen to said thoughts.

"No," I whimpered as he pulled away. I quickly wrapped my arms around his neck to anchor myself to him. "No talking. I've had enough talking."

He grinned. "Hmm, lucky I already barricaded the door, then."

Hmmm, maybe I was beginning to understand the inner workings of his mind because I totally called it. "Make me scream, Sam."

"It would be my absolute pleasure."

CHAPTER FOURTEEN
HER HORN'S A LITTLE BENT

WAKING to an empty bed and tangled sheets wasn't an unusual occurrence. It was something I'd grown used to in the three months I'd been a married woman—time flew when you were having fun, right?—I couldn't believe the amount my life had changed in such a short time. I couldn't believe how much I'd changed either.

If the surf report was good, Sam would get up with Kris and Abbot, then come back a couple of hours later in a fabulous mood, smelling like saltwater and seaweed. I never thought that would be a smell I adored, but it was.

Untangling myself from the messy bed, I stretched languidly, then headed into the bathroom to do the things one needed to do first thing in the morning.

The Cartwright brothers did almost everything together: they worked—not only had they performed a group job, but they also helped maintain many small businesses they used to launder the profits they took—and with the exception of Nate, they played together too. Although, from what Kris had been telling me during our surfing lessons, Nate used to always be with them, only changing his behaviour since Holland arrived on scene.

Holland. We met the year we both turned eight. Her parents had passed away, and she went to live with her aunt who was my next-door neighbour. I always thought we'd be best friends forever because from that moment, we'd gone through everything together. But then, we hadn't—I had gone through everything with *her*. And her behaviour since our combined wedding had shown me how quick she was to leave me behind.

She hated Jasmine with a passion, called her the she-devil when she wasn't in the room and always thought I was being manipulated. When the brothers went on jobs together, Nate brought her around to spend time with us so she wouldn't be alone. *Or maybe he doesn't* trust *her to be alone*. Jasmine tried to make it a great bonding experience by having the three of us hang out in the kitchen cooking a massive family meal for when everyone was home. Holland had spent the entire time with her lips in a pout and her mouth firmly shut, save for a few words here and there that were absolutely necessary. It seemed that she disliked being around the family so much that she was willing to let our friendship go too. It was the cherry on top of my massive realisation pie—Holland only cared about Holland and, like, one other person. There wasn't space for more in her life, and now that Nate was occupying that slot, she didn't seem to need me.

Being cast aside by my friend irked me as I twisted my hair into a messy bun and washed my face. We had never fought, never said a hurtful word to the other during our entire friendship. It seemed so wrong that it should just end and nothing more would happen. But that seemed to be exactly how it worked—she went her way, I went mine, and we simply became two people who used to know each other.

With no contact with my biological family since I left with Sam that day, the Cartwrights had become my family. I was alone, yet surrounded by acceptance and admiration, which was contrary to when I was with my family. I'd always felt alone there too, even when I was around my brother. Trevor was the best part of my family, and I missed him and his kids most of all, but our relationship as siblings was combined with feeling disconnected and disapproved of. He succeeded in an environment where I failed, so I was lonely even when he was around.

Here with the Cartwrights, I was accepted, encouraged, challenged. I was alone in that I was apart from them as an outsider, but I wasn't *lonely*. I could actually feel myself beginning to hope again, hope that maybe, when our relationships were eventually tested as all relationships were, the Cartwrights wouldn't turn away like my biological family did, like my best friend did too. I hoped above all that Sam would stand beside me, and that he'd do it because he wanted to, not because he had to.

As I pinched my cheeks, I let out a sigh, telling myself that there was no sense in dwelling on something I didn't have the power to change or affect. Things were just different now. I was different, just as my life was different.

The smell of bacon cooking tickled my nose. My stomach growled in anticipation, and I allowed my thoughts to file themselves away while I threw on a pair of shorts and a crop singlet before skipping down the stairs. I fucking loved bacon.

Male voices stopped me before I made it to the

kitchen. "So, Jasmine forces you into this marriage and you're suddenly all in love?" Toby. He had a note of disbelief in his voice.

"That's not what I said," Sam replied. I think he had a bowl and a whisk, based on the tapping and scrapping sounds that went with his words.

"You skipped a morning surf to make her breakfast in bed, you walk around with a permanent smile on your face, and I can hear the constant banging you two are doing through the walls half the night."

"We like each other," Sam said. He sounded like he was smiling. I was too, quite liking this conversation.

"Jesus, look at you. You're so whipped."

"Man, I don't know what to tell you. Married life agrees with me."

"Maybe Jasmine should be one of the matchmakers on that *Married at First Sight* show."

"Maybe you should get her to find a wife for you." I thought that was a great idea. Toby seemed lonely to me, something about his eyes that I recognised from seeing it in my own for so long.

"Find? Don't you mean kidnap?"

Way to put a damper on a fun conversation, Toby. I've been trying to ignore that fact.

"I don't think Leesh sees it that way." Sam's tone changed as the pan hissed and sizzled. He was right, I didn't see it so much a kidnapping as a limited choice. And I didn't hate this choice. I actually quite liked it.

"Have you asked her?"

"I don't have to." Something to add to Sam's list of qualities—arrogance. He was obviously also a mind reader.

"Why not?"

"Because I met her family. They're arseholes." I could see why he thought that after meeting my father and being told about my mother. Then there was our discussion about Holland.... "She's better off here where people care about her. We can start our own family, and she won't even need to think about that bigot of a father anymore, or any other fucked-up relative who couldn't be bothered with her. I'll take care of her."

"Back up a sec. Start your own family? As in you want to have kids?" *Holy shit. Kids?*

"Uh, yeah. We're not getting any younger, Tobes. Don't you want kids some day?"

"I guess, but I'm pushing forty. You're only thirty-five."

"And Alesha's thirty-two already. We don't have a lot of time. Women can't have babies forever."

"I'm familiar with the semantics of it all." Toby paused for a moment, and my heart thumped in my ears. *Oh God. He wants kids.* "What's she got to say about this?"

"We haven't exactly spoken about it, but we aren't being careful. She's an adult and knows what that means."

"What if she's on birth control?"

"She's not."

"How do you know."

"Because I know, all right?" Of course he did. There wasn't much of a reason for a virgin with no romantic partner to protect herself from unwanted pregnancies.

"All right. So what, she could be pregnant already?"

"I guess." There was another pause, and I felt like I could hear Toby staring at Sam with an assessing gaze.

"Actually, she might be. We haven't taken a monthly break yet, if you catch my drift."

"Wow. And you're cool with that?" Toby continued. "Having a kid with someone you're not fully in love with? Having a kid when a relationship is so new? She won't be all about you once a baby comes along."

"What's with you and all this love crap? What the fuck is love, Toby? It's just a feeling that comes and goes. It's want, it's attraction, it's something that can grow over time. If she has my kid, if she stands by me and this family, if she keeps being even a quarter of the woman she is right now, then I can handle anything with her."

"You are so whipped." Toby laughed. "And you're going to be a dad. You're too whipped to be a dad."

Sam's laugh seemed to lift from the pits of his belly, a joyful sound that hurt my heart to hear.

If I have his kid.

I closed my eyes, placing my head against the wall, my heart swelling and weeping at the same time. He was saying everything I needed to hear, and better still, he had backed up those words with the way he behaved around me. I knew he cared for me, just as I knew I cared for him. But we couldn't call it love, and there were still problems. I couldn't ignore them and get swept away with my attraction towards him. Not when there was so much we didn't know. Hell, we hadn't even discussed the L-word yet. Just like we hadn't even discussed kids. *Oh fuck. Kids!*

"It's rude to eavesdrop on other people's conversations," Jasmine said, scaring the crap out of me. I turned around and found her a couple of steps above me.

"I'm sorry," I whispered. "It just... it just happened."

"I won't tell if you don't," she said with a wink. Then

she tilted her head to the side and dropped her eyes to my stomach. "Do *you* think you could be pregnant?" There was a tinge of hopefulness in her words, proving she had also been listening for longer than she should have been.

A surge of emotion charged up my throat and hit the back of my eyes. I shook my head. "No," I whispered.

"Are you on something to prevent it?"

"No." I looked down at my hands. It was time to come clean. "I just…I, um, I can't get pregnant."

"Excuse me?" she gasped, slightly shocked, slightly curious, slightly annoyed.

"I… um… I don't bleed."

Her eyes seemed to grow. "You don't get a period?"

I shook my head, pressing my lips together and hoping she wasn't going to toss me out on the street for being defective, or worse.

"Why?"

"My mother. She, um, was a user. Heroine. Maybe other stuff. We thought she didn't have a problem until she went off the rails and left us. But it turned out she was self-medicating while pregnant with me." I swallowed the lump in my throat. "It caused a d— a deformity." It was called amenorrhea—the absence of menstrual bleeding. When I hit sixteen and still hadn't gotten my period, I went to the doctor. After extensive testing, it was discovered that my fallopian tubes hadn't formed correctly and therefore couldn't allow passage of an egg. There was no way I'd ever have children naturally, and even then they didn't know if my uterus could carry to term.

"You can't have children at all?"

"I…." I bent my finger back until the knuckle clicked. "I don't know. Maybe. But definitely not without help."

"Like IVF?"

I nodded.

She took a step back. "I see."

"I'm sorry," I whispered.

Jasmine held up her hand, her head down as if she was trying to regain her control. I held my breath, bracing for the worst. This was the moment I'd been dreading, because at some point in my life, if I married, I'd feared having to tell my future husband that I couldn't conceive a child. Obviously, in this situation, it hadn't come up. I shouldn't have said sorry to Jasmine though. I had done nothing wrong, but still, I felt guilty. I felt I was letting her down, when I really shouldn't feel that way. *Learned behaviour*. It was then that Sam decided to appear at the base of the stairs, a wooden tray in his hands laid out with plates of bacon, scrambled eggs and toast. There was even fruit juice and a plunger of coffee, topped off with a flower from the garden. It brought a tear to my eye. *Here we go, the moment I knew would come. Will he keep me or send me away?* Everything between us felt so fragile in that moment.

"What's going on?" he asked cautiously.

I looked at Jasmine, silently begging her not to tell him. But she didn't even look at me. She turned her head to Sam and deadpanned, "She can't get pregnant."

"What?" The crockery on the tray rattled as he looked at me.

"I can't get pregnant naturally," I confirmed, my voice squeaking a little. "I'm not made right."

"I don't understand." Sam took a step backwards as he looked between us.

"What's to understand?" Jasmine blurted. "You're

wasting your time, fucking her for no reason." She lifted her hands in the air and stormed down the stairs, slamming the front door behind her as she left.

My entire being cracked. So fragile was my sense of belonging, my sense of worth that it took seconds for her biting words to break me apart, reminding me that I was less. Always less. Tears streaked down my cheeks. I looked at Sam, needing some sort of reassurance. Moments before, he'd said I belonged, that he'd care for me, look after me. *If I gave him kids.*

As our gaze caught, my heart lodged inside my throat. There was an emotion in his I couldn't place—betrayal? Anger? Did he think I was a waste of time now too?

Please don't turn me away.

"Is that true?" Sam asked, setting the tray on the step closest to him. My entire body shook. "You can't have kids?"

With a quivering hand, I wiped at my cheeks and sniffed. "Honestly? I don't know." It wasn't my fault, but I felt like an absolute failure. Insufficient. Again.

He looked around, anywhere but at me. The man who was always so sure of himself was completely lost for something to say.

"I need to surf." Each word felt like a stomp, the dismissive heel of a boot grinding all the pieces of me into the ground, telling me I was unimportant and not worth fighting with or for. He turned on his heel and followed Jasmine's cue.

If she has my kid, if she stands by me and this family . . . then I can handle anything with her.

But I can't have his kid.

So he has no reason to stand by me.

It's always been easy to leave me so why should I be disappointed—*devastated*—by this?

Everyone I loved left me.

Eventually.

I gasped, the air leaving my lungs in a punch of emotion. I knew this day would come. Kris's words had just been fanciful. *"Once you become a part of the family, you're a part of it for life. We always take care of our own."* I was sure he believed it, but it'd never truly been tested. They took care of their own because they were all they had. No one had encroached on their precious family fortress before me.

I would never be enough. Not for my mother. Not for my father, my friend. And now, not for my husband or his family either.

No one wants you.

Sliding down the wall, I tucked my knees against my chest and cried. I'd been so strong up until that moment, but I just couldn't anymore. *What's going to happen to me?*

"Hey." I flinched when Toby sat down next to me. "It's going to be OK."

I shook my head, placing my hand on my forehead. "No it won't. I can't give them what they want."

Releasing a heavy breath, he slid his arm around my shoulders and pulled me in a little too tight. The contact and the kindness behind it had me crying even more. But he wasn't the man I needed acceptance from. "Life isn't about getting what you want, Leesh. It's about learning to live with the things you have and making the best of it."

"What do you live without, Toby? Seems to me you all have exactly what you want."

He pressed his lips into a sad-looking smile. "Appearances are often deceiving. In this house, family comes first, our individual dreams a distant second."

"What are your dreams?" I asked, wiping my nose with the back of my hand.

He shifted, taking his arm back before he clasped his hands, forearms resting on his knees. "They're just dreams, fanciful thoughts about being free and unencumbered. I'm no different to anyone else. We all want things we can't have, and we all have to learn to find happiness in what we do have instead."

That was the thing. I had been happy with what I had. I'd accepted everything about my life and what it was lacking. I never expected to end up married at all, let alone to a man who seemed desperate to have children. He hadn't even consulted me. And I had naively never considered that the reason he wasn't using protection was because he wanted me to bear his children. How blind can one girl be. Of course that's what he wanted—that's how babies were made, after all.

Wait. Was that what Jasmine had wanted too? I remembered another moment when I was caught listening on the stairs by Toby. Sam had been telling Jasmine to let him do things his way or she'd never get what she wanted from me. Was that about children too? Was I brought into the family as some sort of breeding stock? It would explain Jasmine's reaction.

Fuck. Now I was questioning everything.

"Am I only here because Jasmine wants grandkids?" I blurted out, the question burning in my gut as tiny pieces of conversations began to fit together.

Toby's light eyes met mine and I immediately knew the truth. "My God, it's true, isn't it?"

"It may have been a selling point."

I was so fucking stupid. Of course they wanted something huge from me. It wasn't just about keeping us quiet and letting Nate have Holland. It was about furthering the Cartwright lineage, producing tiny thieves. And now that I'd been found defective, would I be put out to pasture, sent to the proverbial farm?

"My God, I'm an incubator. A broken incubator."

Toby took my hand and gave it a squeeze. "That's not how we see you, Alesha. We all think of you like family."

"But I'm not your blood, Toby. Sam doesn't love me, you heard him say that yourself. There's no reason for him to keep me if it turns out I can't give him kids."

"Sam isn't that guy."

"Then why did he walk away?"

"Because he had a picture in his mind, and going for a surf will give him some time to change it."

"So he's just going to come back and magically be OK with this?"

He sighed and ran his fingers through his hair. It was the first time I'd ever seen Toby dishevelled. "You need to understand the life we've led. It's not one that ever allowed space for relationships."

"Are you trying to say none of you have ever had girl-friends?"

"No," he said, giving me a look that told me if I'd shut up and listen, he'd make his point. "We've all had girl-friends of a sort, but never anything serious because every relationship was based on a lie about who we were. We all live with our feet straddling different lives—our respectable public life and our behind-the-scenes reality. We couldn't risk falling for a girl and telling her the truth about our family only to have that relationship end badly and her going to the cops out of spite. We learned not to trust in anything that felt vaguely like love, because those kinds of feelings put the family at risk, and the family *always* comes first."

I had to wonder if something like that had happened in the past to make them think like that.

"So none of you believe in love. I get it. But why risk bringing me and Holland into the family? You didn't know us, couldn't trust us. What if we produced these children, then decided to run to save them from becoming criminals too?"

He raked through his hair again. "It's ridiculously complicated. But it mostly has to do with Nate. He's always been the wildcard of the family, playing his own games and making up his own rules. What he was doing with Holland was reckless. Had you two gone to the cops instead of snooping around here, his actions could've brought the entire family to our knees. We needed to give him what he wanted to keep him happy, and I pointed out that you both could produce grandchildren to keep Jasmine on side. Then you were threatened with your lives and the lives of your loved ones to keep you both compliant."

"You knew we'd stay out of self-preservation." It was starting to make sense now.

He nodded. "It's a stronger emotion than love."

I placed my hands on my face and sighed. "This is so fucked up."

"Initially, yeah, it was. But you and Sam are great together. He's legitimately into you. If you heard him saying he wasn't in love before, you also heard him saying how happy you made him and how important he thought you were. He wants you, Alesha, and I'm positive that when he gets over the shock and whatever other shit is going through his head right now, he's going to come back here and tell you he'll take you any way you come."

I shook my head, his words so hard for me to believe in that moment.

"And what about Jasmine? Is she going to be fine with me if I can't give her grandkids?"

"Yes." The voice wasn't Toby's, it was Jasmine's. She was standing at the bottom of the stairs.

Shit. How long has she been standing there?

"I thought you left." I sniffed.

"I did. But then I came back."

"I'll give you two the chance to talk," Toby said, giving my shoulder a squeeze before he got up and took the tray of food with him. Jasmine climbed the stairs and occupied the space Toby vacated.

"I reacted poorly," she said. "I shouldn't have spoken to you or about you like that."

My natural instinct was to want to wear the blame, to suggest that it was all my fault that I hadn't shared something so deeply personal to me.

Cartwrights don't apologise. If Toby was to be believed, that's still who I was. I just hoped he was right and I'd still be one at the end of the day.

"Do you think I should've told you from the beginning?" I sniffled, wiping my hand across my face.

"That wouldn't have been the best idea," she said, smiling a little.

"Oh yeah, the whole death thing." How could I possibly forget?

"It's not on the table anymore. You should know that. You've earned your place in this family."

"I have?" It was crazy that that comment made me happy, but it did. I literally felt lighter, less weighed down.

She nodded. "In the short time you've been here, you've become the daughter I never had. You didn't even hesitate when you helped Kristian get his car back. You've really embraced us. The least we can do is embrace you, whichever way you come."

"Oh God." I couldn't contain the tears. It was the nicest thing anyone had ever said to me—even if it had started with a reminder about the threat of marriage or death. "I don't know what to say." There were tears and snot. I was a blubbering mess.

"Come here," Jasmine said, putting her arm around me and giving me a hug that I so greatly needed. I'd existed so long without much affection that each kind touch felt like the unshackling of chains. "Has Sam told you much about me and where I came from?"

I shook my head, then used the bottom of my shirt to wipe my eyes and nose. I needed a tissue. "Not much. Only that you learned everything from their father, and that he's in prison now."

"That's some of it. Although, I started into this life all on my own. You see, you and I, we have a lot in common."

"We do?"

She nodded. "My mother was an addict too. Heroin was also her drug of choice. She didn't hide it as well as your mother must have and preferred a hit over feeding her child. Which is why I learned to steal to survive. And I got really good at it. So good that it became my business. It might seem like a strange choice of vocation to someone like you, but we all have our place in this world. This is mine, and I won't ever apologise for it."

"Cartwrights don't apologise." I stated, repeating Sam's most ingrained lesson.

She tucked my hair back from my face. "That's right. But we understand and support each other. And *I* understand better than *anyone* what it's like to be the last choice in the eyes of the one person who is supposed to put you first. I want you to know that you aren't the last choice in mine. You are one of us now, and we all want you here. Do you understand that? We want you here."

I sniffed, the tears coming hard and fast. I had no chance in stopping them; she was saying all the things my heart needed to hear and it was bleeding freely. Jasmine was a hard woman. Just by the way she carried herself, I could tell that she had fought for everything she had in this world. But her love for her family was fierce, and I knew she'd do anything for those she loved. Now she was telling me that she counted me as one of them, that I belonged. I had never belonged anywhere in my life.

"Thank you," I forced out through my sobs. "You have no idea what that means to me."

She put her arms around me and held me tight. "I think I have a fair idea."

I nodded and held her back. Of course she understood. She probably understood the feeling of not being enough better than anyone. There was something intrinsically damaging about a mother's rejection, something only another rejected soul could possibly understand.

"What do we do about Sam wanting kids?" I asked

when we pulled apart. I loved that Jasmine wanted me in the family no matter how damaged my insides were, but what about Sam? He didn't come back. How would he feel towards me knowing I wasn't entirely complete?

"When you and Sam are both ready, we'll find you the best doctor money can buy. And if it doesn't work, well, we'll just steal a kid for you."

I lifted my head, gasping in shock.

She laughed. "That was a joke. Get it? Because we're thieves."

"I'm sorry, but that was not even a little bit funny," I told her, completely serious.

Pushing my hair behind my shoulder, she smiled, still amused by her crappy joke and my reaction to it. "I think it's time we got you a phone and a car. I don't want you feeling like a prisoner anymore. I want you to feel trusted."

"I already have a phone and a car," I responded. "You could just give them back, you know."

"Oh, baby." She chuckled. "No you don't. They're long gone."

"Oh." Of course they were.

"It's OK. We'll get you better ones. The best of everything for my kids. You just relax, let your family take care of you."

SAM RETURNED a little before the sun went down. I'd barely eaten all day, barely done anything more than close myself in our room and cry and wait. No one could shake me out of my funk, not even the twins and their comical stories about their landscaping business—Abbot had mowed over a garden gnome, and then Kris had glued its head on backwards. Jasmine had been sure to keep me hydrated, but I couldn't stop worrying about Sam. He'd been gone for so long.

Maybe everyone's wrong. Maybe he doesn't *want me anymore.*

"I'm sorry," I whispered, breaking the cardinal Cartwright rule the moment he walked through our bedroom door. I didn't care, I needed him to know that I really was sorry for not telling him about my condition. Despite Toby's and Jasmine's reassurances, I wouldn't be OK until I knew Sam still wanted me. I'd rather die than feel worthless around him. I didn't want to live in this house and be married to a man who had no desire for me. I just couldn't.

"Don't," he said, his teeth clenched. My chest fell along with my plummeting stomach.

"Oh." I sat up and slid off the bed. "I'll… I'll stay in the guest room tonight, then. We can work out what to do next in the morning." Every word came out as a slight hiccup and a fight against more tears. I stood and looked around, then decided I'd get my things some other time. "I really am so sorry, Sam."

"Stop," he growled, moving in front of me. "Quit apologising, for fuck's sake. You're a *Cartwright*."

"What?" *Why the hell is he saying that to me now?*

There was no response, only action. His hand spearing into my hair, fisting the strands and clashing our mouths together, his tongue forcing entry as his hands tore at my clothes. I responded in kind, the longing inside me manifesting into a white-hot need that sent my skin burning and my insides yearning to connect with him.

I didn't know what this meant. It could be a communication of need or it could be goodbye. It could be the simple taking of what he thought he was owed. The only thing I had any real idea of was my own mind, and I wanted to brand him on my heart and body forever. I pulled him in closer.

Desperation governed our actions, our teeth clashing, fingers scraping. We got his shirt off, then removed my shorts along with my panties. He pushed his board shorts down just enough to release his cock, and then he was inside me. I cried out from the speed of his intrusion, my mouth dropping open as my head fell back and I let out a long moan.

If this was the end, if it was goodbye, I knew I'd never know this type of fucking again. My heart was breaking even though my body felt so alive. So full. So... *God, I want him to want me.* Tears filled my eyes.

"Fuck. I need you," he growled, his hips thrusting, slamming against me. "I fucking *need* you." Each pump produced a noise from me that was more animal than human. I could barely breathe, barely think, the only movement available to me the rising of my hips as I met his thrusts.

"Fuck," I cried as he adjusted his position, tucking his knees and pulling my leg over his shoulder, hitting me deeper. He lifted his hand to his mouth and sucked his thumb before reaching between us and pressing it to my clit. "Oh *God*." The word was slow and low as he pummelled and teased, my entire abdomen tensing, ready to detonate.

"Come, peaches. Fucking *come*. Squeeze my cock as hard as that sweet little cunt can."

"Sam!" My body lifted then shook, the uncontrollable waves pulsing through me, a howling noise climbing up my throat.

Sam reached forwards and grabbed the bottom of my singlet, tearing it open with one swift movement. Then he pulled out of me, his big dick landing against my stomach just in time to spurt hot cum all over me.

"Holy shit," I gasped, watching the creamy liquid leave his body and coat mine. I wasn't exactly sure how to react. Was he doing this because coming inside me was pointless? But then he placed his hand on my stomach and spread his seed all over my skin, up to my breasts, all over my ribs. It seemed like a weird thing for someone to do and I was confused by the action, but oh my Lord, it was hot. Carnal.

"Mine," he said, meeting my eyes. "Do you understand?"

I nodded, my chest heaving. I was pretty sure he'd just claimed me, marked his territory and all that. He'd given me his answer. He wanted me. This man, this big and beautiful beast of a man *wanted* me. Still. I wanted to cry, wanted to climb inside him and live there, because you know what? I believed it. I fucked *believed*.

I settled for tucking my head into his chest while he held me and placed soft kisses everywhere he could. I breathed in his ocean-kissed skin, a scent that had become so comforting to me. It was on the tip of my tongue to proclaim a deeper feeling for him, but I kept it locked down, knowing that wasn't where we were yet. He may not understand what love was, but he understood comfort, understood empathy. Nevertheless, there was something he wanted from me, something I might be incapable of giving, and that felt like a boulder in my heart.

"You want kids," I whispered, tracing erratic shapes on the skin over his heart.

"I do. But I was a dick for assuming instead of asking how you felt about it too. I sometimes forget that you aren't here because you want to be but because we forced you. You probably don't think you can tell me things."

He was right. I'd been careful with my behaviour and the topics I asked about. I never snapped, and I tried to be as agreeable as possible. Still...

"I do want to be here, Sam. I just need to be sure that you'll want me if it turns out I can't give you children at all." Emotion prickled at the corner of my eyes.

He leaned forward, his forehead dropping to meet mine. "Yes, Alesha. Do you really think I'm going to give up my unicorn just because her horn's a little bent?"

"Thank God." A laugh burst through my tears and I placed my hands on either side of his face, my relief making my heart feel set to burst. "But promise me one thing?"

"Anything."

"Please don't ever become a writer. You come up with the worst analogies," I whispered, my entire body singing from the joy of his return. He wanted me. He knew I was broken and he still wanted me.

I thought back to an early conversation I'd had with Holland. *Maybe I really have struck the forced marriage lottery.*

"If I can't be a writer, guess I'll just have to continue being a thief. You think you can handle that?"

I curled my fingers, my nails scraping against the over-grown stubble on his cheeks. "As long as I have you, I think I can handle anything. You make me feel… right."

He chuckled. "Right. I'll take it," he said. "I'll take you too." He grabbed my hips and rolled until I was on top of him, pulling my face towards his in a long, soulful kiss.

While we still had a hell of a lot to deal with in our relationship, one thing had become abundantly clear: we both wanted it, wanted each other. At that point, it was more than enough for me, because we'd managed to jump an enormous hurdle together and he didn't turn me away.

CHAPTER FIFTEEN
EVERYONE HAS SOMETHING TO PROVE

"JUST LOOK AT IT," Sam said, holding his board under his arm and admiring the roiling sea. "It's bloody beautiful."

The water had turned almost freezing, but it was worth donning wetsuits and braving it for the chance to see the sun come up and start my day feeling on top of the world, like I'd wrestled with the power of nature and won.

Surfing wasn't just a sport. It was a way of life.

I'd have laughed at anyone telling me I'd feel that way a few months ago, but since I'd learned, the adrenaline rush that came from a six-second wave was something I lived for.

My surf lessons had become a family affair. Not only was Kris taking me out, but Sam—perhaps from a little jealousy—had taken me too, as had Abbot and Toby at various times. Each of them had a slightly different style, but they pushed me to do more and brave bigger waves. The first day I was invited with them for their morning surf was like my graduation day—I felt like one of the boys, a true member of the Cartwright family.

"I don't wanna admire it, I wanna ride it," Abbot hollered before running into the surf, his long messy hair whipping about in the breeze as he joined the rest of the locals willing to brave the frigid conditions.

I'd met quite a few of the locals over the months. The Cartwright brothers had grown up in Torquay and were well liked. We'd even attended a couple of surfing competitions, which had really opened my eyes to this whole other way of life. The professionals rode waves like they had the ability to walk on water. It was magical to see.

Everywhere we went together, people would stop them to say hi. Girls would smile widely—some would scowl at me—and it was honestly like belonging to some sort of rock star entourage. I may have let admiration by association go to my head a bit, but I'd never been so *visible* in my life before now. People saw me, said hi to me and showed me the time of day. Suddenly I understood those movies where the girl undergoes a makeover to try and get into the popular group at school. Feeling like *someone* was so much better than feeling like nobody at all.

"Who the fuck is that?" Toby asked, a scowl forming on his face as he tilted his head towards a group of three surfers exiting the water. It was obvious that they were talking about us, and their body language didn't seem like the friendly kind. It was Kris who was the first to recognise them.

"Watch your keys everyone. This bitch likes taking cars," he said loud enough for them to hear.

"That's the girl who nicked his car?" Toby asked, and Sam nodded.

I squinted a little to see them in the dim light. It was the girl, the guy called Johno and a third male I'd never seen before.

"Why don't you surf another beach," Sam called out to them. "No one wants thieving scumbags sharing their waves." Ironic, but I'd since learned that the Cartwrights had many rules. One was that they never stole from their own backyard, and another was that they always knew exactly who they were stealing from. They didn't take from poor, uninsured people, those who had kids, or the elderly. It didn't really excuse what they did for a living, but having a moral code certainly made things a lot easier for someone like me to swallow.

"It's a free fucking country," the girl yelled back. Johno gave us one look and started right up the beach.

"You thought finding someone's keys meant their car was free?" Kris said, shaking his head. "Oh, I get it now. You're just fucking stupid."

"Come and say that shit to my face, fuckwit," she screeched, walking backwards behind the men who were with her.

Kris threw down his board and held his hands out wide. "Fucking come at me, then. Send your mates too."

"Ronnie, pick up the pace," the unknown man snapped, and she turned around.

So that was her name—Ronnie. Ronnie the car thief. She didn't look very old. The guy calling her to hurry up was at least twenty years older. A father or uncle perhaps? No, that didn't make sense. He'd be more protective if he was family, considering Kris was taunting them with every step they took.

"At least those dudes are smart enough not to pick a fight they can't win," Toby muttered to Sam.

"After the beatdown we gave the little guy, they'd need balls of steel to take on all four of us." I wondered if the four he was referring to were the brothers including Abbot, or whether he was counting the four of us standing right here—meaning me, the one who'd knocked Johno out cold.

Before they made it to the stairs, Ronnie turned back and cupped her hands around her mouth. "Watch your back, cunts!"

We all laughed while Kris held his arms in the air, flipping the bird. Normally I'd be worried they'd go up there and do something to our cars. But since I'd been given the opportunity to get a car of my own, I'd chosen a beautiful big van that all of us could fit inside along with our boards. It was a lot like driving a fridge around the streets, but the space and convenience made it the favourite vehicle for the entire family.

"Time to hit the waves?" Toby suggested once they were gone. He didn't need to ask twice.

WHEN WE GOT BACK to the house, Nate was sitting at the kitchen counter, drinking coffee and talking to Jasmine. The moment we walked inside, the mood changed. The laughing and joking that was usual disappeared, replaced with something much more serious.

"I see you've replaced me," Nate said with a smile as his eyes landed on me in my wetsuit.

"Not like you can be bothered coming out anymore,"

Abbot responded, striding straight past everyone and going to his favourite place in the house—the fridge. He pulled out milk and a bowl of fruit. That was when the rest of us jumped to action and moved about the kitchen as a unit, collecting bowls, cereal and cutlery. Jasmine poured everyone coffee, cups lined up in her usual manner.

"I'll find the time again," Nate said, sipping his coffee as he watched the hungry mob in front of him. "How do you like it here, Alesha?"

I was mid-chew when the question hit, and I swallowed before I was ready so I could answer, coughing a little and needing a gulp of OJ to wash it all down. "I like it fine," I said when I could speak. There was something about Nate that put me on edge. Maybe it was because when I first met him, he was pretending to be an American called Ben. Maybe I just didn't like the fact that he stole my best friend away from me—but what else did I expect, really. Stealing was what he did best.

"I'm guessing you're here because the job is happening tonight?" Toby asked between scooping cereal and drinking coffee. He kept his head down and made little eye contact.

At first Nate didn't respond. He looked to Jasmine and tipped his head to indicate me instead.

"She's family too," Jasmine said. "You can say anything in front of her. In fact, I've been teaching her how to handle receipts so she can help with the family holdings."

Nate lifted his brow. "Is that so? You've come a long way, Alesha."

The comment seemed condescending and made my cheeks burn. "I guess so," I said. Learning how to run the business had become a point of pride with me. I'd picked it up quickly, and Jasmine said if I kept it up, she'd give me even more responsibility. I didn't like the way Nate seemed to talk like I was just being a *good little girl.* That I wasn't really contributing anything real.

There was a brief moment where no one said anything, but Toby finally broke the silence. "Answer the bloody question," he said to Nate. "Are we doing the job tonight or not?"

"We leave tonight, yes," Nate responded, grabbing a folded sheet of paper from the file sitting beside him. "We'll be gone all weekend."

I looked to Sam. "I thought it was just overnight."

Sam's hand found my knee. It would be the first time since we got married that we'd spend the night apart, and now it was going to be two. I wasn't sure how I felt about that. I'd kind of gotten used to sleeping next to a man who hugged me like a child's sleep aid.

"So did I," he said.

"Change of plans," Nate replied. "They had a breech in security, changed the location."

"Anything to do with our guy?" Sam asked.

Nate shook his head. "He's clean. Some guard had racked up some gambling debt, and they caught him trying to sell the idea to pawnbrokers."

Pawnbrokers. Did that mean jewels? I'd heard tiny whisperings about a truck transporting high-end merchandise. I hadn't been filled in on the exact details, but no one had exactly been quiet around me. I took my chance and pretended I knew more than I did.

"Isn't it really risky to shift jewellery?" I asked. I caught Jasmine's smile before she hid it behind her coffee mug. All eyes landed on me. "Well, isn't it? It's not like the electronics, furniture, and cars you usually take. Jewellery is more distinct."

Kris slung his arm over my shoulders. "Clever, this girl. A good fighter too. We should start bringing her on the smaller jobs. She's got a knack for it."

"I'm fine for it," Sam said with a lazy half grin. "I'd love to see her in action again. It's hot."

"In action?" Nate asked, quirking his right brow.

Abbot and Kristian happily filled him in—even though Abbot hadn't been there—by alternating the highlights of our car re-steal between them.

"Then she kicked him in the nuts and was all 'you need a better boyfriend' to the chick. It was epic," Kristian finished.

"OK," Nate said. "If you want in, and everyone else wants you in, then you're in. Just do me a solid and keep this all far away from Holland."

"You don't trust her, bro?" Abbot asked, and Nate shook his head.

"She just can't handle it. She's… sensitive."

Once again, Jasmine hid her expression behind her coffee mug. That time it was an eye roll.

"You have my word," I said to Nate. "I won't breathe a word to Holland." *Given we rarely speak, that won't be hard.*

"Thank you," he replied before returning to the conversation he was having with his brothers. I couldn't help but notice that my question about selling jewels had gone unanswered.

Later that day, when the men had left, Jasmine filled me in. "We have a buyer who repackages and exports all the good jewellery we find. Our business has many arms, but you can look at us as a supplier of sorts. Electronics go one place, cars and parts go to another and so on. Each person involved operates their own business with its own risks. And we only share information with those we trust implicitly."

It was clever, what they did. No job was done without being thoroughly investigated and planned. Then everything they took went to someone else. All proceeds were filtered through legitimate businesses that were squeaky clean on the surface. Taxes were paid, and in the end, the Cartwrights appeared to be entrepreneurs. I had to admire their moxie. There weren't a lot of people industrious enough to successfully do what they did.

"Have any of you ever been caught?" I asked.

"Besides Derek?"

I nodded.

"Nate went to juvi for joyriding. Sam doesn't like talking about it but he did eighteen months about a decade ago. He went through a tough time in his early twenties. Got into the recreational drugs a little too heavy and was caught trying to steal a safe. The time away set him straight, and he hasn't touched anything but alcohol since. I'm assuming he didn't tell you?"

I shook my head.

"He should've. His time away is the reason they're all so careful now. It's not easy being the biggest guy in a place where everyone has something to prove."

I could imagine it would have been very hard. But something that was also hard was the realisation that I was learning more about my husband from his mother than I was from him. And the more she shared, the more I realised I didn't know Sam at all. We rarely spent time alone outside the family group, and when we did, there wasn't a lot of talking going on. We had a deep connection, I was sure of that much, but what would we be when the physical faded?

"I SAY we just order in some Chinese," Jasmine suggested, looking through a drawer for menus. We'd been discussing what to do for dinner since it was just going to be three of us at home, with Holland staying with us while the men were away. Nate had made it clear that he wanted Holland kept in the dark about the deal, and I still wasn't sure if it was because he didn't trust her. I knew from his family, from how they all related, that he should be someone I trusted, but there was something I wasn't quite getting. Maybe he was just being protective of her. Maybe she really couldn't handle knowing what they did. *Maybe.*

"I like Chinese," I said, sitting on a stool while I drew imaginary shapes on the counter.

"What about Holland?"

"She likes it too."

"Good. Then we'll have Chinese and wine and spend some girl time without all that testosterone in the air." Finding what she was looking for, she lifted it triumphantly.

"Sure." I may have added a slight shrug for dramatic effect. I wasn't looking forward to an entire weekend with Holland, not when she kept going on about how perfect everything was between her and Nate, and I was starting to feel the cracks between me and Sam.

For most of the day, I'd been trying to list all the things I knew about him. He was a criminal. He had a lot of respect for his family. He was easy on the eyes, and amazing between the sheets. An alpha male who was kind to me and made me feel wanted. He loved to surf. He was thoughtful, protective. He loved to eat. He worked hard and didn't have much time for TV.

Outside of that, I had no idea. I didn't know about his upbringing. I didn't know about his school life. I didn't know about any girls before me—had he broken their hearts, or had they broken his? Where had he lived before he returned here with me? I didn't know about his hopes and dreams. I didn't even know whether he preferred books or movies, chocolate or vanilla, beer or spirits. I could take a guess at some things, but we were missing that whole 'getting to know you' phase of a relationship. We met. We got married. And then we just floated along, sustained by the fact that we were attracted to each other.

But desire faded, right? And when that went, what would be left? Surfing? Living in the same house? Stealing shit together? What would become of *us* as a couple? If it turned out we couldn't have kids at all, what would remain? Would he begin to think that there was no more point in fucking me?

"You're not looking forward to your friend coming over for the weekend?" Jasmine asked, looking at me with kind and understanding eyes. She'd been trying so hard to be good to Holland. Since her initial outburst at the wedding, she'd gone out of her way to be pleasant and inclusive, but Holland was blocking her attempts at every turn with short answers and an air of nonchalance. Seeing that kind of behaviour from her piled on top of my own disenchantment with our friendship. So no, I wasn't looking forward to spending time with her at all.

"Is it that obvious?"

Jasmine laid the Chinese menu on the counter between us. "Doesn't take a genius to see something is going on with you two."

"I just don't think she's the person I thought she was," I admitted.

"What kind of a person was that?"

"My friend. Someone who cared about me."

"Why do you think she doesn't care?"

"Because it's always about her. Very rarely about me. I think it's always been that way, but I've only really noticed it since the wedding." I took a breath as I clasped my hands together. "You know, this may seem silly, and maybe I'm imagining it, but it feels like she was so sure I'd be unhappy living here and marrying Sam that she's disappointed that I'm not. And that makes me wonder if our entire friendship has been somewhat based on the fact that she felt sorry for me because I've always been so awkward and pitiful."

"You think the fact that you've come out of your shell is too confronting for her?"

I nodded. "I think so."

She was quiet for a moment. "I can see how you'd think that way."

"So I don't sound crazy and selfish?"

"Not at all. But I am going to ask you to try your best to put those feelings aside. It's so important that all Cartwrights get along so we can work together in absolute trust. I reacted terribly towards her, especially at the wedding. I tend to shoot off before I think, you know that. But she's important to Nate, so I don't want to alienate her and risk alienating Nate too. He's the backbone of this family. We need him and can't jeopardise our family or our working relationship. Do you understand?"

Releasing a sigh, I pulled at my lip and nodded. "I can do that."

With a big smile, she placed her hands on top of mine and squeezed. "That's my girl. We'll have fun this weekend, you'll see."

Sure we would. About as much fun as a thick splinter in my left butt cheek.

TOBY DROPPED HOLLAND OFF, then went to stay on his boat for the night. He'd cited not wanting to get in the way of girls' night as his excuse, but he'd acted far too strangely around Holland in the past for her presence not to be the reason he was bowing out.

"Nate dropped off an overnight bag for you earlier, Holland. It's in the guest room just off the rumpus," Jasmine said when Holland walked inside, still dressed up from her teaching job. She'd always been fond of wearing flared pencil skirts with blouses and colourful cardigans while she twisted her long blonde hair into a bun on top of her head. She looked stylish and put together, as usual.

"Thank you," she said, her lips tight. Then she looked to me. "Hey, Leesh. Nice to see you."

"We're ordering Chinese, and there's plenty of wine," I told her.

She nodded and excused herself, not leaving the guest bedroom until the doorbell rang to signal the food had arrived.

"Your fashion has changed a lot," Holland commented as we sat around sharing fried rice, sweet and sour pork, satay chicken and Mongolian beef. I was also munching on the prawn crackers.

I looked down at my outfit, a pair of navy Spanish pants with a leafy design on them that I'd bought from Tree of Life, and a fitted long-sleeve shirt from Target. My hair had grown past my shoulders and was slightly wavy from all the time I spent in the surf, and I'd given up applying much make-up because I didn't feel the need for it anymore.

"I'm just trying new things, I guess."

She smiled a little as she finished a mouthful of food. "I'm just not used to it, but it looks good. Very boho chic. You're so tan."

"It's all the time she spends at the beach with the boys," Jasmine put in.

Holland just nodded and went back to eating.

The rest of dinner was much of the same. Every conversation starter fizzled out before it could get started because no one *really* wanted to be talking at all. I was relieved when Jasmine told me to stay where I was once we finished, that she and Holland could tidy up. I overheard them planning a day together of shopping and spa treatments.

When Jasmine walked back into the room and excused herself for bed, I mouthed, "Thank you," and she gave me a wink to say I was welcome. I couldn't even begin to explain the weight lifted off my shoulders at the idea of having a day to myself. It had been so long.

"Wow. Did you hear any of that?" Holland asked, coming to sit with me on the couch.

"I did. A girls' day out, huh?"

"I don't know whether to be upset, worried or curious." She tucked her legs beneath her and picked up her wine glass.

"You could try being happy. Jasmine isn't half bad when you get to know her."

She scoffed, sliding her hand over the fabric of her sweatpants as she sipped her drink. "I can't promise much, but I can promise to go in with an open mind. You aren't upset you're not coming, are you?"

"Me? No, not at all. I'm looking forward to a little quiet," I said with a smile, watching as Holland leaned forwards and picked up the TV remote, clicking through to the apps and pulling up Netflix. It took her to the sign-up page.

"Do they seriously not have Netflix?" she asked, looking shocked beyond belief.

"They don't really sit around watching TV at all."

"What do you do all day since you aren't working? Stare at the wall and masturbate?"

"I help out, surf, swim, read. There's plenty to do."

"Let's see if this still works." She keyed in her user-name and password, then smiled when it logged her in. "Yes. Now we can watch that baking show where they mess everything up. I hear it's hilarious."

As the show loaded, I took a large gulp of wine, letting the alcohol dull my senses a little. This was it. This had been the extent of our friendship—basic conversation and binge-watching TV while we waited for our lives to start.

No wonder we were drifting apart now. We were finally living.

"GOOD MORNING, milady. I'm here to escort you to the surfy bumpy water."

I giggled when Toby bowed dramatically. He was waiting outside against my van when I went out the next morning.

"Plus I have your board in the van, right?" I asked, hitting the key fob to unlock it.

"This is true. I do have spares, but that one's my favourite, and surfing is better with company, right?"

"Are you our babysitter this weekend?"

"What gave you that impression?"

I shrugged. "You were going but then you stayed behind. You drove Holland here instead of her driving herself. You're standing here instead of going straight to the beach yourself. Do I need to list more?"

His shoulders slumped a little as he released his breath. "Fine. Nate asked me to hang back and keep an eye on Holland. They've been having a few problems lately, and he's worried about her."

I folded my arms. "What kind of problems?"

"It's not my place to say."

"Are they having problems with each other?" Holland

had been so adamant that they were crazy in love. Had her bravado just been a cover for her own misery?

"I really can't tell you."

I held my key fob up and locked my van. "Then maybe we don't go surfing."

"Jesus, Leesh. That's harsh, especially for you."

"I can't be Miss Nice Girl all the time. Spill."

"No."

Well, I'd give him one thing, he was a man of his word.

"Then I'll guess." It wouldn't be hard. I'd known Holland all my life.

"I still won't tell."

"You won't have to. I'll be able to tell from your eyes."

He laughed at that. "Because my eyes talk for me, do they?"

"Everyone's do." I adjusted my stance so I could look more closely into his eyes, and he adjusted his to assist— as if he didn't believe I'd know the confirmation when I saw it. "Is it trouble in their relationship?" He kept staring at me, nothing in his eyes but a challenge. *OK, that's not it.* "Is it because Holland wants to keep working?" Still nothing. I needed to dive a little deeper. "Is it because she doesn't like kids?" Holland had made it clear to me on more than one occasion that she and rug rats didn't go together. She could only handle kids when they were almost adult-size, which was why she became a high school teacher instead of primary.

There was a tiny flicker in Toby's eyes, but after scrutinising it for a moment, I decided it was more curiosity than confirmation. "Oh God, is she pregnant?" I hoped not, since she'd guzzled so much wine the night before. I knew she didn't want kids but that was just negligent, not to mention hurtful to me. She knew I couldn't conceive.

Toby's expression softened, and he placed his hand on my forearm. "She's not pregnant."

A relieved breath escaped my chest. I didn't even realise I was holding it. "OK." I closed my eyes, feeling a little crappy over my selfish reaction. "Well, what else is there? I've covered them all: the relationship, her job, pregnancy…. Oh, what about Nate's job?" His pupils dilated and his jaw ticked. "She wants him to quit working and he won't. That's it, isn't it?" I found that kind of crazy when she knew exactly who he was when she chased him down and fucked him again. Just like me, she entered the relationship with open eyes. So why was she trying to separate him from his family?

He broke eye contact. "Can we just go surfing before the tide changes?"

"Sure," I said, unlocking the car.

He'd told me all I needed to know.

CHAPTER SEVENTEEN
WHO THE FUCK ARE YOU

I MISSED SAM. Missed resting my head on his chest. The way he brushed my hair. The way his hands roamed my body. Making love until I was at the point of exhaustion every night.

Making love? Did I seriously just think that? Huh.

As if reading my mind, my phone vibrated from a message.

Sam: I'm hungry for peaches.

Smiling to myself, I bit my lip while I tried to figure out what to type back.

Me: That's interesting. I was just lying here thinking how empty I am without your giant cocktail.

Being blunt was going to have to do.

Sam: Take everything off. Send me a picture.

Me: What if someone sees?

Sam: They won't. I'm alone. I'm hard. And I'm thinking about you.

Me: Show me first.

A few moments later, a picture came through of Sam holding his cock.

I squirmed where I lay in the bed. Lord, I was obsessed with this man and what he could do to my body.

Sam: Your turn.

With my heart picking up a few beats, I got out of bed and went into the bathroom to strip. Then I stood in front of the mirror, practicing my pose for a bit to decide what looked more alluring. My back arched? Standing with my hand on my hip? Putting my foot on the side of the tub so he could see a little pink? There was a lot of pressure on.

Sam: I'm dying here, peaches.

Not wanting my husband to die with a giant hard-on, (you wouldn't believe how often this actually happens) I quickly took a shot and sent it through. It was my reflection in the mirror, a hand on my waist and my hip kicked out to the side. Sexy but subtle.

Sam: Beautiful. Now a close-up. I want to see you touching yourself.

How was I even supposed to take a photo like that? Did I just hold the phone as low as I could and hope for the best? Or did I set it up and take the photo with my toes or something?

To make things even more uncomfortable, I still hadn't done any sort of solo touching since Sam and I had been together—he'd always been so readily available.

Jesus, how do I? I tried to work out how to hold the camera first. Standing with my legs apart, then with my foot back on the edge of the bath, which seemed OK, I could work with that. Now I just needed to—*holy shit!*

My phone vibrated and fell out of my hand onto the tiled floor. Scrambling to pick it up, I breathed a sigh of relief when the screen wasn't cracked. Then I sucked my breath in because of the message preview: the tip of Sam's dick with a tiny drop of precum on the end with the caption 'don't be shy.' *Oh my!*

I wasn't trying to be shy. I was trying to be precise. Vag shots weren't nearly as easy as cock shots seemed to be.

Going with the leg on the tub again, I opened the camera and flipped it into selfie mode before I slipped a finger between my folds and took the shot.

Send.

Sam: Keep going until you come.

Sam: Film it and send it to me.

Um. OK. How was I supposed to accomplish *that*? I'd never gotten myself off before, so of course I had zero experience filming it. I supposed I could just mimic what Sam did to me. But the more I thought about it, the more it made me feel uncomfortable. I was doing this for him, not because it was something I wanted to do.

With my thumbs hovering over the keypad, I considered how I was going to word my reply. I didn't want to make him feel rejected in any way, just wanted to convey that I'd hit my sexting limit.

I decided to call instead.

"*Peaches*." His sexy voice sounded delighted to hear from me.

"I'm not comfortable doing that in a video. I'm not exactly comfortable doing that at all," I blurted, a slight edge of panic to my voice.

He chuckled. "That's fine. Why don't you just lie down and talk to me instead?"

"You're not going to try and talk me into it?" I was a little shocked that he'd given up so easily.

"I'm never going to try and force you to do something you're uncomfortable with. I've always told you that."

"Then why did you marry me?" I snapped. I didn't really know why. Perhaps it was because I was uncomfortable over his request, or because of my realisations over the depth of our relationship. Maybe it was because he was gone and I wanted him here. I was on edge.

There was a slight pause. "What's going on, peaches?"

Pulling a cotton dressing gown on, I wrapped it closed and sighed. "I don't know. I just feel messed up in the head."

"Because your friend is there?"

"She hasn't exactly been a ray of sunshine but no, it's not her. It's me. I think I'm just starting to realise a few things."

"Like what?"

"Like how little I really know you."

Silence.

"Sam?"

"I'm here. What don't you know about me?" His tone changed from soft to brash.

I bit my lip. "I found out you went to prison."

"Jasmine needs to learn to keep her mouth shut."

"Don't blame her. You're the one who needs to open up more."

"What, like you? Who the fuck are you to judge me when you don't even know who the hell you are? Were you ever planning on telling me you couldn't have kids? Telling me *anything* about yourself that I didn't have to figure out for myself? You're a closed book. The only person you're showing anyone is the person Jasmine has made you into."

"That's not true," I argued. He was speaking lies. I was trying to fit in, but I was still me.

"Isn't it? Take a look at yourself, Alesha. You don't even know who you are without being told by someone else. You can't sit there and tell me I'm the problem when you're nothing but an empty shell we filled up and forced to behave."

I gasped and he hung up in my ear.

Ow. I wasn't expecting things to go downhill so fast. I contemplated calling him back, but my emotions were high and I probably would have started calling him names if he answered, going for his jugular the way he had mine. Was that what he really thought of me? That I was an empty shell they filled? *What the fuck?* I'd been trying so hard to be the woman I needed to be, the woman he wanted. He'd seemed to be proud of me. Had I been doing it all wrong? How long had he felt that way?

I stared down at my phone, gripping it so hard my knuckles went white. Why didn't he say something? Did he begrudge the time I was spending with his mother? And if it was a problem, why didn't he step in? Why didn't he try to redirect me, *something?* If he didn't like who I was becoming, why—emotion climbed up my throat, closing it off as I hiccupped and sobbed, frustrated and confused. Angry at the way he'd spoken.

In the end, I decided just to go to bed and stare at the ceiling. As time ticked by, I couldn't sleep and switched to watching the numbers change on the clock, counting the moments until he'd return home so I could demand that he explain what he meant, what he wanted. I didn't understand, and it made an aching throb bounce in my head. I needed everything to be right between us again.

I closed my eyes and longed for his touch, longed to rewind time just enough so we didn't fight over the phone. I should have just kept my mouth shut, spoken to him about prison when he got home, been able to watch his face when he reacted. Because that was it, wasn't it? I'd hit a sore point, a topic he didn't want to discuss, and he'd reacted as though I'd attacked.

Jesus.

I sighed and rolled onto my back. He was trying to spend a moment with me and I attacked him. Now I just felt shitty.

I picked up my phone, not wanting to leave things on such a sour note. I didn't want him to stew in anger, then decide we didn't work as a couple anymore.

Flipping on the bedside lamp, I pulled back the covers and propped my phone against them, set to record. Then I parted my thighs and made the video he'd asked for, focusing on how much he meant to me, how much I wanted him in my life until I hit my climax. Then I sent him the video, attaching the caption 'I only care about who I am with you'.

A few minutes later, I got a single word reply: **Peaches…**

I wasn't exactly sure if it was good or bad, but it told me he cared enough to still pick up his phone, enough to give me peace of mind so I could get some sleep. We could talk it out properly when he got home.

Except that wasn't quite how it worked out.

The next time I saw him, he was carrying a bloodied and beaten Toby into the house.

"WHAT THE HELL HAPPENED?" Jasmine demanded as Sam dumped Toby in the nearest bathroom.

He was holding his dress shirt bunched against his face. What was once white was now splotched with bright red. I dropped to my knees in front of him, instantly going into nursemaid mode. It was something that had become natural to me over the years since my mother left.

"Nate," Sam said, not sounding the least bit impressed. "This idiot decided it was a good idea to declare his fucking love for Holland."

"You love Holland?" I asked, seriously shocked. I'd noticed the discomfort between them, but I'd thought he didn't like having her around, not that he hated having to watch her fall in love with his brother. How heartbreaking.

Toby's eyes—what I could see of them through the swelling—met mine. I could tell he knew he'd fucked up. I placed my hand on his knee and urged him to take the shirt away from his face. There was dried blood everywhere, a bright red trickle coming from his nose. His jaw was swollen, his eyebrow split, and his hands and elbows were grazed.

"Looks like he did a number on you." I opened the cabinet to pull out the first aid kit so I could clean him up.

"What's all the blood? Is his nose broken?" Jasmine asked, hovering over me.

Sam nodded. "I already put it back in place. He's going to have a bit of bruising and be really uncomfortable for a while."

"Jesus Christ," Jasmine said. "I don't understand how any of this came about."

"Why don't we go get Tobes some painkillers? I can get you a stiff drink and tell you all about it," Sam said, putting his arm around his mother's shoulders to guide her out of the cramped bathroom.

"How long has this been going on?" I asked when we were alone.

Toby's eyes shifted to the side and he winced as I cleaned his cuts. "I saw her first," he said by way of explanation.

"You saw her first? You mean before all this happened?"

He nodded. "During recon. You know we were targeting you, right?"

"I do," I said quietly, trying to ignore the flash of irritation that flared in my chest at the reminder.

"I was the one watching you, mapping out your movements. I saw her with you, and I wanted her."

Of course he did. Holland always had a special quality that lured other people in. I had and would always be invisible by her side.

"Did Nate know that?"

"No. But I forbade them all to go anywhere near her. I never do that, so I kind of thought they'd get it, you know? Sam got it."

What if Sam had seen her first? I hated the thought.

"Did he want her too?" I made myself ask.

"What? No. He just understood that I was into her, that she wasn't to be messed with."

"But it was OK for them to mess with me?" I wasn't going to lie, hearing Holland was put up on some pedestal while I was considered Cartwright family fodder hurt. It made me feel less important.

His brow creased, and then he winced because it must have hurt. He shook his head, trying to grab my hand. "God, Leesh, this was all before we knew how awesome you were. There's no way I'd let *anyone* mess with you now."

That didn't really help take away my hurt, but I understood the sentiment enough to let it go. Pulling my hand free, I gave him a small smile. "It's OK." I peeled a butterfly strip to hold the split in his eyebrow together.

I cleaned and dabbed with antiseptic, and he winced and hissed like a baby.

"So what caused this all to come to a head?" I asked, trying to distract him from the pain so he'd quit flinching.

"You know I took her to that wedding she was singing at today?" I nodded. "Well, I drank a little too much and when she was singing, I convinced myself she'd be better off with me, so I told her. Then... then I kissed her. Nate saw the whole thing go down."

"Wow," I breathed. "I can't believe you kissed her and got caught. That's crazy."

"Laugh if you need to. It was stupid and impulsive, and I deserved to get the shit beat out of me."

"No, Toby. No one deserves this. Especially not from family. Why does Nate keep doing this to you all? First it was the twins, now you. Has it always been this way?"

He shook his head. "It's just life with brothers. Sometimes we sort things out with our fists."

"It shouldn't be like that."

"But it is."

Sam returned with painkillers and an ice pack. "How's the patient?"

Toby took the pills, then held the ice pack against his jaw.

"He'll live," I responded, sighing as I stood up and started cleaning everything up.

Toby stood to leave. "Thanks, Leesh," he said, pressing a chaste kiss against my cheek. "You're a good egg."

Sam laughed. "Dude, I can't believe you're kissing my wife right in front of me. Didn't you learn your lesson today?" It was all delivered in a teasing tone, along with the jabs Sam directed in the air around Toby.

"Very funny, fuckface," Toby said, smiling a little but obviously in too much pain to laugh. "Do I need to talk to Jasmine, or is she fine?"

"She's fine, man," Sam said. "Go rest. Kris and Abs will be back in about an hour, so she'll be distracted questioning them over the job."

"All right, thanks." Toby tapped his balled-up fist against Sam's shoulder, then ambled out of the bathroom, which gave Sam the chance to turn his attention to me.

"How was the job?" I asked, my voice cool as I focused on zipping the first aid kit before I put it back in the cabinet. I was still hurt by what he'd said the night before, but I really didn't have the energy to rehash it all.

He leaned against the door. "We did good. And when the profits come through, we'll feel a hell of a lot richer."

"Why don't you just steal money so you're paid right away?"

He laughed. "Because big money jobs are filled with risk. None of us wants to get caught. I definitely don't want to get caught again."

There. He'd brought it up himself, which meant I was right, his reaction was because I'd confronted him about going to prison.

"Were you trying to steal money?"

He nodded. "I was taking the safe from a Licensed Post Office. They only cleaned it out once a month, so there were thousands of dollars inside it. I took a risk, didn't take enough manpower, and I was the one who got caught."

"Who *didn't* get caught?" I asked.

"Nate."

"You went to prison and he got away?"

Sam nodded. That explained a lot of the tension between them.

"Oh Sam."

He held up his hand, so I bit my lip and kept the words inside when I wanted to express how hard that must have been for him, locked inside while Nate walked free.

"No one knows," he said. "No one knows he was there except for him, me and now you."

I nodded, astounded that he was trusting me with such a secret. "I won't tell a soul," I promised.

"I know you won't, and after tonight, I really don't

want to talk about this again. I probably don't need to tell you that prison isn't a fun place to be."

I leaned against the vanity and folded my arms. "Did…?" I didn't know if I should ask, but my curiosity won. "Did they do any, um, bad things to you?"

"You want to know if anyone made me their bitch?"

"Well, yeah. You're very pretty."

That earned me a smile. "My arsehole is untouched," he assured me. "But I did have to fight every single day I was in there. And I never want to go through that again. This may shock you, but I'm a fairly peaceful guy. Give me an ocean filled with great waves and a babe like you by my side and I'm a happy man."

"Don't you mean a shell like me?" It was petty, but I couldn't just let his words go unmentioned. They hurt me.

Taking a step forward, he pulled me against him, our hands entwined behind my back, my chest pressed to his. "I regret every word I said to you last night."

"*All* of them?"

He grinned and hugged me a little tighter. "All the shitty ones."

"You were really mean."

"I hated that you and Jasmine were talking about shit I didn't want aired behind my back."

"Why didn't you just tell me yourself?"

"Because it's the worst part of me. I didn't want you to know I'd spent every day of that eighteen months wondering if it was going to be my last. Prison made me feel weak and frightened, and I don't want you to see me as anything other than strong."

"Sam," I started, saying his name like a sigh. I wanted to

tell him I could never view him that way, that he was always strong and fierce in my eyes and that it helped to know he had vulnerabilities too. It made him more human than god. But he pressed a finger against my lips to quiet me.

"I acted like an arse last night, and I attacked your insecurities. And I knew them because even though you think I don't, I *do* know you, peaches. I know you're kind and considerate. That you're fearless and badass. That you're afraid that I'm going to stop wanting you, afraid of being irrelevant to those you care about. I know that you already knew how to cook but pretended that you didn't to get along with my mother. You learned surfing lingo just so you could talk to my brothers. You have a smile that can light up a room, and you make every one of my days better when you're in it. I see you, Alesha. I don't need to know every detail of your past to know what's in your heart. And as for me, I'm not that complicated. I don't want much, just time and freedom."

Time and freedom. They seemed like two of the most important things on the planet—especially to a man who'd been locked up before.

"OK," I said.

"OK?"

I nodded. "You know, for people who never say they're sorry, you sure do a good job of apologising."

He grinned. "I like the way *you* apologise better. But you really didn't have to do that. You'd said the idea made you uncomfortable, and I was cool with that."

I blushed a little. "I was more uncomfortable that you were angry with me. I realised that I kind of started it all by attacking you first. I wanted to make amends."

"There was nothing to make amends for, peaches. It was all on me."

"There you go, apologising again," I said, a grin pulling at my lips as I fanned my fingers across his chest.

"How about we go upstairs and I make it up to you with my mouth?"

"How many times are we talking?"

"Let's see, how many times did I get off watching that clip you shot last night?"

My mouth opened on a gasp. "Did you?" My eyes dropped to the erection growing against my belly.

"Oh yeah." He nodded with a half grin. "Several times. Why do you think I'm so level-headed right now?"

My mouth opened farther. "Several?"

"Keep looking at me like that and I'll give you something to put in that open mouth."

I closed it, then pressed my lips together. "Will you show me?"

He grinned. "You wanna see me jacking off?"

My breathing quickened and I nodded. "Uh-huh."

With a smile on his lips, he held my face on each side, then kissed me while he breathed me in. I could barely stand when he was done. "You're perfect just as you are, peaches. Don't ever change. Don't change yourself for anyone."

CHAPTER NINETEEN
SAMUEL CARTWRIGHT 101

"DID YOU PUT THIS HERE?" I pointed to an old-fashioned metal pail that was sitting in the centre of the dining table the next Friday afternoon. It looked like there was fruit in there.

Jasmine shook her head and walked straight past into the kitchen. We'd been working on accounts all day and she was desperate for a coffee break, perhaps a cigarette or two. "It wasn't there earlier," she said.

Strange. She and I had been the only ones home all day. Kris and Abbot had a landscaping job, while Toby and Sam had a meeting with one of their *contacts*. No one was expected back until dinner time.

As I drew closer, I noticed the fruit was big, fat, juicy-looking peaches. This could only be from one person. "Sam," I said out loud, picking up the largest peach from the top with a smile on my face. I lifted it to my nose and inhaled the sweet scent. I was just about to take a bite when I noticed a small card hanging off the bucket's handle.

Peaches for my Peaches.
A taste so sweet you cannot hate
Please accept this bucket of fruit
As an invitation for a date
Wear something sexy
I'll pick you up at 8.
Sam x
P.S. I know my poetry sucks, but for you, I'm willing to
make a fool of myself if it means you smile.
P.P.S You are smiling, aren't you?

I WAS SMILING ALL RIGHT. I was almost crying too. I hugged the card against my chest and took a bite of the fruit. Together, they were the most delicious moment I'd ever known.

"Peaches, huh?" Jasmine said, coming to stand beside me with her coffee in hand. She placed my mug in front of me. "You and Samuel have a fight?"

"He's taking me on a date." I beamed.

She lifted her brow, looking slightly impressed. "About time you two spent some time on your own. Why don't you take the rest of the day off, go buy yourself something new to wear. Get your hair done, get a wax. Whatever you like."

"Really? You don't need me to help with the accounts?"

"They'll keep. Go pamper yourself a little."

I grinned. "I've never been on a proper date before," I

admitted, using the card to hide the dopey grin that wouldn't quit my mouth.

Jasmine reached out and ran a hand lightly over my hair. "You really are the sweetest girl. I'm glad Sam has you."

"Thank you," I called over my shoulder, grinning more openly now as I rushed out the door, ready to get myself the sexiest damn outfit Sam had ever seen. I was going to knock his socks off.

I have a date!

———

"HOLY FUCKING HELL," Sam breathed, his mouth falling open when I appeared at the top of the stairs. I'd primped and preened to within an inch of my life all afternoon. I was freshly waxed from head to toe, I'd had my hair trimmed and styled in soft curls that bounced around my shoulders, and I'd pulled out my favourite Urban Decay palette and applied the perfect smoky eye with just a dash of glitter. My lips were a nude gloss because I knew I'd be eating—and hopefully kissing). I'd found a perfume with hints of mango, and I'd bought a blue dress that hugged my figure so tight I could barely breathe, with black lace lingerie underneath. I felt a little like a princess. A really smutty princess.

"I should say the same thing about you," I said with a smile as I made it to the landing and moved towards him. He was dressed in a charcoal suit, sans tie, looking absolutely delicious while holding a bouquet of white peonies and pink orchids. He'd really pulled out all the stops.

"Those are for me?" I asked when he just kept standing there smiling at me.

My voice seemed to make him jump to attention, and he practically shoved the flowers in my hands. "Yes. I hope you like them. I noticed you had orchids growing outside your place when we picked up your stuff, so...." His grin seemed to stretch across the whole width of his face as he dragged his eyes up and down my body.

"Should I spin?"

"Please do."

I did a slow turn, pivoting on my heels as he gave a low whistle of appreciation. I also received a couple of wolf whistles from the peanut gallery, Kristian and Abbot watching in the wings. Kris was even filming it for posterity.

"You two are fucking adorable," he said.

Abbot nodded. "I feel like I'm watching a real-life re-enactment of that scene from *She's All That*, except Leesh didn't fall down the stairs and she's way hotter."

"What the fuck movie are you talking about?" Kris asked, his phone still trained on me and Sam.

"You know, the one where these guys make a bet to turn the nerd girl hot?" Abbot replied.

"Are you calling our sister-in-law a nerd?" Toby asked, walking in from the next room.

"No. I said she's hot," Abbot quickly replied, his eyes wide.

"So now you're checking Sam's wife out?" Kris added.

Abbot grinned. "Nah, man, that would be Toby who's into stealing other men's wives."

"Whoa!" all three brothers yelled in unison while Abbot cackled away at his own quip. Toby shook his head.

It was probably way too soon to be joking about it because he was still sporting some terrible bruising, but he was smiling anyway.

"Touché, motherfucker," Abbot said, flipping the bird to his oldest brother. Toby flipped two back.

"All right. My God, you're like squabbling children," Jasmine said, walking into the foyer. "Can't you let Samuel and Alesha have a special moment without stomping all over it?"

The twins looked at each other, then shook their heads. "Nah."

Jasmine smiled, and we all joined her. Then she turned to us and held up her own phone. "Smile," she said, and Sam and I stood together as she took a photo. It struck me that this was literally the first time we'd taken a picture together. It was something that needed to be rectified as soon as possible. We needed at least a thousand more.

"If you've had enough fun ogling my wife, we're going to leave," Sam said, placing his hand on the small of my back.

"We're ogling you too, brother," Kristian said, still filming. "You look like fucking James Bond."

Jasmine took the flowers from me and promised to put them in water. "Have fun," she said, opening the front door for us. Kris and Abbot chased us out, filming until we got into Sam's car. It was chaotic and crazy, but my God, it was fun. I bloody loved those guys, my brothers, my *mum*. I might not have been born to them, but I knew without a doubt that I belonged.

"You look beautiful," Sam said, reaching across the console to take my hand. "If there hadn't been an audience, I don't think we would've made it out the door."

"Oh yeah?" I grinned. "Did this dress get you hard?" I was growing bolder with him as the months wore on. He loved it when I talked that way, and it gave me a sense of freedom to explore what worked for me sexually.

"*You* got me hard. The dress is just pretty wrapping."

I smiled to myself, thinking, *You just wait,* knowing he was going to lose his mind when he saw what was going on underneath.

Placing my hands on either side of his, I turned in my seat so I was more directly facing him. "Thank you for doing this," I said.

He glanced at me and grinned, his eyes shining happily. "I haven't taken you anywhere yet."

I shrugged. "It's already been such fun."

"We're just getting started," he said, picking up my hand and bringing it to his lips. "Did I tell you how amazing you smell yet?"

"No. But I knew you'd like it. Mangoes."

He made a pleasurable noise, then lightly nibbled on my fingertips. It made my insides tingle delightedly, and I kind of wanted to skip the whole dinner thing and head straight for dessert, but I held off. I wanted to spend the whole night talking because sometimes, the pleasure is in the build-up.

We drove for a few minutes, and then Sam pulled the car to a stop in front of what looked like a primary school.

"Here we are," he said, gesturing towards the grounds.

"What is this?" I asked, leaning forwards to look out the front windscreen. "Is this where we're having dinner?" I thought that maybe there was some special event going on, but we were the only car there.

Sam grinned and got out of the car, opening my door for me before holding out his hand. "This is stop one."

"Stop one?"

He slipped his arm around my waist and led me towards the front gate. "You said you wanted to know all about my life, so I'm showing you. This is Get to Know Sam 101. And this is my primary school." He let me through the gate and led me up a path, pointing out buildings of importance along the way. He showed me the mural he'd helped paint when he was in the second grade, the playground equipment he used to climb to get away from the girls who were chasing him and threatening to kiss him on the mouth. "I was worried about cooties at the time," he'd explained before we continued along with him chatting about his favourite memories and the friends he'd once known, some of whom he still did. I actually remembered meeting a couple of them during the summer at the beach.

"And the pièce de résistance." He held his hand out, directing me towards a small picnic blanket that was set up with a single candle burning and picnic basket of food. "Your entrée, madam." He opened the container and held it out to me. Inside were these delicious little meat skewers that were still warm.

I sat with my legs kicked out to the side, looking around the dimly lit school while imagining a tiny Sam running around the grounds, wreaking havoc on all the kids around him. "I'll bet you were a really cheeky little boy," I said, holding out my wine glass as he filled it for me.

He placed the bottle in the basket. "What makes you so sure?"

"I just have a feeling. You're so sure of yourself as an adult. I imagine you were born that way." I sipped the cold crisp wine, noticing he was sticking to water. "You're not having any?"

He shook his head. "We have a fair few stops to get through, so I'm designated driver."

"I'll go slow, then." I smiled and took another sip. "Who was your favourite teacher?"

He screwed the cap back on his bottle and thought for a moment. "Mrs Corroway. I had her in grade three, and she managed to make every day a little fun. I think she's retired now."

"I had a teacher like that in year five. Mr Hodgkin. He played guitar and sang Beatles songs to us, and whenever he read a story, he did the most entertaining voices."

He was looking at me, a smile touching his eyes. "What?" I asked, wondering what it was I did that was so amusing.

He shook his head. "I just like listening to you speak."

I bowed my head and blushed. "We should do it more often."

Grinning, he held out his hand to me. "Come on, there's more I want to show you."

Helping me to my feet, he led me out of the school and back to the car, taking me to his high school next, where he told me all about his dreams of being an AFL player for Geelong. He skirted around the topic of high school girlfriends, but when I pressed, he told me there were a few. He was a bit of a ladies' man, but I already sensed that based on the way local women had responded to our coupling.

"How old were you when you lost your virginity?" I

asked, popping a green bean in my mouth from the second picnic we'd found magically set up and still hot (I had an inkling that he was getting help from someone).

"Geez, do you really want to know the answer to that question?"

I nodded. "I want to know everything about you."

"I was fourteen," he answered with a sigh and a cautious look. I suspected it wasn't something he was proud of.

"Wow," I said. "That's so young."

He agreed. "Way too young. And it was awkward, and it didn't last long."

Reaching across the table, I placed my hand on top of his. "I'm glad I got the expert version of you."

Lifting my hand, he pressed a kiss to my knuckles. "I'm glad for that too. You deserved to be treated like a queen for your first time."

I couldn't argue with that. He'd gone out of his way to make it an earth-shattering experience.

I drank a little more wine, he stuck to his water, and we ate more and conversed.

"What was your best class?"

"English," he said with a glint in his eye.

"That must be were you get all your poetry and writing analogies from," I teased. "English was actually my best subject too."

"Who'd you have a crush on?" he asked in return, causing me to blush again. My crushes seemed so silly next to his stories.

"Oh, I went to an all girls' school."

"There must've been someone," he teased.

"Oh, there was. A boy from the local public school. He

caught my bus and once, when it was full, he gave me his seat. His name was Tim, and he was tall and blond and played the guitar. I thought he was wonderful, but I barely said a word to him. I was far too shy."

"Did you think he wouldn't like you?"

I shrugged. "I didn't really think anyone liked me. I always felt like I was in the way."

He squeezed my hand. "You could never be in the way."

NEXT WE DROVE to the beach. There was no food there, only honesty as we looked out into the night, the moon glinting off the white-capped waves.

"My earliest memory is coming to this beach," Sam said, his gaze faraway, caught in a memory. "Dad was teaching us all how to surf, said we couldn't live so close to the sea without learning. Surfing is the only good memory I have of him. The man was a bastard most of the time, had an awful temper, treated Jazz like shit. They were always fighting, and I hated it. I was actually glad when he went away, relieved the arguing would stop. But she was so sad. For a long time, Jasmine could hardly get out of bed. I was too young to understand it, but she was mourning him, mourning the love she lost. What seemed like a horrible relationship to me was actually Jasmine's everything. He'd gone in there and made her promise to move on and forget about him. She didn't listen, of course, still went there every month and waited to see him, but he'd refused her every time. She was heartbroken. Probably still is, because I've never known her to date. Her focus has always been the family and the business."

My heart hurt listening to his words, for the confused boy he was, and for Jasmine. Perhaps this was partially why they were all so against love. They'd witnessed heartbreak first-hand at an impressionable age.

"How old were you when he went inside?"

"About six. The twins were two. Nate was eight and Toby was ten. He understood everything a lot better than me. He was the rock of the family, even cooked and shopped when Jazz couldn't make herself move. He'd make Nate go with him after school to help carry the bags home. He stepped up, this guy who was just a kid himself, and kept us all going until she could function again. I never understood that feeling, how you could be so heavily reliant on another human that you felt physically sick from being away from them." He reached over and took my hand. "But I think I have a fair idea now. We might've come into this in a messed-up way, but I can't imagine myself without you anymore. I need you," he said, frowning as he pressed a kiss to the palm of my hand.

"Oh, Sam," I said, wanting to tell him that I felt the same way. It had taken me a while to accept that we were real, but he'd come to mean everything to me. I might not have been ready to say it out loud yet, but he had my heart. I needed him as much as he seemed to need me. I hoped he understood that.

"There's one more stop," he said, starting the car and driving towards the main part of town. I thought for a moment that he was taking me to a café or restaurant for dessert, but then he turned onto the Esplanade, parked in front of a big white apartment building and shut off the engine. "This is where I lived."

I looked up at the structure, modern and expensive-looking, sitting directly across from the coastline. It seemed like a beautiful place to reside. "You gave up living *here* to stay at the house in your old room because of me?"

He shrugged. "I actually stayed there a lot before you came along. It's why we were all there on the day you rocked up. But this is the place I used whenever I needed my own space."

"This is one of the family holdings?"

He nodded. "Fake tenants pay fake rent. I get a place to crash when I need it. I thought you might like to crash a while with me too."

I loved being a part of the big family dynamic they had going on at the main house, but time alone with this beautiful big man was too good an opportunity to pass up. "Only if we can walk around naked," I told him.

"You bet your sweet little arse there's a no-clothes policy once we walk through that door."

I unclipped my seat belt. "Then what are we waiting for?"

CHAPTER TWENTY
NEED

"THIS VIEW IS BEAUTIFUL," I gushed, standing on the balcony, dessert wine in hand. The property faced the fore-shore, providing a seamless view of green grass, tall trees and glittering seas as far as I looked from left to right.

"You're right, it is," Sam said, except he wasn't looking at the landscape. He was sitting back from the rail-ing, reclining on a wicker outdoor lounge, staring at me.

"Careful, Sam." I smiled as I turned to face him. "You keep talking like that and I might start to think you've gone soft."

"Come over here and I'll show you exactly how hard I am."

I leaned against the railing, my smile going from teasing to coy. "Maybe I want to stay right here."

"That's a bold choice." He stood and undid each button on his dress shirt, his jacket long discarded and lying over the back of the wicker couch.

I finished the last of my wine and sat the glass on the closest surface. "Am I making you hot, Mr Cartwright?"

With a wicked grin, he walked over to me, gripping my hips before pulling me against him. He was definitely *hard. Nothing soft about this guy at all.* "Burning," he said, just before his mouth landed on mine.

My body sank against his as light moans escaped my chest. It felt so good to be kissing him this way, out in the open without worrying about interruptions or confining what would come next to a locked bedroom. We had an entire apartment, and I hoped to take full advantage of it.

When his hands moved, his fingers searching, my zipper glided downwards and the cool night air brushed against my skin.

"Here?" I asked when he turned me around so I was again facing the sea. His warm chest against my cool back, his lips trailed along my neck as he pushed my dress forward.

"Here," he murmured, obviously not caring that any voyeur with a good pair of eyes could watch us in silhouette. I'd expected we'd at least take this inside, but as his hands and mouth roamed, knowing we were *outside* was quite the turn-on. *Who knew I was a slight exhibitionist?*

I closed my eyes and leaned into him, curving my arse so it rubbed him where he needed it.

"What is *this?*" he growled as he pushed my dress to the ground and found the black lace underneath.

"More fancy wrapping," I whispered, turning again so he could take in the entire spectacle.

He took a step back, his eyes heated with desire as he drank me in, my skin bare save for a pair of black heels and two scraps of lace.

"Fuck me." The words were but a rumble in his chest.

"If you keep unwrapping, I'm pretty sure that's what you'll want to do to me."

"Peaches, that's what I *always* want to do to you."

I smiled and twisted my hips. "Just keep unwrapping. There's more."

Quick as a flash, he was on his knees in front of me, his fingers gripping the lace and tearing.

I gasped. "They were new."

"You said unwrap. I got excited." He placed his palm against my freshly waxed lady parts. "You did this for me?"

I nodded. "The lady at the salon said it's what men like. Do *you* like it?"

He slid his fingers back and forth, slipping between my folds. It was so sensitive and smooth. "Yes. I like it a lot."

Staying on his knees, he teased and played, bringing me to climax with his fingers. I kept my noises low, enjoying the danger of being seen without trying to call attention to ourselves.

"Do you have any idea how much I love making you come?"

Do you have any idea how much I'm in love with you?

Thankful those words stayed in my mind, I touched the side of his face and smiled. "Why don't you show me again?"

His eyes glinting from the challenge, he did just that, taking me from behind against the railing, me gasping as the sea whooshed in my ears.

His hunger for me didn't stop there. He took me on the kitchen counter, licking food from my skin. Then he took me in the massive bathtub, me on top, his hands running soap over my breasts as I moved. Then he carried me to the bedroom, exhausted yet buzzing, and took me again. But that time it was different: slower, more sensual, more tender. My orgasm building in my chest, emotion pushing at my eyes, it seemed like the right time to say it, my heart so full and our bodies so close. But when he pressed his forehead to mine, his body shaking, breath heaving, he whispered the words he'd said before, a thousand times. "I can't stop wanting you."

It was then that I wondered if he wished he could, if he saw his want of me as a weakness, if he kept fucking me because he was trying to chase that feeling away. Oh God, what if that was all this was? I was giving him my heart, but to him, was I merely an insatiable desire? He *needed* me. He *wanted* me. But that didn't mean he loved me.

A pang hit in the depths of my heart, a cry somewhere deep in my soul. That's what I *wanted*. That's what I *needed*. I wanted him to *love me*, and not like he loved his family. I wanted him to love me the way a man loves a woman, all-powerful, all-consuming.

I needed that.

CHAPTER TWENTY-ONE
THE GOOD CHINA

THE HOUSE WAS abuzz in preparation when we arrived home, Jasmine giving orders while Toby and the twins carried them out. "I want everything perfect," I heard yelled from the kitchen.

"Look who decided to bloody show up," Abbot chided, his arms laden with a beautiful set of china plates. He seemed a little put out that Sam and I had been spending more time outside the house than in it over the past month. I got the sense they liked having me around. But we would never get to where we needed to be as a couple with so many people around us. I still felt no closer to that elusive L-word.

"Hey, Leesh. Hey, Sam." Kris followed, carrying a box of crystal glassware.

"What in the world is going on here? The royal family coming to dinner?" I asked, confused by all the hustle and bustle.

"Close." He scoffed. "Nate and Holland. Jasmine

thinks that if the good china is out, Tobes and Nate'll think twice before punching on."

"Here's hoping," Sam said, and I crossed my fingers before we followed Kris and Abbot into the kitchen where Jasmine was furiously rolling out a lump of pastry. "What's cookin', good-lookin'?" Sam asked, leaning against the counter.

Jasmine looked up, but only for a second. There was wild panic in her eyes, and her tense shoulders only added to it. "Thank God you're both here. There's so much to do."

She directed me to the cartons of eggs and told me to separate the yolks from the whites. She was making lemon meringue pie, which was Nate's favourite.

When the pies were done and in the oven, she immediately jumped to the next task.

"Can I ask why we're going to so much trouble when Nate's the one who beat the shit out of Toby?" I asked.

Granted, Toby had kissed his wife, but it was far more complicated than that. I felt they both had things to make amends for, because I didn't believe for a second that Nate had no clue he was cutting his brother's grass.

Jasmine didn't even pause. "Because we always make an effort for family." That was all she'd say on the matter, and I suppose it was all that was needed. Family was everything to her. She would lay down her life for them; cooking a special dinner to bring them all together was the least of it. And since I was family now too, the least I could do was help her, and the most I could do was not take anyone's side. Brothers fought, but they never turned their back on each other. It was something I had to remember because it was so different from my own experience—just because they were pissed didn't mean it had to be over. They gave each other time to calm down, and then they tried again. That's what family was all about.

Funny that it took a family of thieves to teach me what my deeply devout counterpart could not.

Never turn your back on family.

ONE THING I could say for Nate was that he was controlled. Besides the couple of times he'd lost his temper over some wrongdoing towards Holland, he was the picture of calm. Some might even call the man charming (not me though).

That night, however, he was a mess. Every drink placed in front of him was sucked down at rapid speed. I swear the twins had a bet going over how many they could get him to sink since they were the ones keeping him supplied. He spoke in grunts and basically spent the entire meal glaring at Toby. I was seriously worried for the safety of the good china.

Holland seemed to have a handle on him though; a simple touch from her and I could visibly see a moment of calm cross his features. He loved her. Truly, madly, deeply. It was written all over him during each connection.

I watched him carefully, both out of concern and curiosity. Would Sam ever react that same way with me? I didn't know. So far, it seemed it was *his* touch that calmed *me* down. I sighed.

"He'll be OK," Sam whispered in my ear.

I hoped he was right, although I wasn't sure that I'd be OK. Beneath the surface, I was simmering. When Nate and

Holland had arrived, Jasmine had asked me to take Holland out back so they could have a quick word with Nate. I'd been doing a lot of thinking about family and the importance of putting our own issues behind us for the greater good, so I'd leaned into her and said, "I've missed you." Her response left a sour taste in my mouth.

"Really? You wouldn't have known since you never call or text, and when we're all together, you're Jasmine 2.0. I don't even know who you are anymore."

My eyes flashed. It felt like Sam's heated attack all over again. I was *not* Jasmine 2.0. "That's not fair. I'm just trying to make the best of things. You see where fighting against all this gets you." From where I was sitting, she hadn't made a single concession in her attempts to become a part of the family. She simply created wave after wave and acted as though she was above the rest of us.

She closed her eyes like she didn't want to hear it. When she opened them again, she looked at me and said, "At least I'm still me."

It bit into my insecurities. Despite Sam's assurances, I had worried over his words and tried my best not to pick up on anyone else's mannerisms or alter my behaviour to more easily fit in. I was trying to be as authentic as possible, but it wasn't easy when there were so many big personalities surrounding me and my default setting *was* to try and blend in. She'd been so focused on herself, cooped up with Nate that she had no idea of the struggles I faced, or the efforts I was making. I felt physically slapped by her snide remarks and had to get up and walk away so I didn't cause another family incident because I'd *literally* slapped her. By the time I'd made it back to Sam, I was shaking.

It didn't really get much better from there, what with

all the growling and glaring. Then there was the drinking, lord, that man could put it away when he wanted to. Besides the wedding, I hadn't seen any of the Cartwright brothers intoxicated. Nate was my first. Nate could barely stand up by the end of the night.

"Can someone help me get him into the car?" Holland asked when she'd tried and failed to get him out of his chair. The twins and Sam got up to help.

"Why don't you just stay here," Jasmine suggested. "The boys can all help you get him into the car, but then there's no one to help you at the other end when you get home. Just let him sleep it off here, and you can get going whenever you want to in the morning."

Holland considered it for a moment, then relented. "That's probably for the best."

Sam helped her get him settled, and then he and I went upstairs to our room, deciding it was best that we stayed in the big house overnight too.

He flopped on the bed with a groan. "That man has lost his shit."

I climbed on the bed next to him. "I guess love can make you crazy like that. Jealousy makes people even crazier."

"I don't know if that kind of attraction is really love. I mean, it seems powerful and all, but I reckon it's more of an obsession than love. Isn't love supposed to make you happy? Whatever those two have going on is not happiness."

I mused over his words for a moment before my question fell from my lips. "Are you happy, Sam?"

He popped an eye open and studied my expression.

"Are you fishing to find out how I feel about you, peaches?"

I shook my head, embarrassed for asking something so obviously prying. When this all started, I never expected him to fall in love with me—I was forced on him, after all —but as we grew closer, I knew it was something I couldn't be happy without. I had been lacking it for so long that I now knew I *needed* love in my life. "You talk about love like it isn't a real emotion, or you compare it to a weakness. You say you need me, but that isn't quite the same, is it?"

He narrowed his eyes a little. "What makes you so sure I *don't* love you?"

There were a few ways I could answer that question. I could tell him that I honestly didn't know what true love looked like. I had a hope for what it was, but I had no experience witnessing it. I knew my brother loved his wife, knew my father had loved my mother, but their display of such love was very different. Trevor showed controlled respect while my father simply exhibited control. None of that was the kind of love I dreamed of or hoped for myself, the kind of love I wanted from Sam. All I really knew from Sam was that he didn't exactly under-stand love either, so we were caught where we were, with him *needing* me and me *needing more.*

"Because you avoid saying it. You talk around it. And when I heard you talking about me with Toby a while back, it sounded like you don't really believe in love at all."

Heaving out a sigh, he adjusted on the bed and brought a hand up to the side of my face, his fingers playing lightly in my hair. "It's not that I don't believe, more that I don't trust it. It's a strong emotion that can fuck with your judgement. It's messy. I don't want messy. I want this." He pulled me closer and tasted my lower lip. "I want what we have." He wrapped me in his arms and rolled so he was on top of me. "I want you."

As he peeled away my clothing, tasting and teasing every inch of my body, my eyes burned, the unspoken '*I'm not in love with you*' ringing loud in my ears.

I was in love with him, I was certain that's what this was for me. But for him, it wasn't and perhaps never would be. I didn't know if I'd be able to accept that. I wanted the mess.

"TWO WAFFLE IRONS? I can't believe you own two," I said, pulling them out of the cupboard and handing them to Jasmine the next morning.

"When you raise five boys, you need to stock your cupboards like you run a small restaurant that caters to impatient customers."

I laughed as I stood back up and shut the cupboard.

"There're blueberries and strawberries," Sam said, standing at the fridge. "Do we want both?"

"Get the rock melon too. We have extra mouths this morning." Jasmine was already pouring ingredients into a mixing bowl.

I moved across the kitchen and switched on the radio before I plugged in the waffle irons so they could heat. The latest Justin Timberlake song filtered out through the speakers, and Sam took the opportunity to get a little handsy. Lord, how I loved having him near. He stood behind me and held my hips, swaying to the music before he shifted his grip so his fingers slipped underneath my shirt and splayed against the softness of my stomach. He did this move where we both arched backwards and rolled our hips around in a circle before he spun me around, catching me so I was pressed against him. Oh. My. God. It was the most fun I'd ever had moving to music. He had skills, and I was basically just a puddle on the floor. The man made me happy. I just wished that could be enough for me. Was I greedy to want more?

"Enough dirty dancing, you two." Jasmine laughed. "People have to eat in here."

I placed my hand against Sam's chest, heat in my cheeks and desire beneath my skin. "You need to get out of here or we're never getting fed."

I saw the way his eyes moved, basically saying he'd be happy eating me instead. The man just didn't quit. But he did concede enough to take a seat on the other side of the counter while I chopped up all the fruit—although he stole most of the blueberries.

I swatted at his hand. "If you take all the blueberries, there won't be any for anyone else."

He just laughed and took another one with a wink. *Typical.*

"Cheeky." I laughed, just as Holland appeared at the base of the stairs.

"Morning," she said brightly. *She must have slept well.* "Something smells amazing."

Jasmine looked up and smiled. "Hope you brought your appetite. How's that husband of yours this morning?"

"A little hungover," she said with a laugh. "He's taking a shower."

"Well take a seat. These will be ready in a few minutes." Jasmine poured batter into the waffle irons, the sizzle and smell instantly filling the air. "Sam, go get your brothers," she said as she picked up an egg flip and watched over the irons. "We're going to have a family breakfast this morning."

"Anything I can help with?" Holland asked, moving a little closer to us all. This was unusual for her. She was purposely trying to be perky and nice, I could see it in the way she kept resetting her smile.

"Nothing, dear." Jasmine smiled while Sam and I exchanged knowing glances before he left the room. "It's all under control."

Holland stood there looking lost for a moment, then took a big dramatic breath.

Here we go.

"Jasmine, I want to say that I'm sorry about all the trouble I've caused," she said in a rush. It sounded so forced, but I tried to stay out of it.

Turning towards Holland, Jasmine placed one hand on her hip and set her shoulders proudly.

"I appreciate your apology," she said after a breath, being careful with her words. "I hope you can find a way to embrace us as your family instead of kicking out and creating waves."

I stayed silent as I listened on. They would either come to a truce or make everything much worse.

"I can do that," Holland said, seeming surprisingly genuine. "I don't want to be the reason for tension. I just want Nate to be happy."

Jasmine handed me the egg flip she was holding, then

moved to stand directly in front of Holland. "Then you need to make a decision. Are you in or are you out?"

Whoa. I wished Sam would get back so I could see his reaction to this. I didn't think it was going to end well.

"What do you mean?" Holland asked with caution.

"I'm giving you a one-time offer, Holland. If you're unhappy here, you can pack your things and leave. But you'll need to leave for good and never speak to anyone about our family. We won't exist to you."

Whoa times two! I was not expecting that. Jasmine had done everything to be kind and welcoming to Holland for the sake of her relationship with Nate, but now she was delivering an ultimatum, giving Holland the out she had originally wanted. I guessed it was a test of Holland's devotion.

"I don't understand." Holland gulped.

Jasmine actually laughed in a mocking tone. It sent a chill down my spine to catch a glimpse of the woman Jasmine could really be. "I'm offering you your life back. But you'd have to never contact my son again."

Holland's face fell. I actually felt a little bad for her, but even she couldn't have her cake and eat it too. We all had to make compromises.

"I don't want to leave Nate," she responded.

Jasmine smiled. "Then you stay, and you give us something to prove you're in."

"I've already given you two cars and most of my possessions."

"We took those, sweetheart. And you got most of your stuff back."

"True."

"What I want from you is a job."

"A job?" Holland's eyes went wide. "I don't even know how I'd find one."

"You work at a fancy school. Surely you have some sort of information on someone or something that could prove fruitful. You could be our inside man." Jasmine wasn't going to make any part of this easy. It was one thing for Holland to say she would accept the family, but a woman like Jasmine needed proof. Loyalty was something shown by actions.

Chewing on her lip, Holland looked at me for assistance and I nodded, knowing she had information that would make Jasmine and the rest of the brothers happy.

"I...." She shook her head, looking like a stage actor who couldn't remember their lines.

I pressed my lips together. "What about that fundraiser they do every year?" I suggested.

Jasmine's eyes lit up. "Fundraiser?"

Holland cleared her throat. "Er, yes. It's like a, um... festival, I suppose. They put on a fair, lots of games and stalls. There's a silent auction, and the drama students put on a play. This year it's *A Streetcar Named Desire*."

"And they collect a lot of cash from this event?"

Her mouth twisted downwards as she nodded. "Last year they raised over a hundred thousand."

Jasmine actually gasped. "All cash?"

"Some cheques, but mostly cash, yes."

Jasmine stood up straighter and smiled. "Well that does sound like a nice payday. Do you know where the money gets taken at the end of the day?"

"The principal's office. It gets put in a safe, then taken to the bank on Monday."

"Well aren't you just full of wonderful surprises. We

can float this with the boys over breakfast. Welcome to the family, Holland." Jasmine leaned over and kissed Holland on the side of the head.

"WHAT? No. Absolutely not. She doesn't need to prove herself," Nate yelled over breakfast.

Holland had her head down like a beaten dog. *When did she become so morally pious?*

"We don't need your permission," Sam pointed out around a mouthful of waffles. "We know enough to plan it ourselves." He gave Holland a wink, and I knew he was teasing her. The Cartwright brothers lived for the adrenaline rush a good score could get them. And the fact that this one was a lot of cash that wasn't heavily secured meant it would be a thousand times sweeter.

"No," Nate insisted. "Can't we just let one member of this fucking family live a life that doesn't revolve around the next score?"

That comment really pissed me off. She was no better than the rest of us. It was unfair to set her apart. It had already caused enough damage.

Jasmine waited a moment before responding. "She's either a Cartwright or she isn't. We don't allow freeloaders."

"The fact that she works means she's making her own money."

"How does that benefit us?"

Toby cut in, adding his own thoughts to the situation at hand. "Maybe since Holland is the one who gave us the job, she should be the one who decides if it goes ahead."

We all waited for Holland to respond. Did she have the balls to join us, or was she going to continue hiding behind her husband?

"I—" she started, looking down, pausing and gulping.

Stop fighting, Holland! I screamed in my mind.

Then Nate decided to speak. "You don't want to be like us, duchess. You're better than we are. You're good. Stay good."

Fuck you, Nate. He didn't even blink when it was suggested that I get more involved in the family business, but Holland is so *good* that she can't? I was fucking insulted.

"Ain't no room for good people round our table, brother," Abbot put in, always one to say exactly what the rest of us were thinking.

Nate stood up immediately. "Fuck this. We're leaving. Holland, go get your things."

Holland left the table faster than I'd ever seen her move before. She couldn't wait to get out of there.

"I swear to you," Nate growled, holding his finger up while glaring at us all individually, "if you go ahead with this job or do a single thing to hurt her, I will rain bloody hell down upon you all. Family or not."

"Are you saying you choose your wife over us?" Jasmine demanded.

Jaw clenched, his eyes wild, he didn't respond, so Jasmine continued.

"You might want to keep her out of this, Nathaniel. But you should've thought about that before you dragged her into it. You caused this. You lured her here, and you got Alesha mixed up in our business too. She's embraced us. It's time for Holland to do the same."

"I don't want her involved," Nate insisted.

"She already is," Jasmine hissed. "What do you think will happen to her when you get busted for your precious field of flowers? What do you think will happen the year you have a bad harvest and those goons you've mixed yourself up with come to collect? You think you can keep her safe, Nate? You don't even know how to save yourself, you're in so deep."

Nate growled like a wild animal before he grabbed the table and flipped it on its side. Crockery and glass went everywhere, smashing on tiles while the food and drink coated our legs before we had the chance to jump out of the way. In the chaos, he stormed out and slammed the front door, the screeching of his tires the last thing we heard.

"Motherfucker ruined our waffles," Kris shouted, shaking his head at the mess on the floor.

Abbot bent down. "This one's OK," he said, picking one out of the rubble and removing a shard of glass. He went to put it in his mouth, but Toby slapped it from his hand.

"Don't eat it, you knucklehead. You'll be shitting out glass, and I don't want to be the one to explain your bleeding arsehole in the emergency room."

"Let's just get this cleaned up," Jasmine said, looking at the mess on the floor with a tight mouth.

It didn't take long to put everything right again, and the brothers had the ability to turn anything into a bit of fun.

But I couldn't help but feel bad for Jasmine. She'd tried to force family unity and it had all blown up in her face. Now the good china was ruined, much like her relationship with Nate.

CHAPTER TWENTY-TWO
FUCKING FREEDOM

I TURNED my head to catch the sun and the light breeze against my skin. I loved living in Torquay, loved the salty air and the relaxed atmosphere. In the summer, it had been filled with tourists. Now the crowds had died down and a sense of tranquillity descended. "You know, I had no idea this was a café when I first saw it." He'd brought me to this beautiful café that was inside an old weatherboard home not far from the Esplanade apartment. The air was fresh, almost icy, but we'd opted to sit outside nonetheless.

"They've got good food, and since breakfast got so thoroughly destroyed, I thought we could do with a change of scenery and some fresh air," Sam said, picking up the salt from the table, shaking a little in his hand and tossing it over his shoulder.

"That was a bit messed up, huh? Do you think everyone will work it out?"

He shrugged. "Eventually. Maybe. I don't know this time. Nate's never been this bad."

"Do you blame Holland too?"

He met my eyes and squinted. "No. I blame Nate. He's not thinking right."

"Because he's crazy from love, right?"

His jaw tightened a little and he nodded before looking away, watching a couple trying to walk a big excited dog along the seaside pathway. I took that as a sign that the conversation was over. Just as well, since I'd dwelled on that topic far too much of late. I needed to give my mind a break. There was so much more going on around me than my fairy-tale dreaming.

With my stomach rumbling, I looked toward the entrance in the hopes our meals we being brought out. No such luck, I settled on watching a little red-headed girl on the playground where several other kids were running amok. She was yelling for her brother to help her climb a ladder. He jumped down and struggled to lift her, pushing on her butt until she made it safely on the landing. The sight made me smile.

Sam reached over and took my hand. "One day," he said, his thumb moving over my knuckles. He was watching me watch the kids, a topic we hadn't discussed much since he learned of my condition. I felt a pang where my womb was. *When did I start wanting them so much?*

"You know, I thought I had grown used to the idea of a life without children," I started, smiling a little when the girl squealed as her brother took her down the slide. "Now I find myself looking at them and wondering what it would be like."

"Is this your way of saying you want them now?"

"You know, I don't know. I'm certainly thinking about it more. But am I thinking about it because I know you want them and I'm a people pleaser or because I finally have the opportunity? It's hard to get my mind straight sometimes." Holland's words from the night before taunted me. *Jasmine 2.0* I was trying to be happy, but now I was really confused.

"That's why we're going to wait until you're one hundred percent sure that kids are what *you* want. We both need to be on the same page when the time comes."

"Thank you," I said, giving his fingers a squeeze. "I appreciate that. But it doesn't change the fact that my clock is ticking. I don't have a lot of time to decide, and the longer we leave it, the harder it's going to be. Back when I had my initial testing done, the doctors had no idea what my chances would be. They said I'd need further testing when the time came, and that time has never come until now. My insides could be a black hole of nothingness for all I know."

"I'm sorry, peaches," Sam said, his voice so soft it hurt a little to hear.

I lifted my brow at his apology, so against the grain.

"I know, I said the forbidden word." He smiled. "But it's true. We haven't really talked about it much, but I really am sorry that your mother did this to you. Drugs are messed up. Jazz has always been dead against them."

"She said you were using when you got busted." I said the words carefully, hoping we were at a point where he wouldn't launch into attack mode over something he felt I shouldn't know.

Thankfully, he nodded and looked down at our joined hands. "Coke mainly. A little dope to take the edge off when it was hard to come down. It's not a period of my life I'm proud of, and I haven't touched the stuff since. I'm fully behind the anti-drug stance the Cartwrights take now.

They might be easy money, but they're risky, and they ruin people's lives. I don't want that on my conscience."

"What about Nate?" I asked, thinking back to the morning's outburst and Jasmine's comments.

Sam shook his head. "He plays his own game, chases his own demons. I try to stay out of it as much as I can."

"But he's involved, isn't he?"

Sam nodded.

"In what way? Jasmine said something about crops and flowers."

Sam nodded slowly. He wasn't giving me any extra information, but he wasn't going to stop me from putting it all together myself.

"The only flower I can think of is those opium flowers —poppies, right? Is that what he's growing?" I kept my voice really low so no one else would hear.

Sam licked his lips, closed his eyes for a moment and then gave me the smallest of nods.

"He supplies the people who make it?"

Another nod.

Jesus.

I sat back in my seat on a gasp, feeling as though the air had been knocked out of me. Despite the fact that I wasn't currently getting along with Holland, I still cared about her, about her wellbeing, and I worried about her all alone with Nate most of the time. Before now, I'd been worried because I kept seeing signs of aggression, but now I knew he was involved with drug dealers—as a supplier, no less. Was Nate insane dragging her into this? How selfish could one person be?

I closed my eyes as the revelation hit me. Holland had dragged *me* into this without giving my safety a second thought. Looked like Nate and Holland were perfect for each other.

"Tell me something funny," I said releasing the tension in my breath as I opened my eyes. "I need to clear my head and focus on everything that's good. I don't need their shit anymore." I touched my hands to the side of my head and mimed pulling away the bad energy. I'd never tried it before, but it felt like a great way to change my thought process.

Sam smiled and relaxed his shoulders. "OK. You want a joke?"

"Sure."

"You've probably heard it, but here goes. So Superman is flying about, on his way to save the world, when he looks down. Wonder Woman is lying on the beach with nothing on—completely starkers."

I wiggled my brows. "Raunchy. Go on."

"Well, he sees her and he thinks, 'Hmm, I wouldn't mind myself a piece of that.'" This was definitely working, I was already starting to giggle. "He doesn't have much time, but he can't resist. So he flies down there, does her lightning fast, then flies away to continue his mission. It happened so fast that Wonder Woman only sees a blur. She sits up and says, 'What the hell was that?' Then the invisible man shakes his head and goes, 'I don't know, but for some reason my arsehole is really sore.'" His lips twitched as he delivered the punchline.

"Oh my God!" I laughed, loving the lightness taking over in my chest. I wanted more of that, to focus on joy. "Do you know any more?"

He grinned. "I know plenty."

And that's how we spent the rest of our morning.

"WHAT THE HELL?" Sam lifted his head from the shot he was lining up on the pool table. We'd spent most of our day out of the house, exploring the town and discovering places even Sam as a local didn't know about. We'd been tempted to be selfish and spend the night at the apartment, but that wasn't how our family operated. When shit went down, we banded together. Jasmine was going to need us, and we'd done our best to keep her distracted until she decided to have an early night. Now we were hanging out in the rumpus room having a few drinks.

"Did someone just come through the front door?" I moved slightly to try and look down the hall. It wasn't exactly a straight shot, but I'd be able to see if someone was coming our way.

I was expecting it to be Kris or Abbot. They'd gone out about an hour ago, saying they had a couple 'sweeties' to meet, so I wasn't expecting to see them until morning. But hook-ups didn't always go according to plan.

"Um, Sam?" I took a step back, shifting until I was behind him. The arrival wasn't one of the twins, it was Nate. And he looked pissed.

"Where is she?" he demanded, not making eye contact with either of us, rather walking around the marble-topped bar and digging around in the cabinet. He came out with a bottle of tequila, pulled off the cap and chugged back as much as he could before his body forced him to gag.

Sam frowned. "Holland? She left with you, brother."

"I fucking know that. Where's Jasmine?" he growled, sucking air through his teeth before taking to the bottle again.

"Where's Holland?" I demanded, finding my voice in my fear. He was alone and aggressive. He'd left out of his mind. *What has he done to her?*

"Gone," he said, his lips wet from the speed he was drinking. "Left me. That's why I need Jasmine." He lifted his head and yelled at the roof. "To tell her the good news."

"I'm guessing she knows about your flowers?" I asked.

"I showed them to her. That's when she…." Nate paused and looked at the bottle. It was almost full when he started, and now there was only an inch of liquid left. After a moment of study, he opened his eyes wide and shook his head a little, the alcohol obviously taking hold.

"Left?" Sam finished for him.

"Bingo!" Nate pointed in Sam's direction and winked. "Drugs were her deal-breaker. Now she knows and she's gone." He yelled at the ceiling again. "Jasmine should be down here celebrating with me!"

"Jasmine's pissed at you for ruining her china."

Nate frowned as he took another swig. "Of course she is. Stuff was always more important. That's why we're all fucking criminals, right? Taking is easier than earning?" He was still yelling, trying to lure Jasmine down the stairs.

Finishing the bottle, he worked his jaw, his mouth downturned as he warred with the emotions coursing through his mind and body. In his own way, he truly loved Holland. No one behaved the way he had since meeting her without that strong emotion. Losing her was destroying him—a blind person could see that. "No Jasmine? She doesn't want to revel in the success of her plan? Let's see if she'd start to give a fuck if I break her precious *house*." On the final word, he hurled the empty bottle across the room into the glass sliding doors. They shattered into thousands of tiny pieces, then dropped to the ground both inside and out. Miraculously, the bottle was still intact.

"What the fuck is going on?" Toby demanded, hurtling down the stairs. He skidded to a stop the moment he spotted Nate and saw the glass all over the floor. He was only wearing a pair of boxers and had no shoes.

"Toby!" Nate yelled with false cheer. "I have wonderful news for you. Holland is single again. The downside is that Jasmine will never let you have her, and even if she did, you'd be nothing more than a stand-in for me, and you'd be a poor one at that."

"You are out of line," I yelled when Toby just clenched his jaw and stayed silent. I didn't care how distraught Nate was, he didn't get to treat his family like that.

"Peaches, leave it," Sam warned, placing his hand on my arm to keep me back when I started moving forward.

"No. He doesn't get to treat you all like shit just because he's hurting. Your wife left you, boo-fucking-hoo. None of *us* made her leave. She chose that on her own because you obviously fucked up with whatever druggie bullshit you've gotten yourself into. Yelling at your brothers, blaming your mother—none of that is going to fix it for you because at the end of the day, growing those flowers was *your decision*. You fucked up, Nate. You caused all of this. Question is what are you going to do to fix it?"

The room was so silent you could hear everyone's heartbeats. Nate just glared as we all stared. Then Sam stepped forward. "I think maybe you need to lie down, brother."

Nate blinked twice, rocked unsteadily and then

frowned. Jasmine appeared at the bottom of the stairs. "What's with all the shouting?" she asked, still looking half-asleep. She took fairly strong sleeping pills and wasn't easy to rouse. "Nate?" She frowned.

"Holland left," I told her when it looked like no one else would.

She walked carefully around the glass. "Can't say I'm surprised. She was never going to be one of us."

"That's your fucking problem, isn't it?" Nate slurred. "No one's ever good enough. Everyone is forever proving their fucking loyalty." He stopped talking abruptly, clamping his mouth shut as a frown creased his brow.

Oh no.

Seeming to get control, Nate turned his attention back to Jasmine, shuffled slightly and then opened his mouth to speak. Except it wasn't words that came out but a torrent of alcohol and everything he'd put in his mouth that day. Possibly the day before, also.

I clapped my hand over my mouth and dry-heaved.

"That shit is messed up," Sam said, watching with wide eyes.

"Get him in the guest room, in the shower," Jasmine commanded, suddenly very awake and assessing all the damage.

Sam and Toby grabbed Nate, being careful to avoid any glass as they directed him towards the right door. He refused, fighting with haphazard limbs as he said, "Need more alcohol. I just spilt all mine on the floor."

Yeah. And it's fucking gross.

I scrunched my nose up. "I'll get a mop and bucket."

Jasmine looked at all the glass. "That's a good idea. Maybe get the bin and a broom too?"

"On it," I said, glancing back as she went to help Toby and Sam with Nate, who was now hanging between them like a toddler who didn't want to go home. I shook my head. *Baby*. What the hell did he think was going to happen? That they'd live happily ever after? The idea was preposterous, especially considering all the lies in how they'd met.

So now she'd left him. And if Jasmine was to be believed, she'd left with no consequence. That just left me here, the only real casualty in Nate and Holland's love games. I wasn't being let go; what I might want wasn't even being considered. *Isn't that fucked up?*

It wasn't even that I wanted out either. Given the choice, I might actually stay. But it was the fact that giving me an out was never even considered. No one *ever* asked me what I wanted. They just *expected* me to stay, to be a good girl, to jump and hop and skip and do anything I was told to.

What the hell am I doing?

I stood in the middle of the mess, holding the mop and the broom with buckets at my feet, and looked around. *I'm still doing exactly what I'm told.* Inside my chest, I felt this buzzing. It grew bigger and wider with each passing second, swirling through my body until my stomach was churning and I felt sure that I might vomit too. But it wasn't that, it was this clawing feeling scratching at my insides, wanting me to scream, or better yet, to run.

Run.

Dropping the mop and broom where I stood, I knew what I had to do. I didn't run. I walked towards the front door, grabbed my purse and went out into the night.

Like a true Cartwright, I could take what I wanted too.

And what I wanted—me, Alesha—was the freedom to choose. I wanted my fucking freedom. If Holland could have hers, then I could also have mine. If Sam wanted me so badly, he'd have to prove it. I wasn't going to sit there pathetically waiting for him to love me anymore. Finally, I found my backbone.

It was love, or it was nothing. I wouldn't come back for anything less.

CHAPTER TWENTY-THREE
FIGHT FOR IT

THE PROBLEM with being an inherently anxious person was that when you finally made a decision and stood up for it, you questioned yourself from that moment on. The hour-and-a-half drive from Torquay to Caulfield East was fraught with moments of *What am I doing? Am I insane?* as well as the struggle not to turn around and go back with my tail between my legs. Worse was when the phone calls started. Sam, Jasmine, even Toby. They were all trying to get in contact with me, and I had no choice but to turn my phone off to save my own sanity. I was doing this for me. For once, I was being the selfish one.

And perhaps I was doing it for Sam too. He'd never done something for himself either. In a lot of ways, we were the same, he and I. We both did what we were told, didn't create waves. We slotted into the mould other people made for us. But what would we be if everything else stopped? What would we become if the only decisions we had to make and the only paths we had to take were our own? Would we walk together, or would we walk apart?

With so much external pressure, I didn't think either of us could answer those questions the way we were. Something drastic had to happen to blow us up.

I was being the bomb.

Arriving back at my place, I entered the communal drive and sat in front of the dark building with my van still running. After all these months, returning to the tiny home I'd been so proud of was surreal, like the excitement of buying a villa off the plan had happened a lifetime ago. Back when I was another person entirely. When I didn't believe I'd ever marry. When I didn't believe I could possibly want children. Before I believed in anything, really.

Cutting the engine, I sighed. I was finally home.

Home. Was that still what it was to me now? I owed it to myself to find out. However, one thing stood in my way —I was without a set of keys.

I got out of the van, looking at the weeds in my garden bed and wishing I'd thought to put one of those plastic rocks in there with a key hidden inside. My spare key lived at Holland's place and had been stolen in her first altercation with Nate. I'd never thought to replace it. Now I guess the Cartwrights had all my keys. Well, that wasn't going to stop me from getting inside. I had skills, and I could work this out.

Switching my phone on and into airplane mode, I used the flashlight to shine on the windows. Surely I'd left one open. I hadn't exactly left that day thinking I wouldn't come back. The villa was only two bedrooms and tiny, so the search didn't take long. Thankfully, I'd cracked the window in the bathroom.

Unfortunately for me, that was probably the smallest

window in existence. It was high up and not much bigger than an oblong pizza box, but I was pretty sure my hips could fit through.

Holding my phone between my teeth, I dragged a potted plant off my front porch, then pulled it down the side of the house, giving myself enough height to reach the frosted window.

Popping the screen, I slid the window open as far as it would go, tucked my phone away and pulled myself up. It was a tight squeeze and involved angling my body by slipping one arm through and then twisting diagonally so my shoulders slotted through.

"OK. I can do this," I coached myself, one arm pressed against the wall while the other touched the ceiling and my feet scraped against the brickwork, pushing myself farther inside.

"Come on," I grunted, getting past my chest and then leaning towards the cistern, ready to catch my weight as my hips came through. Except they didn't come through. My chest and my stomach made it, but as I tipped my weight forward, my arse and hips got wedged.

Shit. I'd tipped farther forwards than I could go back, which meant my legs were sticking straight out in the air, and my torso was upside down against the wall with the blood rushing to my head. Worse still, my phone was in my back pocket, so I couldn't get it out to call for help. And voice commands wouldn't work because I'd set it to airplane mode.

Just bloody brilliant.

Spreading my arms out against the wall, I kept pushing against it, trying to pull my body the rest of the way in. I tried rocking my hips, wriggling my arse, kicking my legs. None of it was working.

Fuck. Fuck, fuck, fuckity fuck. How was I going to get out of this one?

I lifted my head. "Help," I called out, hoping maybe one of the neighbours would hear me. "Heeeeelp!" I tried louder, then listened to see if I could hear movement. There was nothing, but I wasn't going to give up and become that girl who died of starvation because her arse got caught in a window frame. I kept yelling and wriggling, crying out and pulling. Then somehow, by the grace of God, someone came.

"What the hell have you done to yourself?"

Quitting my baneful cry, I lifted my head to the voice, finding Sam standing in front of me with his hands folded across his chest.

"Wait. The front door was open?"

He nodded.

"Holy fuck." Why hadn't I even thought to check that?

I let out my breath and held my hands out to him. "Do you think you can help a girl—owww!"

All at once, the window broke free of its fittings, sending me tumbling forward, my hand going straight into the toilet bowl before Sam caught me.

"Whoa there." He set me on my feet and helped me remove the window accessory I was wearing around my waist. Somehow the glass had survived with only a slight crack.

"This is disgusting," I said, shaking off my wet hand and grabbing toilet paper to dry it.

"Hey, at least you flush," he pointed out.

I moved into the bathroom and pumped about forty

spurts of hand soap into my palm, scrubbing my skin up to the elbow. When I turned on the taps, I was relieved to find warm water. Setting up a direct debit for all my bills was definitely the best thing I ever did.

"What are you doing here?" I asked as I dried off my arm and found Sam waiting in the doorway.

"I was planning on asking you the same thing."

"I live here," I said. "This is my home."

"No, your home is with me. This is just a place you *used* to live in."

"I didn't agree to give up my place and live with your family. I didn't agree to any of the things that have been decided for me."

"Is that why you left? Because you want to make your own decisions? Have I not given you *everything?* What more do you want?"

"The same consideration Holland gets."

He frowned. "Is this some pissing contest? More of your jealousy over your friend?"

"I'm not jealous of her. I just want to be as human as her."

"You don't feel treated like a human?" He looked as though I'd slapped him in the face.

"Why did you do it, Sam?"

"Do what?"

"Marry me. Why did you do it?"

He held his hands out to his side. "Because—"

"Because you had to, right? Not because you wanted to. Not because you were in love with me. Because your mother told you to do it. Do you even want me now, Sam? Or have you just gotten used to having me around? Did you come after me because you wanted to, or because

Jasmine said 'go get her'? Don't you see, we're *both* the people she shaped us into. We're playing a part, pretending everything is OK when it isn't fucking OK. I don't know who the fuck I am anymore. And I don't think you know who you are either."

With his jaw clenched tight and his shoulders set straight, he filled the entire door frame of my tiny bathroom. "I don't know what you expect me to say or do."

"I expect you to fight, Sam. I expect you to say what you feel, tell me what you want. I don't give a fuck what's expected. Just be honest. What do you want? What the fuck does Samuel Cartwright want in his life? Is it a marriage he was forced into? A job he was groomed for? A life governed by other people's rules? What, Sam? What?"

He released his breath through his nose and closed his eyes for a moment, maintaining his control. "You're obviously upset over tonight and this morning. Why don't you come home and get some rest. We can talk about this properly in the morning. Maybe a surf will clear your head?"

"What?" My brow knitted so tight I felt the skin fold between my eyes. "*This* is my home, Sam."

"Peaches," he said, a hint of warning in his tone. "Please come with me."

"Or what? Mummy will lose her shit? I won't be allowed to have my freedoms and privileges anymore? No van, no surfing, No dessert for a week? What will happen, Sam? Why can't I be free with no consequence too?"

"That's what you want?" he asked, a slight shake in his voice. "You want to be free of me?"

"*I don't know!*" I shrieked. "I don't have a fucking clue what I want, Sam. I just want to have a *choice*."

His teeth ground together, and a contained rumble went

through his chest. "Fine. I'll give you a choice. Stay here and leave me, or come home, be with me."

"That's it? It's that easy for you? After everything we've been to each other, you're just letting me go. No fight, nothing."

He pressed his thumb and forefinger against the bridge of his nose, closed his eyes and growled before he spoke. "What the fuck else do you want? I'm giving you exactly what you asked for!"

"Are you? Or are you saying what you think you should? Don't *give* me what I want, Sam. Fight!" I shoved his chest. "Fight for what *you want!* I want you to be honest with me. I want you to tell me how you feel. I want you to *choose* me. *Fight* for me, Sam, because if you can't fight or you don't want to, then what the fuck are we doing?"

Two breaths. He took two breaths before his eyes flashed he cracked. "You want me to fight?" he yelled. "You want me to break down, confess my devotion and tell you all the secrets I'm holding deep inside me? Fuck you. I married you. I cared for you. I did everything right, every-thing that was asked of me. Why isn't that enough? I'm not playing games with you. Choose *me,* Alesha. Choose me or fuck the hell off."

"I want to choose you, Sam. I really do. But when your argument is that you 'did everything right', how can I? I'd rather be lonely without you every day than be with you, knowing you were settling for me because I was forced on you."

His eyes flashed, and before I knew it his mouth was on mine, his tongue pushing, teeth hitting and bodies buzzing. My hands grabbed his shirt, then gripped his hair, pulling slightly. I could barely breathe, but I couldn't stop. I wanted him to devour me, pull me inside himself.

"Does that feel like settling to you?" he demanded, his chest heaving as he pressed his face into mine, like he couldn't get close enough.

I shook my head. "No. It felt like *wanting*."

"Yes," he whispered, kissing me again. "How many times do I have to say it before you believe it? I want you, Alesha. I *need* you."

Need.

Lifting me in his arms, he carried me to my bedroom and placed me back on my feet next to the bed. "I don't want you gone," he whispered, reaching down to pull my shirt over my head. "I want you with me." He pressed soft kisses over my shoulders, up my neck. "Don't you understand that? You're my wife, my family. I need you."

Need.

Peeling the rest of my clothes off, he laid me back on the bed and climbed over my body, his mouth teasing and tasting along the way. Then he kissed my mouth, his passion and tension brimming. I let myself fall into it. Allowed myself to quiet my mind and just *feel* everything he was trying to convey with his movement and his body. The way his hands touched my skin. The way his fingers teased my sensitive areas and brought me to climax. The way he paused when he pulled his shirt off because he knew I liked to run my fingers over his abs. And the way he locked eyes with me as he pushed inside me.

He took my hands in his, intertwining our fingers before he held them above my head, his hips rolling as he thrust inside me, causing my mind to go numb and my body to cry from pleasure.

"This," he whispered. "This is everything I have." He thrust his hips a little harder, his voice gruffer. "Isn't this enough for you?"

Need. Not love.

A tear formed in the corner of my eye. I felt so much when I was with him. My body surged and heated beneath his touch, my heart beat quicker when he entered a room and my mind went quiet at his closeness. I wanted to believe that we were put in each other's paths for a reason, that perhaps divine intervention did exist. But I struggled to believe that a man as beautiful as Sam could possibly want me, could want to be with me. Sex was wonderful, and I felt a deep connection whenever we lost ourselves in each other. But the physical faded. I might not have had a lot of experience with relationships, but I did know that. This heat we were experiencing, one day it would fade. And then what would we be left with? I didn't want to become his obligation.

I felt the tear slide down, so I closed them and turned away.

Immediately Sam stilled. "Am I hurting you?"

I shook my head, unable to stop the emotion that was bubbling up inside me. He released my hands and pulled out, collecting me in his arms and wrapping us both in the warm covers.

"I don't know what to say, peaches. I don't know how to make this right."

I pulled his arms tighter around me, pressed harder against his chest. "Just h-h-hold me," I sobbed, and he did just that. He held me until I cried myself to sleep.

"Hey." He pressed a kiss to my shoulder as I woke up still wrapped within him. It seemed we hadn't moved all night.

The moment I realised he was still there, emotion pricked my eyes. *Why on earth am I still crying?*

He shifted his weight and pulled me towards him so I rolled on my back. I covered my eyes because they wouldn't stop leaking.

"Are you still upset with me?"

I shook my head.

"Do you still feel like I don't want you enough?"

Again, I shook my head.

"Then what? What do you need from me?"

I wiped my eyes and looked up at the ceiling. The answer had been a screaming voice in my mind for months. I'd tried to ignore it, tried to reason it away, but it was eating away at my sanity. I wouldn't be OK until I knew if it was possible.

I inhaled a shaky breath and forced myself to meet his eyes.

"I need you to love me," I whispered. Then I felt my heart crack as I watched his face fall. That was the only answer I needed.

Jumping out of bed, I grabbed my old robe from over the door and wrapped myself in it as he called my name.

"You need to go," I said, my arms folded around my waist and my eyes focused on the floor.

I could hear the tension in his breath as he slid out of bed and got dressed. It was the longest minute of my life.

He stopped in front of me. "Will you look at me?"

I shook my head, keeping my eyes on the floor.

"Please," he said, hooking a finger under my chin until I caved and lifted my head, my gaze to the side. "Alesha."

I forced my eyes to his. His weren't filled with joy. With love. No, they were filled with something much worse than that. In his eyes, I saw pity.

"Why are you still here?" I asked, my voice hoarse.

"Because I don't want to leave you like this."

"Well, I want things too. It doesn't look like I'm getting it either."

He pressed his lips together and closed his eyes. "I'm not saying I don't love you, peaches. I'm just not going to say I do."

"That doesn't make any sense. Do you or don't you love me? We've spent the best part of a year together. Surely you have some clue."

"I'm sorry," he said, and I shoved his chest.

"Don't say sorry. You're a Cartwright. Just say what you mean."

"Fine. I don't know how I feel. I want you. I don't want to be without you. That's all I know."

"So you like fucking me and you're not bored yet? That's not good enough for me."

"That isn't what I said."

"That's what it sounds like."

"Jesus, Alesha, what the fuck do you want from me?"

"I want you to love me! I just fucking told you that."

"And you can honestly say you love me? The man who essentially kidnaped you and forced you into a life of crime. You're in love with that man?"

I lifted my chin and met his eyes. "Yes, Sam. I'm in love with you. And I'm not going back with you until you can say the same."

His eyes searched mine and his jaw tensed, his breath

coming hard. "If I leave, I might not be able to come back. This could be it for us."

"If that's the case, Sam, so be it. I don't want to get you in trouble with your family, and God forbid you stand up for yourself and go after what you want."

"That's not fair."

"Maybe. But it's the truth."

He stared at me, and I could see the war of his mind behind his eyes. "I don't want to leave without you."

"I'm not spending my life with a man who doesn't love me. It's not fair for either of us."

"I could put you over my shoulder and force you to come with me."

"I'd only run away again."

"I could lock you up. Keep you so you can't leave."

I placed my hand on his chest. "That's not the kind of man you are."

His brow knitted and he looked away. "Just come back with me."

I shook my head. "How about you come back *for* me. Fight, Sam. Figure out what you want, how you *feel.* Then fight for it."

He withdrew from me in a flash, striding through the living room in a few steps. Then he opened the door and slammed it so hard the windows rattled.

I dropped to the floor and cried.

Why can't he love me?

CHAPTER TWENTY-FOUR
PERFECT JOB

"ALESHA WARD?" The courier stood at my door with one of those handheld machines, the stylus dangling off it.

"Yes?" I sniffed as I opened the door a little farther.

"I have several boxes for you," he said, looking at me warily. It was understandable. My eyes were swollen from crying all day and barely sleeping. I also hadn't brushed my hair. I must've looked a fright. He either thought I was horribly contagious or that I'd break down in front him and claw at his shirt like a maniac.

"Several? What are they?" Considering they were addressed to my maiden name, and I hadn't been back in my own place long enough to order anything, I was at a loss.

"I don't get to see inside them. I just deliver 'em," he said, returning to his van and opening the back door. When I heard him click open a trolley, I knew he was going to be a while. I propped the door open with a little statue of the Virgin Mary—my father's idea of the perfect gift—and went into the bathroom to wash my face and make myself look somewhat decent by pulling my hair back into a knotty ponytail.

When he finished piling them up inside the door, I signed his tablet and he left, leaving me to stare at the pile in front of me. When I'd chewed my thumbnail down to the quick, I decided to open the box on top. The first thing I saw was the dress I'd worn on my date with Sam. My heart actually stopped beating.

They'd sent me my things. They'd addressed them to Alesha Ward. *Ward.* I wasn't a Cartwright anymore. Sam wasn't going to fight for me. He didn't want me anymore.

He doesn't want me.

Picking up the dress, I held it between my hand, the anger and injustice of never being good enough rising up and manifesting itself in a blinding rage.

"*Motherfucker,*" I screamed, holding it above my head and tearing it to pieces. Once I started, I couldn't stop, I kicked and shoved, threw and stomped on every single one of those boxes, crying and screaming the entire time. It wasn't fair. I'd loved him. I'd been a good wife, a good daughter-in-law, a good sister-in-law, and the moment I stood up and said 'what about me', they turned around and walked away.

Putting my hands over my face, I stepped back until I hit the wall and then slid down to the floor. Too upset to cry, all that would come out was an open-mouthed gasp. I could barely breathe.

What is so horrible about loving me? Why am I never enough?

IF A PROFESSIONAL WAS to break down my personality and align it with the events in my life, they'd probably diagnose me with an anxiety disorder stemming from the fact that my mother abandoned me when I was young. They'd probably say that I also had trust issues, never believing other people's words and actions, always expecting the worst from them. Because why wouldn't I? Even my own mother didn't want me, and my own father didn't trust me. I didn't see my own self-worth, which was why I was so easily moulded. I wanted people to like me, and I was willing to change myself for their validation. And why wouldn't I do that too? The first time I demanded to have my say, I lost everything I'd grown to care about, proving once again that I was worthless. Nobody needed or wanted me. They let go far too easily.

Was it too much to ask for someone to fight for me? Was it too much to want someone to love me above all else? Or was I the one who was too much? Did I expect more than I deserved?

I probably should've gone to see a professional, but I chose to spend the next couple of months self-diagnosing via articles I found through Facebook and Google. It seemed like a productive use of my time, something to fill the hours when I wasn't working.

That's right. I'd gone back to work. Gone to my father with my tail between my legs, begged my uncle for another chance, assured my brother that I was fine and of course I was eating—if eating cereal straight from the box could be considered a meal. Essentially, I shut myself down. It was like my heart didn't work anymore.

At least I finally had something in common with my

mortuary clients—I was as dead inside as they were. Suddenly, it was my perfect job.

"I'M GLAD YOU'RE BACK," Trevor said as I helped him dress a corpse before we placed them in their silk-lined coffin. It was a woman who'd died of old age. She didn't have a lot of family, so they weren't doing a viewing. She was being buried in her favourite pair of pyjamas, a framed photo of her and her late husband in her hands. It was taken on their wedding day, and the way they looked at each other melted my heart. They seemed so happy. I hoped their marriage had been a happy one too.

"Hmm," I said, slipping the frame beneath her hands.

"It hasn't been the same without you. No laughter."

I straightened the cuffs of her sleeve and stepped away, surveying our work before I helped Trevor close and seal the lid.

"I thought Jenny was doing my job while I was gone?"

"She was. But it's hard working with your spouse all day and then going home to kids."

"Do you think that's why Mum and Dad couldn't make it?"

"Mum and Dad couldn't make it because she was an addict," he corrected.

"They fought a lot."

He shrugged. "At least they cared enough to fight. Being kind all the time isn't the ideal either."

"Are you and Jenny having problems?" I asked, reading between the lines.

"Don't all couples have their problems? Jenny and I aren't perfect. We fight. And sometimes we feel like giving up."

"But you don't." I sprayed sanitiser all over the work area.

"No. Because at the end of the day, we love each other."

I put far more effort into wiping down the stainless-steel surface than was necessary, trying to keep my thoughts even. "I guess that's the difference between your marriage and mine. You love each other. Sam doesn't love me."

Finishing up, I turned to walk away and put an end to the conversation. Trevor had been trying to get me to tell him what happened between Sam and me for weeks. I didn't think he could believe my marriage wasn't salvageable.

"Did he tell you that?"

"He wouldn't say he did. That's pretty much the same, right?"

"I don't know. Some people struggle with the words even though they have the feeling."

I shook my head. "He doesn't have the feeling, Trevor. He never did."

"Then why did he marry you?"

I met his eyes. "Because he had to." Then I turned around and walked away. That was all I had to say.

"I'm heading home. I'm done for the day," I said at my father's office door.

He remained focused on the paperwork on his desk. "Is Mrs Barnett ready for tomorrow?"

I nodded. "So is Mr Henry. The morning services are all ready to go."

"I'll need you to help Jenny pick up flowers in the morning."

"Sure. We can use my van."

"That's fine." He waved me away but I didn't move, just stood there until he finally looked at me. "Do you need something?"

I twisted my fingers around each other, struggling not to slip back into the obsequious daughter I was before. Part of walking away from the Cartwrights was fuelled by my desire to learn exactly who I was and how I fit into this world. And to do that, I needed to revisit my past and understand why everything went so wrong. One thing I'd learned from the Cartwrights was to be bold, to unapologetically go after what you wanted.

"What happened to Mum?"

He froze completely, perhaps even stopped breathing. Then he looked me in the eye. "She left," he said, a hint of defensiveness in his tone.

"And then what happened?"

He looked down. "We never saw her again."

"I don't believe that."

He picked up his pen again. "Well, that's what happened."

I took a step forward, that clawing feeling taking over

my chest again. "You're lying," I said in a harsh whisper. "I don't believe that. I don't believe you never looked for her. I don't believe you don't know where she is or what happened to her. Maybe you've been keeping that information from us to protect us, but we're not kids anymore. We deserve to know what happened to our mother."

Suddenly Trevor appeared beside me. "Is she right, Dad? Do you know?"

Dad took a deep breath, then placed his pen back on the desk before clasping his hands. He let out a heavy sigh. "We tried to save her," he said. "Did everything we could, spent everything we could in the hope she would recover. But she was sick, and not just from the drugs. She was just never right in her mind. Chronic depression. We couldn't save her." He pressed his fingers to his eyes.

"What does that mean?" Trevor asked.

"You were both so young," he said, lost in what I was sure was grief.

"What does that *mean*?" Trevor demanded, his eyes wide.

I swallowed the lump that had formed in my throat. "It means she's dead, Trev. It means she overdosed."

"Fuck." I'd never heard my brother swear before. He placed his hands against his forehead and released a sob. "Fuck."

Dad met my eyes, his shining with emotion. "Now you know."

Trevor shook his head, his voice quivering as he spoke. "You should've told us. We had a right to know." He stormed out of the office, and I heard the back door slam.

I closed my eyes to the sound. "He's right, you know. You should've told us."

"You were already so heartbroken. I thought it best...."

"You were wrong," I said, turning to head out the door.

"I'm sorry," he said to my retreating back. I turned around, the apology seeming almost as strange as Trevor swearing.

"What?"

"You're right. I'm sorry."

"Where is she?" Even as I said it, I think I already knew the answer. "And what happened? I need to know everything you know."

He gave me a tiny nod. Then he began.

GROWING UP, you could frequently find my father working in the garden of our home, specifically the roses that grew underneath our kitchen window. I had a memory of my mother planting them when they were but tiny shrubs in pots. That's where he'd spread her ashes. Turned out, he was out there talking to her. Why? Because despite everything, he loved her.

Sitting on the wooden bench that had been there for as long as I could remember, I stared at those bushes, my eyes brimming with tears. My mother was dead.

I'd always assumed, but to have it confirmed was so much bigger. Dad had told me that she'd left to spare her children the anguish when things got too bad. She checked herself into rehab and then a private mental hospital. There were times when they thought she may be getting better, but then she'd take a turn for the worse and they'd be back at square one with her self-harming to try and end whatever demons she carried in her mind. In the end, she saved up her medication, hid it inside her toothpaste tube. Then she took it all and never woke up.

That was when I was fifteen. Dad had known where she was for five years before she took her own life. And he didn't tell us, didn't take us to see her, or tell us she was OK. He just let us think she'd abandoned us. *How fucked up is that?*

She'd been dead for seventeen years. Seventeen years and I didn't know. I couldn't even pinpoint a memory from that year where I could say then, that must have been when it happened. Because I didn't feel it, I didn't notice any change. You'd think the universe would shift just a little when someone as important as a mother died. But it didn't move at all.

Wiping my eyes on the back of my hand. I took a deep breath of the fragrant air and looked around the backyard of my childhood. It was mostly the same, save for a few trees that had grown taller. The palings on the fence were still broken, left over from a time when Holland and I had tried to make a secret passage between our yards. We failed, and I got grounded for breaking the fence.

Holland.

I was missing her more lately, I wondered how she was coping without Nate, if she felt as empty without him as I did without Sam. I wanted to call her, but at the same time I didn't. I still needed time on my own, time to work out exactly what I wanted and why I wanted it. Reconnecting with Holland didn't feel as though it would help, seemed more like reaching for an old habit. 'Holland's best friend' didn't feel like part of my identity anymore.

Sam's wife. Now that was something I would be happy to call myself. I missed him most of all, and wondered if there'd ever come a time when my heart didn't ache so bad without him, or a day where I didn't consider calling him or texting to say I was wrong, that I didn't need him to love me.

But I did.

A tiny mewing sound caught my attention just as a tiny tabby cat slid through the fence. It was cute and still a kitten. "Hey, little fella," I said, making kissing sounds and rubbing my fingers together. "Are you lost?"

Without hesitation, it bounced over to me, jumping at my moving fingers and swatting them with its tiny paws. It gave me a chance to check the silver tag that hung around its neck on a pink collar. "Blanche Dubois," I read out loud, smiling at the formal name. When I flipped it, I saw the address for next door. Holland's aunty had obviously gotten herself a cat.

"Let me guess, you have a sister named Stella?" I scratched it behind the ear for a moment. Then it sat up, alert, and scampered back through the fence where it had come from. "See ya."

"Tea?" My father pushed through the back door, holding two mustard-coloured mugs with the strings of the teabags hanging out. I didn't realise he'd gotten home. I must've been sitting out here for quite some time.

Giving him a smile, I reached out and took a mug, pressing the warm ceramic against my cold hands. "Thanks, Dad," I said, taking a sip while he took a seat beside me.

"I've had a lot of deep conversations out here," he said. "Whenever I didn't know what to do or which way to turn, I'd come and talk to your mother." He gestured towards the rose bushes.

"I always thought you were one of those crazy gardeners who talked to their plants to help them grow."

He pressed his lips together as he swirled the teabag through the milky water in his mug. "Your friend is living next door again. Did you know that?"

I looked over to the house, spotting two kittens in the window on the second floor. I smiled inwardly because I was probably right. Two cats, Blanche and Stella, named after the characters in Holland's favourite play. "I didn't know that."

"You two have a falling out?"

I shook my head. "I think we just finally grew apart. It happens sometimes."

"I suppose it does. Family seems to be the only thing that lasts." He had no idea how much those words hurt me. I felt like I'd lost an insurmountable number of people I'd attributed that word 'family' to. But then it was different when someone was blood related. The link of blood was the very reason I was sitting in my old backyard, having an awkward conversation with my father. He was my blood and I couldn't change that. I could only grow to accept and understand because I didn't want to lose anymore. So much was already gone.

"Did you really think I was going to be like her?" I asked, pointing to the roses so he didn't think I was still talking about Holland. Growing up, I always thought he was worried about me becoming an addict, but after learning more about my mother, I now realised he was worried for my mental health.

"I was worried about both you and Trevor. But more so you. You were so withdrawn at times, and other times you had this wildness behind your eyes that reminded me of your mother's free spirit. I was afraid of losing you to the same sickness."

"That was called being a teenage girl," I said, sipping my tea.

"Perhaps. I just knew I needed to keep you close. Maybe too close sometimes."

"Do you realise that you lost me anyway? All those rules, all that pressure to behave a certain way. I felt like I couldn't be myself around you, and I hid who I was because of it."

"I wasn't trying to stifle you, only guide you. Medicine never helped your mother. I turned to God for help with you."

Playing with the string of the teabag, I looked into the liquid warming my hands. "Do you feel like He helped?"

"You're strong and healthy," he said, as if that explained everything and excused even more. But I understood the sentiment. In his mind, his prayers and his rules helped guide me into the woman I was now. In a way they did, but more than anything, I think my upbringing was responsible for everything that was messed up about me. I wondered what he'd say if I told him that it was the bohemian thinking of a family full of nonconformists who helped me become as strong and mentally healthy as I felt today. *I miss them so much.*

Instead of telling him, I simply leaned in and nudged him gently with my shoulder. "Yeah, Dad. I'm OK," I said, giving him a more genuine smile than I had before. Then we sat together in the quiet, listening to the birds and drinking our tea. I didn't think we'd ever have a great relationship, but I understood him a little better now. At least there was that.

CHAPTER TWENTY-SIX
STARVATION

BY THE TIME December rolled around, I'd progressed somewhat, primarily to eating cereal from a bowl with milk added as opposed to straight from the box. It still wasn't the best diet, but it was easy when cooking just made me think about the Cartwrights and all the meals I was missing out on being apart from them.

My own family had shared a meal or two of late, with Trevor and Jenny inviting me and Dad around for Sunday dinner. We were trying to make it a thing, though I wasn't sure how long it was going to last. It wasn't exactly the most rollicking meals I'd ever been party to.

With my feet up on the couch, I spooned Special K Berry into my mouth, flicking through the latest full catalogue of Bobbi Brown make-up. After finding out about Mum, I spent a few days reflecting on my own state of mind and realised that while working in the funeral home paid well, it was never what I wanted to do with my life. So I dialled my hours back to part-time, sharing the load with Jenny while also teaching her a few more techniques.

On the days when I wasn't working with my family, I was at the make-up counter at David Jones, fulfilling my adolescent dreams one customer at a time. I loved it there, and every shift I worked gave me a little extra bounce in my step. I was finally doing something that was just for me. And when I thought about who I was, I could take a deep breath and feel OK.

I was OK.

Just as I slurped the last of my cereal off the spoon, there was a knock on my door. I'd thrown myself pretty heavily into online shopping of late and I was expecting a package from Tarte to arrive any day now.

Getting excited by the prospect of new make-up to test, I set my bowl on the coffee table, uncurled my body and padded to the door, my heart stopping for a moment when I saw a familiar large shape.

"Oh my God."

I touched my hand to my hair, checking it wasn't doing anything out of this world. Then I held my hand in front of my mouth, breathing into it and then sniffing my breath. It smelled like special K and berries. Not my preferred mouthwash scent, but at least it wasn't horrible.

The knock sounded again. *Oh God. I should change.* I was wearing a pair of leggings and an oversized shirt that I was pretty sure I'd just dripped milk on.

Another knock.

What the hell is he doing here?

"OK. You can do this," I whispered to myself, placing one hand on the handle while the other flicked the dead-bolt. My heart rattled my ribcage and my breath shook as I steadied myself, then pulled the door open.

"Peaches." Sam held up a literal bucket full of them.

They were better than flowers, and reminded me of his silly poem. Oh, he was a sight for my love-sore eyes. His hair was a little longer and his skin sucked against his jaw a little tighter, but it was still him, still beautiful, still huge. He filled my entire doorway looking like perfection in a leather jacket. I glanced over his shoulder and saw a motorbike next to my van. He hadn't had that before.

Reaching out, I took the bucket from his hands and met his eyes. They looked tired. Tired and empty. The light, that sparkle he always had, wasn't there. *Could he possibly be hurting as much as me? Does this mean...?*

I didn't even want to think it.

"Thank you," I whispered, stepping aside so he could come in. He ducked his head and stepped past me, not moving much farther before he stopped and ran his fingers through his hair. I closed the door and leaned against it, waiting as mixed emotions ran across his features. My fingers itched to touch him, my arms longed to wrap about him, my mouth wished to taste him and my whole body cried from wanting to be held by him.

I love him.

Not a moment went by when that feeling had been any less intense than it was when we were together. So I waited. The seconds ticked by. I let out my breath, then held it again.

He cleared his throat. "I, um... I fucked up."

I didn't know what to say or how to respond. I didn't even know if he was talking about us or if something new was happening. So I waited, and I continued to hold my breath.

Frowning, he lifted his head and looked out the window. Then he sucked in some air and dropped his eyes to his hands. "I never should've said yes in the first place. I should've made them let you go, stood up for you. I should've done things with you the right way—dated you, learned everything about you, met your family, proposed. But we rushed into things with this crazy plan of Nate's and now... now he's—" His voice cracked and his face scrunched up. It took a couple of breaths before he could go on. "he's dead."

"Oh God," I gasped, dropping the bucket of peaches and closing the distance between us in an instant. I wrapped my arms around his neck and he buried his face in mine, his arms encircling my torso so tight I almost couldn't breathe. His body shook against me, breaking down to the point where I almost had to stop him from falling.

"Please don't tell me to go," he begged.

I ran my fingers through his hair and kissed the side of his face. "I won't."

Catching my face in his hands, he kissed me roughly, his movements filled with emotion and grief as he walked me to the couch and started pulling at my clothes.

"Wait," I gasped. "I'm not sure we should do this." I didn't want him to fall into me like an old habit.

He stopped and looked into my eyes, holding either side of my face, his hands shaking. "When I found out about Nate, the first thought I had was of you. The only person I needed to be with was you. I love you, Alesha. This is a shitty time to tell you, but my life isn't worth a dime without you in it."

He said them. The words I'd been wanting to hear. Why wasn't I jumping into his arms? Why wasn't I swooning at the sound? Had I given up on us? Was it too late now?

No. I loved him. I loved him so much that I was scared to believe this was true. We had obstacles to overcome, and just because he was grieving didn't mean those obstacles were magically gone.

He moved to kiss me again and I placed my hand over his mouth, blocking his access. His eyes seemed shocked, but there was one thing I needed to know. Something important before I allowed myself to get caught up in everything that was Sam. "What about the rest of your family? What are they going to do when they find out you came here?"

"I don't give a fuck about what they think. Didn't you hear me? This is about me and you. I need you. I love you. Please, peaches. Don't turn me away again. These last few months have been shit, and I don't think any of it's worth it if you aren't there to share it with me. Ask for anything and it's yours if you'll just come back to me. I'm not even living anymore, I'm just missing you."

That was it. My heart was full. "I love you," I whispered. "I just want you."

"I love you."

With hungry mouths and hungry hands, he took me right there on the couch, barely breathing from his need to kiss me, to taste me, to be inside me. My entire being rejoiced at his return, but my heart wept at the reason behind it. I hated that it took something tragic to make him see what he was missing.

"I've missed you so much," he gasped, pushing inside me, his fingers digging into my hips. "You feel so amazing."

I dared not speak, afraid to break the spell as we moved together, reclaiming our bodies, the connection even more powerful than it had been before. I cried out of joy, I cried out of relief, I cried because his brother had died and the only comfort he'd wanted was me.

"I love you," I whispered as my body shuddered and his did too. He groaned against my neck, a muffled cry filled with sorrow and release. When I touched his cheek, I found it damp. My heart had never been so full and so broken at the same time. This man, this beautiful and powerful man, was trusting me to see him break. I knew he'd see this as a moment of weakness, but to me it showed nothing but strength and honesty.

"I love you so fucking much," he murmured, holding me even tighter until his breathing slowed and then evened out.

I couldn't help but smile as I ran my fingers through his hair. He'd literally fallen asleep while still inside me. I didn't know guys could do that.

Letting myself sink into his warmth, I kissed him gently and then closed my eyes as well, knowing it wouldn't be long before I joined him. I hadn't slept a single night in peace without him.

Just as I drifted off, my phone rang, startling me awake.

"Oh God," I gasped, looking at the time. "I'm supposed to be at work."

"Ignore it," he murmured, shifting a little to get more comfortable before realising we were still connected. He moved his hips. "Yeah, you really need to ignore it." He was still semi-hard from before, but I felt him stiffen with each thrust.

"Oh God," I moaned, gripping his biceps as he picked up speed. The first time had been filled with emotion; this time was pure need.

Thankfully, my phone stopped.

"Fuck," he hissed, sitting back and gripping my hips. "So tight. I missed... fuck."

My phone started ringing again.

"I have to answer," I gasped. "They'll—oh!" His thumb pressed against my clit and started making circular motions.

"They'll what?"

"They'll just come looking for me."

He paused his movement and grabbed my phone from the coffee table, hitting Accept before handing it to me.

"Hello," I said, out of breath.

"Are you all right, dear? You sound puffed." It was my aunt Miranda, who generally dealt with all things employee related.

"I'm just not feeling well. I meant to call but I've been, uh." Sam thrusted unexpectedly. "I was, uh." Another thrust.

"Are you going to throw up, dear?" Miranda asked.

Sam rolled his hips, his thumb doing magical things to my clit. "Uh-huh," I gasped, almost whined. Then before I could say any more, Sam grabbed my phone and ended the call, flicking it to the side before he brought his mouth to mine.

"I need you today. I need you all day, every day."

Placing my hands on either side of his head, I ran my fingernails through his thick hair. "Why do you need me?" I whispered.

"Because I love you."

I nodded, almost crying. "I'm right here. I was always right here. You just had to want me enough to come get me." And thank God he did. I'd missed him beyond words.

"Peaches," he murmured, wiping a tear that slid from my eye.

"I'm OK," I assured him. "I'm just glad you came back."

Then his lips returned to mine, and barely left until it felt like starvation was setting in.

"WHAT HAPPENED?" I asked as we sat in my kitchen, eating from my cereal selection.

"Fire. Tore right through his property. They suspect arson."

"You think it was those dealers he was involved with?"

He shrugged and swirled his spoon in his bowl. "He's been AWOL since you and Holland left. I know he wanted out of the life because Holland was against it. Maybe he tried and they retaliated?"

"Does Holland know?"

"I'd assume so. The cops would've told her like they told us. She's his wife."

"Oh God. How horrible. How'd Jasmine take it?"

"She lost it. Toby crushed her sleeping pills into a vodka tonic just so she'd rest."

"Everyone else?"

"Devastated. We're all fucking devastated. This wasn't supposed to happen. He was supposed to get old with the rest of us and continue to be the bossy pain in the arse he's always been."

"I had to make up a six-year-old boy who lost his fight with leukaemia the other day. It felt so wrong to be preparing someone so small. The only thing that working with the dead has taught me is that life is fragile. It can be over in the blink of an eye, so we have to live our best one. We owe it to all the people who didn't make it this far."

He nodded slowly, his brow creased in thought. "It just doesn't feel real, you know?"

I placed my hand on his thigh and my head on his shoulder.

"I know. I'm so sorry you lost your brother, Sam," I said, shocked he was gone. I didn't have a huge amount of contact with Nate, and he wasn't really my favourite person, but that didn't mean I didn't feel his loss. I hurt for the absence of a heart beating in this world. For the loss of a brother, a son, my friend's husband. "It's OK to say sorry in this instance, isn't it?"

He kissed the top of my head. "Yeah. It's OK."

"When's the funeral?"

"I don't know. We only found out early this morning. I kind of flipped out and came to you as soon as I could get away."

"Do you think we should go back? Make sure they're all OK?"

He moved slightly so he could see my expression. "We?"

I nodded. "You're all grieving. I want to help. If you think they'll let me."

"They'll let you. They've missed you. You're still a part of the family."

"Then why did you send all my things addressed to my maiden name?"

"Because you had to sign for them, and we never officially changed your name on your ID."

Tears hit the back of my eyes. "What? I thought it was because you never wanted to see me again."

His eyes went wide. "No," he breathed. "We were just giving you space and the time to choose to come back on your own."

"You thought I'd come back without hearing those three massive words?"

He gave me a mournful half smile. "I kind of hoped you would. But I'm glad you didn't. We needed this time to realise that what we had was the real deal. The kind of love that makes you physically sick without the other person."

I nodded. "You got skinny."

He chucked me under the chin. "So did you. But my God, you're beautiful whatever way you come."

Taking a deep breath, I tried not to cry again. I had him back. "Let's go home."

Packing an overnight bag with a few things, Sam and I headed out to the van and adjusted the seat configuration so his bike could fit in. Then I handed him the keys and he hugged me tight against his chest. "I can't believe it took my brother dying to make me say I love you."

"I can't believe you didn't fall in love with me instantly," I said with a sad smile.

"Is that when you fell for me?"

"Honestly?"

"Yes. No more games."

"Yes. The moment you smiled at me, I was smitten."

If it was possible, he managed to hug me tighter. "God, I love you. How did I get so lucky to find you?"

"I suppose we should thank Holland. She's the reason I was there."

"And Nate," he whispered, his voice growing hoarse.

"And Nate." Pulling back a little, I took the keys from his hand. "I think I'll drive. You rest."

Before going back to Torquay, I took a slight detour past my father's house. Since I was only just starting on speaking terms with him again, I didn't want to ruin that by disappearing without explanation again.

"You're talking to your dad again?" Sam asked, and I nodded.

"It took a couple of months, but he ended up telling us what happened to my mother, and that opened the lines of communication."

"Your mother? What happened to her?"

"She overdosed. But I found out that she left because she was mentally ill. The drugs were kind of a side effect. It doesn't really fix things, but it provides some context."

"I'm sorry," he said, brushing his fingers against the back of my neck.

I shrugged. "At least I have closure now."

The moment I unclipped my seat belt, my eyes flicked towards Holland's aunt Maya's place. The lights were on inside, and Holland's car was in the driveway. While I'd skipped going over there the last time I was here, this time it wasn't about me. She'd lost the man she loved; my feelings could be pushed aside.

"I just want to go next door first and check on Holland. Want to come inside, or do you need a moment to yourself?"

"I'll wait in the van. I'm not capable of playing nice right now."

"I understand." I leaned over and gave him a parting kiss. He held on for a little longer, then let out his breath. "I love you so much, peaches."

"I love you too."

Despite our circumstances, it felt so good to be finally saying it.

———

WALKING UP THE FOOTPATH, I took a deep breath and knocked on Maya's door. She answered it dressed in a terry robe with her hair and make-up done from the office. She was in her late fifties now, with hair more grey than blonde. She had sharp honey-coloured eyes like Holland, and the wit to match. She smiled when she saw me. "Alesha. It's been so long."

"It has," I agreed. "I heard about Nate. Is Holland OK?"

Her expression flickered with confusion before resetting itself into the picture of concern. "Oh, it's terrible what happened. She's devastated, gone away for a while to recover from the shock of it. I'm not sure when she'll be back."

"Gone away? Where?"

"Oh, a spa or something."

"A spa? But her car is here."

"In Queensland," she added. "Shall I let her know you called in?"

"It's OK. I can call her. Thank you, Maya."

After saying our goodbyes, I walked away with a

strange feeling. Why would Holland leave for a spa on the day her husband died? She loved him, and knowing her as I did, she would've been beside herself. It didn't make sense.

Heading next door to my dad's, I blew Sam a quick kiss, then ran up the path and knocked on the door. Dad answered like he was standing there waiting—I actually wouldn't put that past him.

"I thought you were sick," he said as he pushed his glasses up the bridge of his nose. My father was in his sixties but he dressed like he lived through the Great Depression, wearing beige trousers, a white button-up shirt and a beige cardigan. There were actually a couple of women at the church who'd been after him for years, so despite his terrible fashion sense, it seemed my father was quite the catch.

"Just a twelve-hour bug, it seems," I lied, leaning against the doorway. When he stepped back to let me inside, I declined.

"Does this visit have something to do with that husband of yours who's skulking in your van?"

"He isn't skulking, Dad. His brother died. He's upset."

His expression shifted. Having worked in a funeral home for years, he understood more than most what it meant to lose someone. "Is that why he was here this morning?"

My eyebrows jumped together, confused. "He was here?"

"Well, not here. Next door. He turned up in an old station wagon and left with that friend of yours."

"Holland? Are you sure?"

"As sure as the stars in the sky. She left in her pyjamas right after a police car was there."

"She was married to Sam's brother."

"I see. He's the one who passed?"

I nodded. "I'm going to go back to Torquay for a few days, help with funeral preparations and take care of things around the house. Can you manage without me?"

He nodded. "Jenny's not as good as you, but she's got a good eye for detail."

"Tell her I'm thankful for her."

"I will. And give Sam's family my condolences. I wouldn't wish that kind of loss on anyone. If there's anything we can do, help with the funeral or advice on the best prices for flower arrangements, give us a call."

"Thank you, Dad. That means a lot." I moved to leave but he called me back.

"When Sam is feeling up to it, bring him for dinner. If you two have patched things up, I'd like to get to know him."

"You would?"

He nodded. "I'm not against interfaith marriage. I was against losing my daughter. And well, like you said, my rules made me lose you anyway. I feel that in these past weeks I've gotten you back somewhat. I don't want to drive you away again."

I flung my arms around his neck, hugging tight and probably shocking the hell out of him. "Thank you, Dad," I whispered.

He hugged me back. "You grew up good, baby girl."

I smiled, not about to set him straight on that one.

When I got back into the van, I made a quick call to my supervisor at David Jones and let them know I needed time off for a family emergency. She was wonderfully understanding, which meant that I was able to completely focus on the man I loved. I clicked my seat belt and casually asked Sam if he went to see Holland that morning.

He shook his head and frowned. "I came straight to you, why?"

"No reason," I said. "My dad thought he saw you. He must've been mistaken."

"Maybe it was Toby?"

"Do you think he'd try to swoop in like that?"

Sam shrugged. "I don't think he'd swoop in. But he loves her too, so he'd want to make sure she was OK."

I started the engine. "You're probably right."

RETURNING to Torquay in the wake of Nate's death, I wasn't sure how warm or cool my reception would be. Sam said they'd missed me, yet I worried they'd be upset that I'd been gone for so long. Jasmine could yell at me to get out. Toby could refuse to speak to me at all. And the twins might feel betrayed; they'd been the most welcoming to me, and I'd left without even saying goodbye.

But the moment I walked through the front door and heard their voices in the back room, I felt at ease. They were sitting around drinking and telling stories about Nate, a sad warmth in all their tones.

Sam walked ahead of me, announcing, "I got our girl back."

Kris and Abbot rushed me, picking me up and hugging

me at the same time. "We've missed you, babe," Abbot said.

"The morning surf just hasn't been the same," Kris added, pinching me on the cheek.

I touched his head. "Your hair has grown."

"Time for a proper haircut," he said with a wink.

"I like it. And I've missed you guys too. I just…"

"You needed some time. We get it." When they released me, Toby had already walked over.

"Does this mean the team's back together?" He looked between me and Sam, and I nodded.

"Bonnie and Clyde ain't got nothing on us," I told him as he hugged me tight.

"I'm glad you're here. We've all missed you a hell of a lot."

When he released me, I was getting choked up. I'd expected some animosity, perhaps magnified by the freshness of their loss. But they were all just so relieved to see me, I ended up feeling guilty for leaving and convincing myself that they never really wanted me at all. There were times I really hated my brain.

"Alesha." I turned to the sound of Jasmine's voice. She was sitting on the couch with her legs folded beneath her and a gin and tonic balancing on her knee. Her eyes were glassy and red-rimmed, a mixture of sorrow and alcohol. She held out her free hand. "Come and sit by me. I've missed having my daughter around."

That did it. I started crying and pretty much dashed towards her, hugging her like a little girl so desperate for a mother's love. "I'm so sorry, Jasmine," I whispered. "I'm sorry about Nate, sorry for leaving. I'm sorry for everything I wasn't thankful enough for."

She ran her hand down the length of my hair and pushed it behind my shoulder. "Don't be sorry. We all have our own journeys. And I knew you'd come back. I just had to wait until this knucklehead son of mine got his shit together and told you how loved you are." She looked up at Sam, who leaned down and kissed her on the side of her head.

"How you feeling, Ma?" That was the first time I'd ever heard him refer to her as anything other than Jasmine or Jazz.

She patted his hand. "I'm OK. Just sad. We've been sharing stories about your brother, remembering happy times."

"Let's see," he said, sitting on the other side of her, sliding his arm around her shoulders and placing his hand on mine, effectively hugging us both at the same time. "Remember that fishing trip we took when I was about eight? You were trying to do manly things with us to make up for the fact that Dad wasn't around anymore. We were all squabbling in the small space, and Nate kept eating food off my plate whenever I wasn't looking. I got him back by filling his ears with Vegemite while he was sleeping." Sam smiled, shaking his head. "He was so pissed."

"I remember that," Toby said with a chuckle. "We tormented him by singing 'Happy Little Vegemite' for the rest of the trip."

"Remember that time he shot you in the eye with a water pistol full of wasabi and water?" Abbot asked, his question directed at Toby.

Toby laughed. "How could I forget? I had to have my school picture taken the next day, and I looked like a rabbit with myxomatosis."

We kept going like that well into the night. And as much as the loss of Nate was hurting the Cartwright family, pulling together to remember him was the thing that was going to heal them. I knew they'd make it through. I knew Nate would always be alive in their hearts, even though his loss hurt like hell.

It's a shame Holland couldn't be here to hear this. It would've helped her feel a little less sorrowful too.

NATE'S FUNERAL was held almost two weeks later, when the coroner released the body after ruling out any foul play. It was thought that Nate was driving away from the fire when it engulfed his car. He was unrecognisable.

The service was far larger than I expected. It felt like everyone in Torquay knew and loved the Cartwrights and mourned along with them. Even my father was in attendance. Holland, however, was not. I didn't know if it was because she thought she wouldn't be welcome, but I thought she should have been there. He was her husband. She loved him. That was all that should have mattered.

After the funeral, I tried calling her while we were gathered in a function room at the local surf club. The call went straight to voicemail, so I left a message and tried to focus on those in attendance. Despite the sombre mood, it was much like any other gathering. Drinks flowed, speeches were given and stories were shared. Nate was loved and received the perfect send-off. I wished I knew him better, as I thought I probably judged him too harshly due to our circumstances. Now it was too late to make amends.

"I think Jazz needs some quiet," Sam noted, watching her force yet another smile while someone else offered their condolences. She'd been so strong the entire time, refusing to be the spectacle, but now her edges were looking frayed.

"Let me take her home," I said. "You stay with your brothers and wrap things up here."

Nodding, Sam kissed the side of my head. "Drive safe," he said. "I'll follow as soon as I can."

Jasmine blew out a charged breath the moment we got into the car. "I need to go home. I need to drink myself into oblivion and wake up when this is all over."

I pressed my lips together in an understanding smile. I didn't need to point out that the grieving process was never really over. Loss just got easier to live with.

Pulling into the circular drive of the Cartwright home, I killed the engine and frowned when I could still hear it running. I looked in the rear vision and noticed a black SUV pulling in behind me.

"Someone's here," I said.

Jasmine turned around and set her jaw, her eyes hardening. "Stay here," she commanded.

I did as I was told, cracking the window and keeping an eye on her at the same time. Two men got out of the SUV. They appeared normal enough, but by the look on their faces and the set of their shoulders, I didn't think they were there to offer their condolences. This was business.

"I just buried my son," Jasmine said, placing her hands on her hips. I thought that was a good move, because I'd read that folding your arms meant you were intimidated and keeping them open like that showed you wouldn't be messed with. "This couldn't wait for another day?"

The smaller of the two, a man with one of those undercut hairstyles that were popular these days, was the one to speak. I assumed the bigger guy with the bald head was there as the muscle.

"And I'm very sorry for your loss. But business doesn't stop just because you're sad. Your son was a big part of our business. That fire took out our best crop. That's going to seriously affect our profits. Now we need something, I don't know—life insurance, the proceeds from his estate—to help us cover *our loss*."

Oh. I knew who they were. These were the guys Nate was in bed with. The drug dealers.

"I don't have any control over that. He was married, so everything legally goes to his wife."

"Is that her?" The drug lord nodded towards the van, and the muscle came straight for me. I didn't really know what went through my head in that moment, but I unclipped my seat belt and jumped out of the car before he could reach me. Like I wanted to be ready or something.

"No. His wife wasn't at the funeral. I don't know where she is."

The muscle grabbed me by the arm anyway and jostled me over to his boss.

"That's a pretty ring you're wearing there, sweetheart. Who gave it to you?"

"Your dad when I was sitting on his face," I responded. "I'm your stepmum now." The words shocked me more than anyone else. It seemed when confronted with a situation where I felt in danger, I got really mouthy. The drug dudes found my response mildly amusing, but not amusing enough to let my arm go.

The drug lord smiled. "Well, the next time you're in that position, do me a favour and suffocate the bastard. He always was a cunt of man."

"Sure. I didn't like him much anyway," I said, and the guy laughed.

"I like you," he said, waggling his finger at me. "You've got fire in you." He leaned in so close I could smell his breath. Ew. "But not enough to distract me from my task. Your husband owes us money for the fire that ruined our crop. Since he's left this earth, it's going to be on you to get that money to us."

"I've already told you, she's not his wife," Jasmine insisted. "She can't give you anything."

Drug man smiled. "I don't give a fuck whose wife she is. You're the family matriarch. You work out how to get my money. In the meantime, Bruno." He clicked his fingers, and Bruno tightened his grip and started dragging me towards the SUV.

"What the hell are you doing!" Jasmine demanded, leaping to my defence before the drug dude put his arm out and stopped her.

"Just taking a little collateral. I'll return her to you unharmed when I get my money."

"How much do you want?" Jasmine asked in a hurry.

"Considering how much revenue we'll be losing, I think it's only fair to ask for... all of it."

Jasmine gasped. I had no idea how much 'all of it' was, but judging by Jasmine's reaction, it was a lot. I really didn't want to be collateral while they worked that one out.

"Is your name actually Bruno?" I asked the muscle as we neared the SUV.

"Yes," he said, his accent heavy. Greek, I thought.

"I guess your career options were pretty limited, then."

"Why?" He totally didn't understand that his name was a clichéd hired muscle name.

"Never mind," I said, twisting my body around with enough force that when my open palm hit against the base of Bruno's big nose, I both felt and heard the bone snap. Blood started spurting everywhere and he stumbled back. But the motherfucker didn't let go. He just opened his eyes wider, growled from the pain, then placed his big hand on the side of my head.

"Shit," I said, knowing in the microsecond before it happened that I was going to have an almighty headache.

My head collided with the side of the SUV, pain slicing through my brain and blackening my vision. He tossed me in the back seat, causing more rattling in my head. I gasped as I tried to right myself, touching my head to check for blood as I blinked to clear my vision. "Ow."

As I sat, intent on trying to scramble out the open door while Bruno attempted to stem the flow from his nose, I heard a growl followed by a grunt. Bruno's body arched backwards as a thick arm wrapped around his neck and yanked.

Bruno may have been the drug dude's muscle, but Sam was mine and he was bigger. Angels sang an exultant chorus, a big brass band blew trumpets and beat drums, the crowds cheered, all rejoicing in my rescue—although that noise could have also been the concussion, I was pretty sure I was developing.

I jumped out of the SUV just as Bruno slid into a heap on the ground, passed out but definitely still breathing.

"Samuel!" Jasmine's scream came at the same time we heard the click.

"He'd better not be dead," the drug dick said, crouching to check Bruno's pulse while keeping his gun trained on Sam and me.

"He's not," Sam said, shifting me until I was slightly behind him. "Just sleeping."

"You're out of your depth here, son. All I want is compensation. I won't be going away until I get it."

"You *won't* be getting it," Jasmine said, her lips curling as she came up behind him. The moment he turned to address her, she raised her hand and plunged what looked like a pocketknife into the side of his neck.

If I'd thought Bruno's broken nose had sprayed a lot of blood, a knife to the carotid artery produced a waterfall. I'd seen the amount of blood that came out of a human body before, but never like this. I'd never watched a man bleed out before.

"Holy hell," I gasped.

As he gripped his neck, Sam grabbed his gun and uncocked the hammer, shoving it in the back of his pants as he tried to use his body to shield me from the sight. Jasmine just stood there with the bloodied knife in her hand, staring at the douche as he tried in vain to stem the flow.

"I know it was you," she ground through clenched teeth. "I know it was you who set that fire and killed my boy." The drug man shook his head wildly, gurgling and choking on his own blood as he dropped to his knees. "How dare you come here demanding money and making threats. You think I wasn't expecting you? You think I wasn't ready? I didn't become who I am by lying down and getting fucked over by miserable cunts like you. I know who you are, Simon Ferezis. I know where you live and who your friends are. And most of all, I know everything there is to know about your business. You underestimated a grieving mother, and now you're the one losing everything."

He coughed on the ground, struggling to keep a hold of his life. It was taking way longer than in the movies. They took seconds while this was minutes. Not a lot of them, but still, minutes. Enough time for another car to pull into the driveway. Enough time for Toby and the twins to rush over and mutter things like "Holy shit" and "What did you do?"

When it was over, and the drug man I now knew as Simon had lost his fight, Jasmine looked over to Bruno and pointed to him with her bloody knife. "He needs to die too," she said.

"Fuck!" Toby yelled. "Fuck." Then he stormed over to Bruno, pushed him into a sitting position and kneeled behind him.

Oh no

Toby took three quick breaths, the fight evident in his face as he placed his hands on either side of Bruno's head. I literally witnessed a piece of Toby's soul crack, the sorrow and pain flitting across his face before he roared and twisted Bruno's neck so far it snapped. He was dead—I heard the crack, saw the way his face went slack.

Then I threw up on the ground.

"WHAT ARE we going to do with the bodies?" Kris asked as we sat around the table, each with a stiff drink in hand. The house was dark except for the light overhead, like we were in a secret meeting. In a way it was, the lighting fit the mood. It was one thing to steal, another entirely to take a life—well, two. Thankfully, the Cartwright property was secluded enough that no one could've seen what went down unless they were flying directly overhead, so witnesses weren't our problem. Hiding the evidence was.

"Someone's gonna know they came here," Abbot added. "Someone's gonna come lookin'."

"And we're going to say we never saw them," Jasmine concluded. "We'll dump the car into a gully, drop the bodies in the ocean for the sharks to get. No one will ever find out."

"Bodies have ways of turning back up," I whispered, my shaking hands clutching the glass of straight vodka in front of me. I took a sip, making a slurping noise because all of my finesse was locked away in the numb part of my brain. "They bloat, animals find them and drag them free, they get hooked on fishing wire, caught in a boat's propeller, eaten by a shark and discovered in its belly."

"Take them out far enough and deep enough, it'll never be a problem. No one ever found Harold Holt," Toby said.

"Yes, but there are so many theories surrounding his disappearance. There may be no body to find," I added.

Jasmine pressed her fingers against her eyes. "Then what do you suggest?"

"There's only one real way to completely dispose of a body."

"How's that?" Sam asked.

"Fire. And not just any fire. We need to cremate them."

"And how are we going to do that?" Kris asked.

"Yeah," Abbot added. "We can't just walk up to the funeral home and say, 'Chuck this in with our brother, will ya?' Get a three for one deal."

"You're forgetting something," Sam said, his eyes on me as his lips kicked up at the side. "Alesha's family owns a mortuary. She has keys."

"And alarm codes, and working knowledge of the chambers," I added.

"I say we do it," Toby said, downing his drink. "Kris and Abbot can deal with the car. Don't dump it, take it to the chop shop in Sunshine and sell it for parts. They'll take it no questions asked. Me and Sam will deal with the bodies. Jasmine and Alesha, stay here and bleach the driveway."

"I need to come with you," I said. "The cremator isn't just 'push a button and it's done'. There's a whole process we have to go through that takes a few hours. We have to leave the place looking like no one was ever there."

Jasmine looked at her watch. It was almost 9:00 p.m. "Then you best be on your way." On our way. Such a casual order to dispose of two bodies. It made me sick to think about what we had to do, but it *had* to be done. Had to.

How did my life get to this point?

Right, I married a thief. Fell in love with him *and* his family.

And I'd do whatever it took to keep them safe.

CHAPTER TWENTY-NINE
FUCKING SELFISH BASTARD

SAM DROVE. After loading the bodies into the back of my van, hidden in surfboard covers with boards on top, we were on our way. Every car that followed us, every car that sat beside us at a set of lights, it all felt like they were looking at us, that they knew we had murdered two men.

"I don't want to keep this van anymore," I said after a while.

Sam reached over and took my hand. "We'll get you a new one tomorrow."

"Why did she do it?" Toby asked from the back seat. "Why'd she kill him? What did he want?"

"He wanted money," I said. "He wanted any sort of insurance Nate had. Jasmine killed him because she believes they were behind the fire."

He pressed his lips together and shook his head. "I fucking knew something like this would happen."

"What do you mean?" I asked. "That they'd come looking for a payout, or that Jasmine would want revenge?"

He sighed so heavy that the weight of his thoughts filled the cabin. "All of it. The whole thing is fucked up."

When he looked out the window, working his jaw as he bounced his leg, I turned back around in my seat and watched the road through the front window. For some reason, I kept thinking about what my dad said about seeing someone who looked like Sam leaving with Holland. Was it Toby? Was he trying to hide her because he knew the men Nate was mixed up with would come looking? It made sense. What didn't make sense was that he hadn't done the same with his family. He'd left the rest of us in harm's way.

"Did you go see Holland to tell her about Nate?" I asked suddenly, never one to curb my need for an answer or to figure out a puzzle.

Toby frowned and shook his head. "I haven't seen her since I got Nate's car back for him."

Sam seemed surprised by the information. "When did you do that?"

"Couple weeks after she left. Nate asked me to do that and give her all her stuff back. I was just a messenger."

"I didn't think Nate was talking to any of us then," Sam said, glancing in the rear-view mirror. "Least of all you."

Toby shrugged. "I guess we found some common ground."

"Look out!" I shouted, slapping my arm against Sam's chest as a kangaroo bounded across the highway, right in our path. He swerved, and there was a sudden pop that made the van fishtail as he hit the brakes and steered us into the emergency lane.

We jerked to a stop. The kangaroo bounced off, seeming unharmed.

"Did we hit it?" Toby asked.

"I don't think so. That felt like a blowout." With a sigh, Sam got out of the van and walked around it. "Rear left," he said. "Gonna have to change it."

"Fuck," I said, knowing we didn't have time for this. The look on Sam's face told me he agreed.

With all of us piling out, I kept watch while Toby and Sam made quick work of the tire. I was grateful that we've gone to the effort to conceal the bodies in the first place, because without those surfboards covering them, retrieving the spare from the boot would have revealed our crime to any car passing by.

"You guys need a hand?" A man driving a courier van slowed beside us, his hazard lights on.

"We're fine," I said, my palms sweating as a prickling crept over my skin. "Just a flat. They've got it under control." I thumbed towards Toby and Sam, who was swearing and sucking on his thumb.

"Clearly," the guy said. "Why don't I give you a hand? It'll only take a few minutes."

I smiled, insisting, "It's really not necessary." But he was intent on being the Good Samaritan. *Great. Just what we need.*

"What the fuck is this guy doing?" Toby hissed as I walked towards the van.

"Helping," I told him, hooking my fingers on the open back door and pulling it down. The surfboards may have hidden the bodies from a distance, but close up it was obvious there was something more there.

"Fucking do-gooders," Toby grumbled before putting

on a false smile and giving the guy in question a friendly wave. "G'day, mate. We're actually all good here."

"It's cool. I'm an old hand at this. Spend half my life on the road." He kneeled next to Sam and asked if he could take over. Reluctantly, Sam handed over the tire iron. The guy flicked it around like he was a member of a pit crew and as promised, the whole thing took a couple of minutes.

Less time than it took that guy to die. I closed my eyes to push away the thought.

Once the jack was released, the guy—who was chatting away at a mile a minute about how hard it was to drive all night then go home to kids who were hyper and just wanted to play—collected the tools and headed towards the back of the van. Toby was quick to block his path and relieve him of his burden.

"I've got this. Thanks, mate. Appreciate it."

The guy smiled and nodded, wiping his hands on the back of his dark pants. "Yeah." He looked up at Toby, as if he was suddenly figuring out how tall he was. Then he did the same to Sam. "Wow. You boys are big, huh? Brothers?"

"We are." Sam nodded. "Thanks for your help," he said again, holding out his hand to shake the man's, trying desperately and calmly to get him to leave.

The man shook his hand, then thankfully wandered back to his own van and left. I didn't think I took a breath the whole time.

"My God, I thought he'd never leave," I said, placing my hands on my face as Toby opened the back of the van to put the tools in. I walked to the front, swearing I heard him muttering to himself, something like "I knew this was a stupid plan. No retaliation if they thought it was an accident, my arse. No one gets out scot-free."

When we got back into the car, I met Toby's eyes. He held mine for a second and then looked away, clearly pissed.

"Are you OK?" I asked.

He met my gaze, his eyes wild. "No, I'm not," he said simply. It broke my heart. He was such a gentle soul, and now he had all this on his conscience.

"Let's get out of here," Sam said. "We've already lost enough time."

"Go around back," I instructed, pointing to where it was normal for the funeral home to receive bodies. I got out of the van first and went inside, deactivating the alarm before heading downstairs to open the dock from the inside. I pushed one of the wider trolleys we used for our larger clients, figuring it'd be big enough to put both bodies on.

Sam had already reversed the van into place, making the unloading much easier. He and Toby heaved the surfboard bags and the bodies inside them on top, and I directed them through to the crematorium.

"What do we do if there are already bodies in there?" Sam asked.

"We never cremate bodies at night. It's a fire hazard, obviously. Someone has to be here to monitor the chambers."

The doors all swung open to allow easy access when pushing heavy trolleys, but I held them open anyway, stopping once we got to the cremator.

"So we just throw them both inside?" Toby asked.

"No," I said. "It'll take too long if they're in together. There are two cremators, so one can go in each."

I opened the hatches on both, and they got the trolley into position in front of the rollers. "Now we slide one of them inside," I said.

I stood to the side as Sam and Toby did just that. Bruno went first, although I couldn't be sure. It was just that the first bag seemed a bit more bulky than the other. Everything was moving along perfectly until the bags caught and the remaining one twisted just enough so it started to slide off the trolley. Purely by reflex, I reached out and tried to catch it. But I was a tall skinny woman, incapable of catching a fully grown man. We both went down.

"Holy shit," one of them said. Then there was a crash and the trolley shot across the room, hitting the wall on the other side with a crash. Bruno went down too, taking a swan dive off the rollers and joining me and Simon on the floor.

I couldn't get up.

"There… th-there's a-a b-body on me," I stammered, my arms and legs flailing as I tried to roll or slide from beneath him. His foot was in my face, and with rigor mortis setting in, I couldn't get it to move out of the way. "Get it off. Get it *off.*"

Within moments, Simon was removed from my chest and I could breathe again. Sam offered me his hand and a sympathetic smile. "You OK, peaches?"

I shook my head. "Not even a little."

He touched my cheek with a commiserating look in his eye. Then he and Toby made quick work of filling the chambers before I started the cremation process. There wasn't much left to do but wait.

I found some food in the break room's refrigerator and made us all a light meal even though I didn't think any of us were hungry. It was simply something to do. It sat in the centre of the table untouched.

"He needs to come back," Toby said all of a sudden, his eyes taking on this faraway quality.

"Who does?" I asked.

"Nate," he said, his lips drawn tight as he looked between Sam and me.

"Oh, Toby," I said, reaching over the table to touch his hand. "Nate's dead." *Poor guy. It must really be hitting him now.*

Toby's expression furrowed and he shook his head. "He's not."

"Excuse me?" Sam said, his eyes wide in disbelief. I couldn't believe what I was hearing either.

"What the hell are you saying?" I demanded, struggling to comprehend what he was telling us.

"Nate's alive." Toby said it with closed eyes. "The fire. The body. It was all a ruse. He wanted out because he knew Holland couldn't love him if he stayed in. So he faked it. I helped him."

I guess that answers the question about who my dad saw.

Sam's mouth twisted downwards. Then he stood and leapt across the table, punching Toby in the side of the head. Toby's seat tipped back and he landed on the floor, out cold, arms out wide like he'd decided to sleep like that on purpose.

"Holy shit!" I covered my mouth.

Sam straightened up and shook his fist, hissing from the pain. "Fucking ow. His face hurt my hand."

"I think your hand hurt his face." I looked down at poor Toby. It must've been incredibly hard for him to help his brother chase a happily ever after with a woman *he* was in love with. My heart went out to him. But I also understood Sam's position. We'd been crying for weeks. We'd attended his funeral, killed his enemies, and now we found out it was all a lie. Nate simply ran away.

Cartwrights don't run, even when they want to. Arsehole.

"I'll get you some ice," I said, grabbing a pack from the freezer to put on his knuckles. I was sad to say that this wasn't the first time it was required for the same reason. Sometimes death brought out the absolute worst in people, and we needed to be prepared for all situations.

"I can't fucking believe this," Sam said, pacing the room. "He's *alive*? I just went to his fucking funeral. We're killing people in his name. *Fuck,*" he yelled. "That fucking selfish bastard. Do you see what he's done? Do you see? Did you... did you see what we... what we *did*?"

Sam's hands went to his hair and he dropped into a seat. I sat right behind him and wrapped myself around him as best I could. "What do you want to do?" I asked, rubbing my hand up and down his back soothingly.

He shook his head. "I don't know. Find him. Drag him back. Make him clean his own goddamn mess."

"Good," I said, pressing a kiss to his temple. "I think that's exactly what we should do. The last I heard, running wasn't the Cartwright way. And we certainly don't make our loved ones pay for our mistakes."

ONCE TOBY CAME TO, he explained that Nate had wanted to win Holland back. She could handle the fact that he was a thief, but she couldn't forgive him for helping supply drugs.

"She mentioned the downward spiral of your mother and its effect on you as her reason, Leesh," he said, making me wonder if perhaps I'd been reading Holland all wrong these past months since we'd met the Cartwrights. I knew I had a tendency to do that. I'd assumed so much, and I had doubted Holland's intentions all along, hadn't I? I'd twisted them into actions fuelled by jealousy and unkindness when maybe that wasn't the case at all. To find out she left her marriage because she witnessed how awful it was for *me* to lose my mother to drugs… wow. Maybe *I* was the one who needed to get the log out of *my* eye. Perhaps her concern all these months was real and not the twisted bragging I'd taken it to be. She'd been my only friend for years, my shield to the outside world, and I'd loved her like a sister.

I thought she didn't have room for me in her life anymore. Showing compassion over something that had so deeply affected me told me she did. I felt like I'd been a horrible friend, and for the first time in months, I really wanted to make amends with her.

Toby continued telling us how Nate organised new identities for them both and bought them a house in a city called Portland. I'd heard of it before—it was the location of the state's oldest European settlement and had once been a busy fishing town. Now it was a quiet little seaside town, a perfect place for a woman like Holland to shine in.

"And what does he plan to do down there? Go straight? He hates earning an honest living," Sam said.

"He wants to open a bookshop. He and Holland are obsessed with reading."

"He is?" Sam asked, looking like that was the first he'd heard of it.

Toby nodded. "The man *loves* books. He'll read anything with a good story."

"Wow. I had no clue."

"I'm starting to get why Holland fell so hard for him," I said.

Sam gave me a fast look. "You wish I read more?"

I smiled and threaded my fingers into his hair. "No, you're fine. I just never understood what Holland saw in him. But I'm starting to. She loves to read, she's always dreamt of owning a book store, and she always wanted a man who would make her the centre of his universe. It looks like she got it."

It seemed I'd also judged Nate far too harshly too. When we saw them again, after we've sorted out our drug dealer problem, I promised myself I'd make more time for them. They were family, after all.

It WAS about three in the morning when we were finally done cremating the remains. We left with them in a snap-lock bag that we emptied inside a storm water drain, figuring that was the best place for men like Simon and Bruno.

Exhaustion didn't even come close to describing our state when we made it back to Torquay. We'd stayed awake by talking about everything and anything. Toby told us of his dream to own a fishing business that was in no way connected to the family 'business'. Sam admitted to feeling lost most days, wondering what the point of every-thing was because it seemed like there'd never be an end.

"I think that's part of the reason I was so keen to have a family in the beginning. I feel like this life won't end for me until I have kids to pass it all on to. I don't want to be sixty and climbing through windows to steal shit," he'd said.

It made sense. I wasn't sure how excited I was at the thought of having children for the purpose of growing the criminal empire, but I supposed there were worse things to be in life—like a drug dealer.

"What are we going to do when more drug dudes turn up here, looking for the ones we got rid of tonight?" I asked Sam once we'd showered away the day and fallen into bed. We didn't even have the energy to make love, which was a first for us.

"Drug dudes?" He chuckled and then grew serious,

drawing small circles along my arm with his fingertips. "We're going to Portland in the morning. We're going to make Nate come back and clean up his mess."

"Do you think we're going to have to kill them all?"

His fingers stopped and he let out his breath. "I hope not, peaches. This family has had enough death for a while."

CHAPTER THIRTY-ONE
I'M NOT SORRY

TOBY STAYED BACK with the twins and Jasmine while Sam and I drove down to Portland. We didn't tell any of the others that Nate was still alive. Sure, it would've eased their grief, but it've have increased their suffering—especially Jasmine. It would've devastated her to learn that her own son would rather have her believe he was dead than trust her with his scheme. No, it was better if we went alone. Sam could convince Nate, and I could convince Holland. We hoped.

"This is quite the house," I said when we pulled up outside the large sand-coloured home directly across from the ocean (those Cartwrights certainly loved their ocean views). It had taken us almost four hours to get there.

"You interested in a place like that?" Sam asked, leaning down to take in the view.

"It's not too different from the Torquay place, really. Just a little smaller. And it would all depend on the surfing. If we ever buy a place all of our own, it has to have great surfing and lots of one-way windows so we can walk around naked all day."

He bit his lip and groaned. "You're making me hard. Maybe we should go find a hotel or something, deal with this after some alone time."

I grinned. "I think we should do this first. Waiting makes that other thing so much sweeter."

He sighed. "OK, but don't be shocked if I punch my brother in the face."

That's exactly what he did.

"The *fuck*," Nate yelled, clutching the side of his face. He didn't stumble from the force of it, so I'd give him that.

"The fuck?" Sam responded, his voice booming. "The *fuck*? I don't think I need to tell you what that was for, brother." Placing his hand on Nate's shoulder, Sam stepped inside, pulling me along for the ride. His hand on his face as he worked his jaw, Nate shut the door behind us.

"That right hook of yours could use some work."

"Fuck you," Sam growled.

"Nate? What's going on?" Holland's frightened voice floated down the stairs a few moments before she came into view and answered the question for herself. "Oh shit." She had a vase in her hands that she lowered to her side, for protection or decoration, I wasn't sure.

"Toby blabbed," Nate informed her.

"He didn't just *blab*," I snapped. "Don't you fucking dare put this on him after the shitstorm we've just come from. A shitstorm *you* caused."

"Shitstorm?" Holland repeated, looking slightly alarmed. "What the hell happened? Nate?"

"Simon and Bruno paid us a visit," Sam answered.

Nate's jaw flexed. "What did they want?"

"They wanted everything you ever owned," I told him, the pressure of my mixed emotions taking over my stomach. "They showed up right after your funeral and tried to strong-arm your grieving mother. How could you do this to her, Nate? Do you have any idea how distraught she's been? We've *all* been?" He needed to know he fucked up.

"Don't blame him, Alesha." Holland stepped forward. "He did it for me. Jasmine would never let him go if he didn't do something drastic."

"Are you mental?" Sam said, looking at her like she had two heads. "How is this Jasmine's fault?"

"You told me yourself, Sam. *No one* walks away when they know shit that can get someone put away."

"I was talking about *you,* you fu—" Sam stopped abruptly, pressing his mouth and eyes closed as he took a calming breath. Then he levelled his furious gaze on Nate, rising to his full height, almost an inch above his brother. "Cartwrights don't run," he forced through his teeth.

Nate's jaw ticked.

"You're being naïve, Holland," I continued for him. "Jasmine isn't your enemy. She let you walk away, let me walk away, and she would *die* for her sons. Everything Nate did, he did for selfish reasons because he wanted you. *Everything* that has happened over this past year is because of him. He shit the bed. And now we're all fucking *murderers* because of him. So I hope you two are happy!"

"Holy shit," Holland gasped, her hand going to her mouth. "Nate? What did we do?"

Sam swallowed hard, then raked his fingers through his hair. "You really want to know, Holland? You really want to lower yourself from your almighty pedestal and get dirty with the rest of us?"

Nate's arm shot out, grabbing the front of Sam's shirt. "Don't you fucking dare speak to my wife that way."

Charged breathing mixed with testosterone-laden actions. I got that Nate wanted Holland protected, that he wanted to keep her good, but having no idea what we were up against wasn't going to help her. Besides, she was already tarred by the same brush as the rest of us, she had a stack of knowledge about their various crimes and not reporting them was a crime in itself. Whether she liked it or not, she was a Cartwright too.

"Jasmine killed Simon," I announced, my gaze moving between Nate and Holland. Nate's grip loosened on Sam's shirt as his eyes widened. "She thought they set that fire and murdered you, so she retaliated. Toby had to kill Bruno so there were no witnesses. Sam and I had to help dispose of the bodies in my family's crematorium. Now that you know all about it, you're an accomplice after the fact." I clapped my hand on Holland's upper arm. "Welcome to the family, sister."

Holland's eyes filled with tears as she shook her head. "No," she whispered. "He said we were free. We were going to be happy here." I stood and watched her shattered dream slide down her face in silent tears.

"You can still be happy. You just need to quit fighting what you are."

She wiped at her cheeks. "An accomplice?"

I shook my head. "A Cartwright. There's pride in that name, Holland. It means family above all else."

She swallowed hard but nodded. While she didn't look convinced, she at least seemed to understand.

"AT LEAST IT makes sense now why you weren't at his funeral," I said later while we both sat on her front porch, looking for whales in the ocean. Sam and Nate were inside 'discussing things', and since Holland seemed to need a moment to digest the fact that their actions had resulted in two deaths—albeit bad guys—she and I moved outside.

"What was it like?" she asked, squinting against the sun.

"It was sad. What else could it be? Everyone he ever knew or cared for him was there. He was so loved, Holland, and they were all beside themselves. I don't think you understand what he left behind for you."

She slid lower in her chair and scowled. "I feel so incredibly selfish now. I know he did all this for me. I wanted him out, nagged him for months. Because he loves me, he did something drastic to give me what I wanted. I'm sorry you got caught in the middle of it all." She reached over and grabbed my hand, giving it a squeeze. "I feel like I got everything I wanted and you've been thrown in the shark tank."

I touched the tender spot on my head were Bruno had introduced me to their SUV. *She isn't wrong. But I thrive in the shark tank.* I'd become a whole other person since the Cartwrights had come into my life. A stronger one. A happier one. I'd found myself because of them.

"Holland, you need to stop looking at his family like they're some sort of demons. They're not. They're good people, they really are. They make me feel more welcome than my own family ever did, and all they want in return is loyalty. They have shitty morals, sure, but they're *honourable.* They would die for each other in a heartbeat. If you'd let them, they'd feel that way about you too."

She scoffed. "I don't think Jasmine could *ever* feel that way about me."

"Well, it's not like you've really given her a chance. She's been trying, and you keep constructing walls to keep her away. You're being pig-headed and pious. And it's you who's driving the wedge in this family. Not her, not Nate—you."

"Did you rob the school?"

I shook my head. "We don't steal from kids."

"We." She took a deep breath and held it for a moment, staring out to the sea. "You've changed," she said, turning to study me. "You've got this *joie de vivre* you didn't have before." I sat proudly under her scrutiny. "It's a good thing. You seem tired and stressed, but you seem happy too. Are you happy, Leesh?"

I nodded. "I'd be happier if I still had my friend. But yeah, I'm happy."

"You didn't seem to need me," she admitted, taking a sip from her coffee—Irish, to help calm her nerves.

"Why wouldn't I need you? I was thrown into this new world where I had *no one*."

"You don't think I felt that way too?"

"How could you possibly? You still had everything that was yours. You got to keep your job, your apartment, your connection to your family. I lost all of that."

"I was still forced into a world that wasn't mine."

"A world you wanted, Holland. Don't lie to yourself and say that when you dragged me out to that house, you weren't doing it because you wanted Nate. You were obsessed with him, just like he was obsessed with you."

Her mouth twisted slightly and her eyes glistened. "It

was never my intention for us to get caught," she whispered.

"But we did get caught. I feel like I made the best of things and you just kept trying to run away."

"I never wanted to run from Nate. Never wanted to leave you. I stayed because I cared."

"But then you left anyway."

She nodded. "You fit in there so well. Flourished, even. I was willing to go through with that job. I wanted to fit in too. Then Nate showed me the flowers and I couldn't. I just couldn't. Not after what we saw with your mum. Not with how much her leaving affected you. You lost your light when she left."

I took a breath. "She's dead, you know."

Holland's eyes filled with tears. "Oh, Leesh."

"It's OK. It happened a long time ago, and I always had a feeling."

"I remember you saying." Holland placed her hand on my forearm, giving it a squeeze.

A wayward tear drifted down my cheek and I wiped it away. "You remember how my dad was always talking to the roses?" She nodded. "That's where she is."

"That makes a lot of sense," she said. Then I filled her in on the rest of the tale, how I left when she did, made amends with my family and finally started working in cosmetics.

"What made you leave?" she asked when I was finished. "Was Sam not being good to you?"

"Sam was wonderful. He always had been. But I wanted it to be real. We got married and then floated along in this attraction we had for each other. We needed time to work through our feelings. I needed time to work out who I was."

"You wanted the fairy tale," she stated with a smile.

"I did. But mostly I wanted to be his choice instead of his obligation. I wanted him to love me."

"Looks like he does. You wouldn't be here if he didn't."

"Yes." I looked over my shoulder to where I could see the shadowed outline of two brothers sitting together in deep discussion. There was so much going on inside my head from the events of the last few weeks, and I had to really concentrate to keep it from overwhelming me. Having Sam made it so much easier. "We love each other very much."

"Remember when we never thought we'd marry?" she said, joining me in watching the men.

I smiled. "Remember when we promised that we'd only marry brothers so we'd be sisters?"

She laughed. It was the first hint of joy I'd heard from her in what felt like forever. "What were we, nine?"

"I think so." For a moment we sat quietly, thinking of a shared past filled with childish dreams. Some dreams came true. "But we did it, didn't we? We're sisters now."

Meeting my eyes, she nodded. "I'm sorry, Leesh. For everything."

I took her hand. "I'm not sorry, Holl. This all happened for a reason. I think we're exactly where we're meant to be."

CHAPTER THIRTY-TWO
RENEWAL

"HAPPY ANNIVERSARY, PEACHES," Sam said, kissing me awake. It was one minute into our wedding anniversary and he was sneaking into my bed. That was the problem with being married to a thief. He probably stole my room key when he was in here earlier—though I may have left it out on purpose as a temptation.

"I don't think you should even be in here." I smiled. "Isn't this bad luck?"

He slid his hands beneath my negligee, worn because it was white and lacy and the first piece of sexy sleepwear I ever owned.

"The superstition isn't valid when you're renewing your vows. We're already married, and you know how much I need you."

I could feel that *need* pressing against my butt.

"You know most men are past the honeymoon period by now, right? They're too busy watching sports or something to maul their wives."

His hand moved over my stomach as his mouth

worked along my shoulder and against the curve of my neck. "Is that what you call this?" he whispered. "Mauling."

"My word power isn't the best when you're doing that."

"Doing what? This?" He ran the tip of his tongue around the shell of my ear. "Or this?" He slid his hand down to my mound, stopping just before he got to point where I'd begun to throb.

"All of it," I whispered, causing him to chuckle lightly.

"What can I say," he said, slipping his fingers in the waist of my lace panties. "Most men don't have a wife who mews like a virgin and looks rock-star hot in their underwear like you do." He'd taken me to that fancy underwear store that got in trouble for their raunchy Christmas displays, and we'd gone a little wild with the purchases. He struggled to keep his hands to himself before the sexy underwear, but ever since, he was constantly hooking his finger in the waist of my pants to check which ones I was wearing. It was possessive and made me feel so damn sexy and wanted. It did wonders for my self-esteem. And not that it needed it, but it had even done wonders for our sex life. He wasn't the only one who was insatiable.

"Mews like a virgin?" I repeated as he pushed the panties down my legs and flicked them off the bed.

"Yes. When I touch you—" He slid his finger between my folds, placing the perfect amount of pressure against every sensitive spot. I moaned. "—you mew. Just like that."

"I like it when you touch me like that."

"I love it that you're already wet from waiting for me. You knew I was coming, didn't you?"

"I was counting on it," I whispered, wriggling back against him until he moaned from the friction of my butt against his cock.

"I remember the first night I took you. The way you blushed and moaned, so eager to experience everything I could give you. You were so perfect." His fingers teased and probed, his mouth kissing my skin between his words.

I moved against him, reaching back to slide my fingers in his hair. "Your touch has always felt so good. I'm glad I waited. I'm glad it was you." I turned my head towards him, kissing him hungrily as his hand brought me to climax before he slid inside me, taking me in the spoon position, the angle so perfectly deep that I almost came a second time after only a few strokes.

"Not yet, peaches. Wait for me this time," he whispered, pressing his fingers into my hips as he rocked within me.

"But you feel so good," I gasped. "So good. I can't."

I really couldn't. I shuddered around him, my muscles clenching and releasing, body shaking, breath hissing. With a moan, he followed me, his fingers tightening on my hip as his cock pulsed inside me.

"You feel *so* good," I repeated, breathing hard.

"You know that's my line, right?" He chuckled, kissing me with slow force.

"I was just telling the truth," I said when we pulled apart.

When he left to get something to clean me up, I took a moment to admire the beautiful ring he'd given me at Christmas. It had been a turbulent time for the family with

Nate coming back. I would never forget the look on Jasmine's face when we brought him back home that day.

———————

"Jazz." We'd entered the house through the sliding door, going straight into the kitchen where she was alone preparing coffee. She froze.

Then she turned.

The coffee pot fell from her hand with a loud *crash*.

"Nate?" Her wide eyes welled with tears as she stared at him in disbelief.

Toby came running at the sound of the breaking glass, skidding to a stop the moment he set eyes on Nate. He swallowed once, shook his head, then turned away.

"Tobes," Nate called after him, his voice imploring. Toby just kept going, his shoulders hunched, having lost their usual pride.

"Leave him, brother," Sam said. "You made him lie for you. Add he had to kill for you. He needs time."

Nate nodded, the rest of us breathing in the sorrow in the air. This family was heavily bruised, and only Nate could fix it.

"What the hell have you done?" she whispered, shaking her head.

"Mum." He stepped towards her.

She backed away. "Do you have *any* idea what you've done?"

"I was trying to break free."

"You started a *war*."

Nate's tongue peeked past his lips, wetting them, and then he swallowed hard. "I'll fix it," he promised.

The silence stretched into a vast ocean of unspoken words as mother and son stared at each other, hurt and anguish in their eyes. "You do that," Jasmine said finally. "And don't you dare come back here till you're through."

I HAD NO IDEA HOW 'FIXED' everything was, but we hadn't had any further visits from anyone connected to Nate's flower business, and Nate and Holland spent the week between Christmas and New Year's with us at the house. Holland even made a huge effort to be friendly with everyone. It seemed things were dealt with, at least to Jasmine's satisfaction.

Toby, on the other hand, was not OK. He'd gone through a lot at the hand of his closest brother, forced across that invisible line he'd never wanted to cross. He'd killed. He had a scar on his soul now, and I didn't know how we were going to fix it. Most days, he acted like he was OK, but there were times when I'd spot him sitting alone outside, throwing the ball for Rogue until even the dog grew tired of it. Then he'd just continue sitting out there, staring off into the distance, looking lost. Sometimes I'd sit with him, and other times I'd find Sam, Kris or Abbot sitting with him. We were all just trying to be there, trying to let him know that he wasn't alone; we were there on that day, and we were there for him now. We just hoped that time would help him find that light inside of him again so he could come back to us.

Speaking of the twins, they were the most adaptable men I'd ever known in my life. They'd been pissed when they found out Nate had faked his death, even left and returned with bruised knuckles after hearing the news. But once they got the shock out of their system, they were right back to being their crazy, light-hearted selves. Sometimes I thought they were the glue that held this family together. They made anything heavy feel lighter.

My relationship with Holland had definitely grown stronger. I wouldn't say we were the best of friends again, but we were definitely on the road to becoming something else—sisters perhaps, the kind who still loved each other even when one of them was being a pig-headed arse (I was talking about Holland, here. She was trying to embrace the Cartwrights, but she still had a long way to go).

Jasmine, well, she was Jasmine. Strong, capable and centred. That woman would keep walking forwards in the middle of a cyclone. You simply couldn't put her down. I found myself taking pride in any comparisons people made about me and her. She was fierce, and I was cool with being seen as fierce too.

Despite the messed-up year we'd had, Sam and I had come out of it stronger, and during that same Christmas, he wanted to show me how much I meant to him by getting down on one knee.

"What are you doing?" I'd asked, looking around the room at our gathered family. They just smiled knowingly, and my heart beat even faster as I realised what was going on.

Holding out that little blue box that every girl dreamed of one day owning, he looked up at me, his eyes filled with all the love I felt in my heart, and said six very important words. "Peaches, will you marry me again?"

I didn't have to think. I immediately said yes, ecstatic for the chance to renew our vows and reset our marriage, this new day planned to perfection so we could put the disaster of our first wedding behind us. I wanted to look at our first year together as an overzealous form of dating, our true married life starting after we said 'I do' without any sort of coercion. That way it would be real. That way I would forever believe it.

That's not to say I didn't still question Sam's motives and his devotion to me. My brain just wasn't adjusted enough to believe that someone could possibly love me at my best, let alone at my worst. But he was tireless in his efforts to show me that I was his very reason for waking up each morning. And when he presented me with a seaside cottage with the tinted windows I'd wanted for my birthday, I'd spent a week walking around naked to prove to him how happy he made me. Granted, the nakedness was a little uncomfortable when the mailman came knocking, but we quickly learned that a robe hung on the back of the door was a great solution for unexpected visitors.

Now he was treating me to my dream wedding. We had booked a local hotel and filled it with our guests. I had chosen my perfect dress, and my father was ready to give me away. Holland was my pregnant matron of honour, a piece of information she'd only dropped a few days before. It was very early, so no one knew outside the family. It was a bit of a shock for me since she'd never wanted children, but once she and Nate went back to Portland in the new year, she was suddenly bit by the baby bug.

I was sure they'd make beautiful book-loving children, but I couldn't help feeling a little tug of longing at how easy it had seemed for them. Sam and I still wanted children, but we were going to have to embark on a very frightening, very expensive journey to make that dream happen. But that was OK. We'd do whatever it took, and we'd do it together. United, we were strong. And on the upside, Holland being pregnant meant she couldn't get stuck into the champagne this time and cause a whole new family incident since we were all still on tenterhooks with each other.

When I made my way up the aisle later that day, Sam's side of the altar was going to be a little crowded. He was going to have all four of his brothers as his collective best man. There had been a lot of questions about Nate's resurrection, but once we explained that the coroner had made an error and Nate had simply gone on holiday, the questions slowed. I'm not sure anyone really believed that lie, but it was the best story we had for them—simple was more believable than complicated.

On top of the bridal party, all of our friends and relatives were invited, our vows were written and a reception was ready to go. We were making all that went wrong last time go right, reclaiming the day as our own. Sam was giving me my fairy tale, and I loved him even more for it.

"Don't tell me you're going to kick me out of your room now that you've gotten want you wanted from me," Sam said once he'd carefully bathed away our mess. "I agreed to the whole separate room thing, but I never agreed to separate beds."

"That makes absolutely no sense." I laughed. "And no, I'm not going to kick you out. Turns out I can't sleep too well without that big chest of yours wrapping around me."

"You mean this one?" he asked, pumping his pecs so they danced.

I nodded. "Yeah. I *really* like that chest."

"Do you like it, or do you *love* it?"

I laughed. "I love it." He slid into the bed and I snuggled in close, sighing from the happiness of being close to him. There was no such thing as perfect, but I was pretty sure this love I shared with Sam was as close as it was going to get.

"Sam?" I whispered just as his breathing started to deepen.

"Hmm?"

"I can't wait to marry you again."

"I can't wait either. I love you, peaches." He kissed my shoulder.

"I love you too."

The end.

Sign up to the Lilliverse Newsletter to discover more titles, limited offers, and upcoming releases by Lilliana Anderson
https://www.lillianaanderson.com/newsletter

NEXT in the Cartwright Brothers series, *Foolish Games*, featuring Kristian and Veronica.

I didn't have an easy life. Waiting tables for a function centre was about as good as life got for me. There were no tips—unless telling me I had a great arse could be considered a tip—but it was enough for me to live on, barely. Everything else I needed, I took. And I was never caught, except that one time when these brothers and some weird chick busted me for stealing their car. It was their fault I took it. They shouldn't have left their keys where I could find them. And it was a sweet ride; I chucked a couple of donuts in that thing and it smoked up like a charm. Good times.

Anyway, those guys took the car back, turned my boyfriend into a pussy and ended up making me homeless. When I saw that same car again in the function centre parking lot, I couldn't resist. I pulled out my keys and started scratching. *C*... *U*... busted. I should've known it was a bad idea, but I never was one to listen to my conscience. Suddenly I was locked in a room while a family of five ridiculously hot brothers argued over what to do with me. Their mother wanted me dead, but they were insisting that stealing and vandalism weren't necessarily grounds for a beheading. I was on their side. I quite liked my head—even though it seemed like I'd just gotten myself in way over it.

But do you know what was crazy? The brother I'd stolen from, the one who'd caught me defacing his car, was now watching me like a lion watches a big juicy steak. Hmm, maybe I could spin this in my favour after all....

Preorder here - ***books2read.com/u/47877R***

ALSO BY LILLIANA ANDERSON

Cartwright Brothers

Fool Me Twice

Fools Rush In

Foolish Games

47 Things

47 Things

One More Thing

Standalones

In the Wind

Till There Was You

Never Again

Drawn Series

Drawn

Drawn 2 – Obsession

Drawn 2 – Redemption

Drawn to Fight

Zac & Evie

Hugo & Meg

For more information on upcoming releases visit

www.lillianaanderson.com/preorders

ABOUT THE AUTHOR

Bestselling Author of the Beautiful Series, Drawn and 47 Things, Lilliana has always loved to read and write, considering it the best form of escapism that the world has to offer.

Australian born and bred, she writes New Adult Romance revolving around her authentically Aussie characters with all the quirks you'd expect from those born Down Under.

Lilliana feels that the world should see Australia for more than just it's outback and tries to show characters in a city and suburban setting.

When she isn't writing, she wears the hat of 'wife and mother' to her husband and five children.

Before Lilliana turned to writing, she worked in a variety of industries and studied humanities and communications before transferring to commerce/law at university.

Originally from Sydney's Western suburbs, she currently lives a fairly quiet life in suburban Melbourne.

For more information on Lilliana and her work:
www.lillianaanderson.com
info@lillianaanderson.com

To join her Facebook reader group and talk books
https://www.facebook.com/groups/438800699591852

facebook.com/LillianaAndersonAuthor

twitter.com/confidante_lili

instagram.com/lilliana_anderson

ACKNOWLEDGMENTS

AS ALWAYS, there are people to be thanked! Many sets of eyes go in to the creation of each of my books and I am very grateful to every person who takes time out of their lives to help me.

To **Julie Chippendale** and **Cyndi Hart-Duplessis,** thank you so much for beta reading and giving me excellent feedback to work with. I can't tell you how much I appreciate your sage advice. To my editors at **Hot Tree Editing**, and **Marion Archer** of Making Manuscripts, I thank you all for your keen eyes and funny comments. **Helena Cullen** and **Margaret Neal,** thank you for helping to proof the final copy—hopefully we got them all!

To my team of sharers, you're all so wonderful. I don't ask you to do what you do, but you see something I post and share it far and wide. I'm eternally grateful. Thank you all so much. I love you all!

To every blogger and reviewer who has an ARC or has signed up to post about my book – I thank you too. You are the first step to announcing my work to the world. No author can do this without you xoxox

Also, a big thank you to my husband for putting up with my bitching and moaning and his unending support and encouragement.

Thank you to my kids for being so patient while I stare at a computer screen and finish typing out a thought. I love that you all come and sit with me while I work just to spend a bit of extra time with mummy!

And of course – thank you to all of my readers. You are the most important of all. Without you, I would be writing to the crickets.

Mwah! xoxox

www.ingramcontent.com/pod-product-compliance
Lightning Source LLC
Chambersburg PA
CBHW031128120726
47905CB00006B/1608